Yellow breasted
Chat

...dge shad...
... song

Oyster
...ll
...redatory snail
—that drills holes
—through its prey

...derband

...to be
... slowly

Golden Winged
Warbler
...rare find! Was
...hing oddly...

THE DEADING

THE DEADING

NICHOLAS BELARDES

EREWHON

an imprint of Kensington Publishing Corp.

erewhonbooks.com

EREWHON BOOKS are published by:

Kensington Publishing Corp.
900 Third Avenue
New York, NY 10022
erewhonbooks.com

All Kensington titles, imprints, and distributed lines are available at special quantity discounts for bulk purchases for sales promotions, premiums, fundraising, educational, or institutional use.

Special book excerpts or customized printings can also be created to fit specific needs. For details, write or phone the office of the Kensington sales manager: Kensington Publishing Corp., 900 Third Avenue, New York, NY 10022, attn: Sales Department; phone 1-800-221-2647.

Erewhon and the Erewhon logo Reg. US Pat. & TM Off.

This is a work of fiction. All of the characters, organizations, and events portrayed in this novel are either products of the author's imagination or are used fictitiously.

ISBN 978-1-64566-129-0 (hardcover)

First Erewhon hardcover printing: August 2024

10 9 8 7 6 5 4 3 2 1

Printed in the United States of America

Library of Congress Control Number: 2024932748

Electronic edition: ISBN 978-1-64566-131-3

Edited by Diana Pho
Map design by Alice Moye-Honeyman
Interior design by Kelsy Thompson, images courtesy of Adobe Stock

For Jane

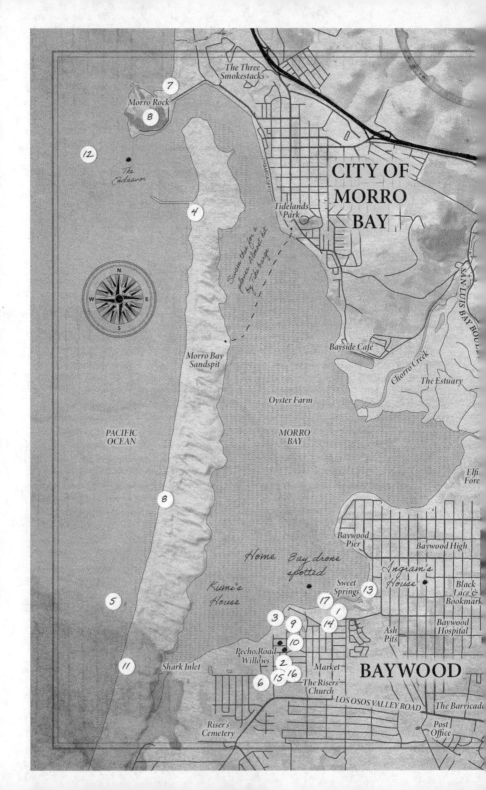

MONTAÑA
DE ORO
STATE PARK

The Hidden
Farm

18

Islay Creek
Campground

Dead of Night

Valencia Peak

COON CREEK TRAIL

The Faceless
Forward
Operating
Base

1. Summer Tanager
2. Red-Eyed Vireo
3. Pacific Golden-Plover
4. Common-ringed Plover
5. Pigeon Guillemot
6. Townsend's Warbler
7. Peregrine Falcon
8. Mountain Plover
9. Great-crested Flycatcher
10. Yellow-billed Cuckoo
11. Snowy Plover
12. Red-footed Booby
13. Northern Parula
14. Yellow-throated Vireo
15. Chestnut-sided Warbler
16. Magnolia Warbler
17. Ruddy Turnstone
18. Hooded Warbler

Before

WE HEAR ABOUT the old man rising at Sweet Springs lookout. We also learn of the magic cat in Coon Creek, and the police officer resurrection on Pasadena Drive. We gather to talk and laugh about them. We sneak booze. We suck down spliffs. We call our get-together the Dead of Night and have a real rager down in a hidden cove away from all the MDO park rangers. That's Montaña de Oro, the state park where you can walk on beaches, trails, and hike to Valencia Peak and stare at the stars and ocean. Nothing about our party is serious. It's just an excuse to be together soon after it all started.

Days go by. Weeks. Now, all kinds of adults are pretending to die. *Deading.* That's what we call it, have been calling it, because, well, we've done it before, like more than a year before the adults ever thought to start their stupid version.

Thirteen months ago, to be exact, Mr. Nuño's entire English class deaded two days after Kaylee Jones deaded in an elevator. Blas really likes her, we all know. Anyway, we acted like we'd been in some awful school shooting. No fake blood though. We weren't about to get gross. Half of us sprawled on the floor. Some slumped over desks. Chewie Miller hung over the portable tablet cabinet.

We did it to make fun of ourselves. We did it because we die and it isn't fair.

You see, we'd already held GUN CONTROL rallies, BLACK LIVES MATTER rallies, EARTH DAY rallies. Those always got us nowhere. Adults don't listen. We know that.

Whatever.

Truth?

Already told you. We group deaded as a *joke*.

That, and because we knew Elisabeth Garcia's social media accounts would blow up. We all wanted to be famous.

We deaded because we wanted to shake people up. We did it because deading is hilarious. We wanted to see our own expressions, our fake dead faces fresh out of the oven, and we did it before any of that fake deading while drinking Grimace shakes. We wanted to see the comments. We wanted to start a trend, okay? We'd all seen what Kaylee Jones had done two days before. We had to be a part of that.

What happened with her? She deaded on the campus elevator. Mr. Rocha was about to head to the second floor when he caught her lying there. Julie Moore was straddling Kaylee's thin twisted frame, smart phone out, thumb snapping images.

"Best ever," she said in her singsong way at Kaylee's blank stare. "Everyone gonna wonder who took dead photos of you," she sang. "Too bad we can't make your face blue, maybe add some purple. I think that's what *dead* really looks like."

Julie kept on going, like her teacher hadn't been standing there, listening, half horrified at Kaylee's blank stare. She snapped another shot before acknowledging his presence. "Sorry, Mr. Rocha. For a post. You know."

"No, I don't know," said Mr. Rocha.

Julie giggled like she didn't care, like she didn't want to explain, though she did. "She's deading."

"Oh."

Kaylee's eyes came back to life. She sat up.

"Your dead . . . thing is over," said Mr. Rocha. "Get to class. I need the elevator."

And that was the beginning, though what we did started sooner, somewhere else. Larry Lincoln said *he* read something on *Bustle* and told *Kaylee* that deading started somewhere in Russia. They were deading like crazy in Moscow. Freaking out friends and family over and over. Deading in schools. Deading in parks. Deading in parked cars. Deading while driving. Deading while crashing.

The article wondered if Putin had been deading all along.

From there it spread across other parts of Europe, then Japan. For some reason the Japanese kids really loved to dead. We all wished we could join them at pachinko parlors and beautiful temples. And then it spread to China, people unhappy that they couldn't get jobs. It was a kind of rebellion. We loved that.

Anyway. We began deading at Baywood High.

We teenagers anyway.

We started the deading here.

Deading. Deading. Deading.

And then we stopped. It got boring. It was over, for months and months.

But then this thing happened. It started with the adults. Something completely unrelated. Something similar. Everywhere in Baywood, people lying on sidewalks and streets. In living rooms, in restaurants. Next to cars and on the beach. In hotel lobbies. In school hallways. Around the administration building. In the gym. Really old people started doing it, then our little sisters and brothers.

People in their forties, thirties, twenties, teens . . .

We'd deaded long before the adults. That's the thing. We'd DONE IT. We were already over it.

But that shit was a joke. We were just playing around.

Whatever started happening, whatever is really happening, is messing us all up. We knew this almost right away, can tell from that look in each others' eyes, from the stories we started to share. No one is going to be a social media star this time, not the way this has been playing out. It's beyond what we ever imagined, what we could comprehend. It doesn't feel real and we're all scared. We're not even sure if anyone will make it out of Baywood alive.

Chapter One

CLOSE TO ONE in the afternoon the scare happens: a single snail found drilling into an oyster. By itself the snail isn't a threat. A wash of yellow. An amber spiraled jewel. Ten thousand, on the other hand, could wipe Bernhard's oyster farm from existence.

He pinches the shell, drops it in a baggie to take ashore.

Tidelands swell out here along the back bay where Bernhard's floating dock and office rocks with the rush of water. Oysters feed off this sudden transformation between high and low tide, their beds buffered by a long harbor, by breakwater walls and sandspit dunes. The danger of what the open sea can bring can still slip through the narrow harbor mouth, Bernhard knows this.

Chango Enriquez and Deb Ochoa, both hired hands, peer at the zipped bag. "Got to be a one-off, yeah?" Chango says. Deb nods. Chango has always cried wolf about something. Strange algae colorations. Bizarre giant sea slugs. Slithering octopi found while raking grit, slime, and bony sealskin remains atop the rows of mesh bags. This one is no apparition. He'd spotted the glittering amber shell. Plucked it from an oyster, even flicked its little tentacle eye. "Can't believe it let go the shell," he says, eyes still roaming the beds, potential victims everywhere. "We're searching for more, boss. We'll get these little *cabrones*."

Bernhard grunts, his stomach a knot of potential lost product. The snail slithers in the baggie, tentacles outward, explores every edge of its new universe. Eyes like specks of stars against a thin wall of plastic. Bernhard wants to crush it right here. Instead, he leaves Chango and Deb to search the beds a second time, while he brings the specimen to the Center for Coastal Marine Sciences of California Polytechnic State University, San Luis Obispo. Best to confirm what it is or isn't.

An hour later, Dr. Beth Magaña grins. Says she hasn't seen an Atlantic driller in ten years. "This could be a one off," she adds. "You never know. But the fear is real. Coastal ecosystems have reached a crisis point. More than your oysters will fall victim if there are others. And where there's one, could be half a dozen, maybe more."

Bernhard isn't pleased with that stupid grin, or this kind of talk about ecosystems and timelines. The tidelands have always been tough, harsh, filled with nutrients that could pump life into massive numbers of shellfish, a lot more than his farm holds. At the same time he considers the strangeness of this snail, how nature's ability to make spirals is a mesmerizing aspect of the sea. Maybe that's what throws predators off, why this single snail hasn't been eaten by something bigger than itself. Complex shell patterns and colors. Fibonacci sequences. He's about to complain about its camouflage when Magaña goes on about some ocean blob, waves of seabirds washing ashore.

"A million starved murres, with little body fat, empty stomachs," she says. "All white fluff beneath. Nothing in their guts."

He feels what she's saying, though he doesn't believe this tale of swirling sea-tundra, feather and bone. His head fills with static. What does he care about bird die-offs?

Dr. Beth Magaña seems to enjoy this part of the conversation. "This is similar to all those birds dying in New Mexico a few years ago. Tens of thousands of passerines found in the sand, starved after fleeing forest fires, then a cold front. All that insect loss due to drought. Destroy one food source," she says, "everything falls to pieces. Here, look . . ." She flips through her tablet, scrolls to a report from someone named Jotaro. "He studies ocean biomes south of us, in and around Channel Islands."

Her fingers highlight a section:

> The Blob is a result of unseen explosions like the atom bombing of Hiroshima, transforming the seas with 228 sextillion joules of heat. No doubt ocean food chains are affected. Fish numbers in Pacific coastline estuaries are already down. Salinity is up (I've attached a chart). What you can do: Harvest shellfish and plant crops early. Monitor for predators. Consider other methods of growing over the next few years. Consider more protection from tides. Consider what might happen if the worst comes. No one can predict how bad this will be.

A muscle twitches below Bernhard's left eye. Why hadn't he already received this report? Should he even believe it? Aren't all those El Niño numbers a lie too? Someone surely messes with those buoy sensors. He's seen those warming trends. Little orange heat blobs all over the map. It's cyclical. So what? Big deal about those hundred-degree ocean surface temps off Florida too. Probably happens all the time.

He reads more:

> I know it seems like an obsession with water temperature, but this is pretty unusual and perhaps to the land-based, it needs the context. We do get warm water offshore around this time in an average year. What is different this time is that the warm water has entirely displaced the colder inshore water. Our charts usually show yellow and orange offshore (warm) and blue/green inshore (cool). But now it is beyond orange into the brown (68°F) in

some areas, and no cool water at all inshore. This is unusual in two respects: 1) the warm water has lapped up right to shore; and 2) the warm water is several degrees F higher than what we usually consider warm around here. This is very warm for us. Note that an unexpected Least Storm-Petrel was netted on Southeast Farallon Island last week. That suggests a marine heat wave, rather than El Niño, but as the latter strengthens and warm water shows up from the south, the entire situation will unite. The current sea surface temperature anomaly map shows a cold region to the south of us, separating us from the El Niño. Interesting if at the same time troubling. I guess as we fry on this earth, we will be happy enough seeing all the bird vagrants brought in by the doomsday scenario. Fascinating but terrible. This will mean gigantic red tides and *demonic acid outbreaks*. Say goodbye to crab season and expect more mass bird die-offs.

He admits what could happen if there was a danger. A decrease in micronutrients means less meat per shellfish. A decrease in customer satisfaction. He can't expand his oyster farm if meat quality heads to the toilet. Some of his fishing friends predicted this would happen. Thank god these marine heatwaves go underreported. He bites his tongue. Magaña. She has it out for him, he thinks, for oyster farmers in general, has for a while now. He doesn't believe he's destroying habitats, no way, not for a minute. It can't be what she thinks. Plenty of tidewater nutrients to go around.

"I'll email this to you," she says. "Mind if I keep this specimen? I don't come across this species every day."

Chapter Two

BERNHARD SITS ACROSS from his wife Katherine at Bayside Café, a harbor restaurant just off the back bay. He's already been to the oyster farm and back. No report of any snails so he sent Chango home. Deb promised to work until dusk, said she could use a few extra hours on top of her twelve-hour shift. That's good because Bernhard doesn't feel satisfied. A weight sits in his gut about snails in the silt and slime, how Magaña has it out for him. He doesn't like when things come at him from multiple directions.

Katherine picks at her dinner, starts to say something about the fish being too dry. "You know, we really should have gone to the Quarterdeck in Arroyo Grande," she says. "You proposed to me there."

He talks over her, complains how Magaña is helpful one minute then spies on him the next. "She lurks in the marina with her binoculars," he says. "I've seen her mingling with Harbor Patrol when she's on a kayak. They whisper things. She's not looking at birds or waterlines when she's out there. She's spying on me, on the goddam oysters."

The sun has melted its orange eye into the darkness of Morro

Bay's tidelands, spreading a dust haze into lavender blood. A heater next to the table glows and flickers. Katherine's face has become a haunt of propane light. Reminds Bernhard of her great-grandmother Mary staring ghostlike from Katherine's library photo shrine. That flowing drift of white cotton, that narrow, starved face. Gone for decades, Mary's judging eyes continue to examine anyone who sits and reads.

Almost always alone in the photos, as if she never knew a soul, Mary sits on a couch, on steps, bent and thin in a kitchen, eyes sideways to the lens. You forget the camera eye, that she only *seems* alone—that great-grandfather Katherine never mentions with his finger on the shutter—or maybe her rumored Dunite impressionist lover from a seaside cult. A dune vortex worshipper, he illustrated shadowy hellscapes, underworlds filled with heaps of burning sand that melted into disturbing forms.

A photograph of the sandy communal home of Moy Mell hangs amid the shrine. Some say the painter had a bedroom next to hers after she left her husband, that they visited each other in the middle of the night. Her pale form next to a white porch surrounded by tents and clotheslines repeats itself along the wall. Bernhard can imagine them all, the house shifting in angles and shadows, sometimes thin and tall, other times white and tilted, sinking into sand.

Some photos haunt Bernhard more than others. A reflection or shadow in one window feels like a slice of darkness that crept from the sea, that lodged itself in a plane of glass, come from beyond piles of distant dunes and shrubs. In the same image Mary smiles at something inward, distant.

Images play through Bernhard's mind, a stillness in them springs to life, cracks open amid faded black and white. The great-grandmother, a dark line next to an oak or cypress. Sometimes a blur on a sand dune, ocean in the distance, her body dwarfed against a black band of seascape. She stares from a wraithlike portrait like she knows something about how this will all end for Bernhard. Wallpaper patterns resemble a crypt. Walls close in. The sea closes in. Death closes in. Shadows and shapes where the old woman's eyes should be. Their blackness pulls him into a void where he imagines a starless drift. He can only escape along an edge that releases him into a swamp of roots and mulch. Katherine has stepped from a similar monochrome nightmare. He thinks maybe she was born of some tree of blood, squeezed amid tangles of roots within some dark hollow.

Bernhard wonders when this happened to Katherine, when this transformation took place. Some nights he doesn't even think it's her in his bed, but Mary, resurrected, a leather-skinned thing pulled from the soil, skin coarse against his, bony skin to skin, breathing curses against his back, whispered from tangles of deadfall.

Her hand creeps to her glass, edges lit by a tiny flame, the candle-dusk having slipped to midnight blue. Bernhard slurps down his entire martini to rid himself of how sunken Katherine's cheeks have become. Desperate to pull himself away, he continues talking, avoids eye contact. "These local marine biologists are always accusing me of operating poorly within the tideland ecosystem. Any minute they're going to say I'm harming the birds, the water. And if I harm the birds, they'll think I hurt the fish, snail, and crustacean populations. I just know they're going to say that every goddam thing in the tidelands is at risk because of my oysters. And now this Blob? A warning to make me paranoid. A way to get me to reduce size. Saw a report from this guy, Jotaro. Then *she* sent me a letter. Listen to this."

He starts reading from his phone screen. "Higher water temps from the Blob mean forage fish are replaced by warm-water varieties. That means lower nutritional value. The fish they feed on go deeper where the murres and auklets can't catch them. Not only that, predator fish are eating the good stuff. Cod, flounder, and walleye come in because they're hungrier too. The entire ecosystem has shifted. Murres starving mostly. Warmer waters affect more than seabirds and fisheries. They bring invaders up and down the West Coast like that Atlantic oyster driller your worker found. This means your harvest runs the risk of predation, or at the very least, a decrease in intertidal micronutrients. The overall quality of your oysters are at stake over the next few seasons."

Katherine isn't listening, he can tell. She starts talking about their son Michael who studies law at Pepperdine. Her voice drones through the salt air. "Michael's new girlfriend is from Newport Beach. I think she has a disorder of some kind. She's all bones. I never see her eat."

Bernhard doesn't want to talk about this. He doesn't want to point out the irony. He's got a one-track mind to enlighten her, to pound some sense about what's eating at him into that cold stare. "Four years straight of quality oyster meat, Katherine. This isn't the end of the world. I see dollar signs. Exceptional oysters with each harvest. We have to expand. We've got the perfect tumble method. It's all peaches and cream. These scientists and biologists—they operate on fear. It's Blob paranoia. They want me to think I'm harming the environment or that we can't withstand the Blob." Then he lies: "I've seen other reports. Fish numbers have been holding steady in the estuary. Salinity levels too."

"Can we step away from the oyster farm for an hour?" Katherine says. "I drove down here to be with you." She pops open a mirror, stares at her shadow in the heater glow. She's always staring at those cheeks, her thinning lips, her eyes and eye makeup.

"Takes five minutes to get here," Bernhard points out.

She changes the subject again: "I don't like having two homes so close to each other. I can't maintain them." She takes a gulp of wine. "Michael says you haven't called all week."

"I thought you liked sleeping apart sometimes." Bernhard

wants to call her ungrateful but doesn't. He knows he uses that word too much. It causes them to hate each other for days on end. But he can't manage to stop thinking how unappreciative she's been the past year. He tries to focus on their son though he can only think about her rudeness, those cheeks, that damn snail again. He glances into the darkness as if he can see his floating dock consumed by gastropods.

"Can't Michael see I'm busy?" he says. "I mean, with this snail issue and everything? What does he want?" Bernhard has spent most of the week driving up and down the coast for TV interviews, promoting his upcoming harvest by promoting safe oysters. He has nothing but pride in his farm though by the look on Katherine's face it's about to cost him his marriage. What does he care? He gets hit on all the time these days, which is why that second home comes in handy. Wealthy man of the bay. "Mister Shellfish" they call him on KSBY and in the papers. He's got more respectability than any oyster farmer on the coast. Photos and videos of his weathered face in front of piles of oysters pop up anytime anyone googles *California oysters*. Narrow glasses over pinpoints of eyes. Tousles of grey hair. Big forehead. Teeth white as whalebone. He wishes they had snails on the menu. He'd eat every goddam one.

Katherine's green eyes have melted to grey pits in this light. They meet his. "He's dropping out of the law program."

This hits Bernhard out of the blue. More ungrateful family shit is what this is. He bites his lip. Swallows. Now he's craving bourbon. Lots of bourbon. He tries to lower his voice with some measure. "Our son can't do that."

Katherine's face seems to have grown thinner. She drones in a steady line of disappointment. "He wants an MBA. He wants to be like you. Sad as that sounds." Her mirror still open, she glances at herself again. "God, I hate all of this."

"You should like having multiple homes, cars, vacations," he says. "Maybe our son would benefit from being more like me. God knows I could use some support from this family."

Katherine peeks at herself. Maybe she wants to disappear into the mirror. He wants to throw the damn thing and her into the bay. She sinks into her drink, drains her glass. "Feels like we live in lighthouses," she says. "I'm just home to stare at the sea, to wait for something, never for you anymore."

Chapter Three

KATHERINE ASKS IF Bernhard will be in their bed tonight. When he doesn't answer, she slams the car door, starts the engine. Seconds later she makes a sharp turn onto Main Street, her haunting form a blur, taillights dwindling to pink dots.

Bernhard watches her pass Windy Cove alongside Great Blue Heron silhouettes in a eucalyptus rookery, branches fingerlike over the bay. In them, giant shaggy birds, their plumage lined with ritual markings, long bills sharp and deadly. They're haggard witches casting spells on the cars beneath them.

He walks over to the marina, tries to forget his wife's image, her voice, but sees nightmare images. Glimpses of her great-grandmother standing atop the night sea, slowly sinking, asking him to join her.

He still sees the apparition while slipping into a dinghy and piloting toward the oyster farm's floating dock. He ignores the ghost, really a tidal marker that he soon passes, tells himself he can sit in his office and crunch numbers. He'll smell the sea, let the lull of the bay cradle him, and that will be that.

The moonless boat ride makes him feel blind while he cuts across windless waters. Images of Mary fade, though his anxiety is replaced with a new reality. Magaña. Jotaro. The Goldilocks Zone. Poisoned streams. Large die-offs from estuarine organisms, microalgae, tainted plants, chemicals. He knows deep down there really may be a connection. Won't stop him from growing shellfish. He'll never cease production. He'll keep those oysters right where they are, let them tumble and churn in muddy bay water. He doesn't care. His oysters act like both filter and sponge. They'll steal the bay's nutrients until nothing is left. Other organisms can just leave the tidelands if they can't find anything to eat, if they can't handle the silt. Let them die if they must.

A few dim lights on the floating dock guide him. Above those, the Milky Way shoots its arm along the bowl of night, looms like an open wound revealing the scintillating white-and-blue blood of starlight. Behind the boat, Morro Bay glitters, as does Baywood across to the south. Car lights east of the estuary move in a distant line along San Luis Bay Boulevard.

Frigid air seeps into the bay while he moors the boat and climbs to the dock. Something about the cold feels comforting. He likes the slight breeze, the cold moisture settling on him, in his lungs. And right now he likes the chill and isolation. This aloneness reminds how he can be a forgotten thing trapped in darkness and seawater. He thinks how a lone sea lion might feel foraging in the protective harbor of the bay. No great white sharks here. No predatory whales.

Walking across the dock, he sees something—another ghostly form, this one standing amid oyster bags. He shudders before realizing who it is. Deb should be leaving about now. Doesn't matter. If she wants to rake bags he'll pay. He knows she's desperate like Chango, trying to save money to rent an apartment in Baywood. Bernhard is sure most of his workers have roommates—probably five or more in a two-bedroom unit. No one can afford to live alone on Bernhard's shit pay. You can't really make it around here unless you're a business owner, lawyer, supervisor, manager of some kind, administrator, doctor or nurse practitioner. A simple home in Morro Bay or Baywood can easily cost a million. He knows Chango lives with his mother and brother, and she owns a salon. She's not rich and probably needs him to help pay the mortgage. But what man wants to live with his mother forever?

The rush of tidewater slips past the dim-lit dock. Salt tickles Bernhard's nostrils. He waves to Deb's dark form, calls out, "Any snails?" For a moment, he leans over the rail, admires the sound of his farm, the churn of oyster bags, seawater flushing them. He really does love the system he's set up to take advantage of nature's forces, the moon, and tidal movements. Ever since he was a boy he's felt this way, that he needed to master nature's forces. His father mastered waterways, built dams. Those obstructions destroyed diadromous spawning grounds until fish ladders were installed. Hell if Bernhard was ever going to help any bay fish. Let them gulp for air.

Oyster bags placed more than a year ago have been covered by the incoming tide. Each bag contains 120 oysters, once merely larval seeds, now mounted in areas around the dock. Each shellfish needs air, needs to squeeze its muscles, needs to be tossed and turned, agitated while the tide washes in and out. Buoys tied to their rise and fall hold them steady.

Fully grown oysters sell in bulk to seaside restaurants and markets in Las Vegas, San Francisco, Sacramento, Los Angeles, San Luis Obispo, Bakersfield, Fresno, even small towns like Delano, Arvin, and Hanford. He distributes quickly and efficiently. At harvest he has five hours to pull bags from the water and refrigerate them to prevent each oyster from sloughing into a warm mass of guts inside each shell.

What really makes him proud is the demand for his shellfish. His oysters have developed a unique flavor from the quality of estuary water, from stabilized temperatures, from phytoplankton that Morro Bay oysters feed upon. He knows this one-of-a-kind bay turns over faster than others, leading to more nutrients for each shellfish. The fresh water flow from Chorro and Los Osos creeks shifts the taste to a sweet underpalate, a green melon rind, he calls it. This year he increased his oyster farm size. When he did, some of the local fish stopped migrating into the bay. Didn't bother him. His worry has always been growth-stunted oysters rather than snails. Only a few bags have turned out smaller shells. He blames that on seed oysters bought from a hatchery in Kona, Hawaii. That won't happen again, he's told himself. He goes with a different supplier these days.

He ignores whether Deb answers or not and slips into his office, wishing he hadn't left that snail with Magaña. She'll probably publish some related paper, make sure to blame his oyster farm for attracting the damn thing to the back bay. One snail. One stupid snail. He'll deal with Magaña in his own way, in his own time. His profits will speak to that. Simple fact: He helps fuel tourism that pours money into oysters, not to mention all the taxes and permits. The entities that be? They need his money to pay their damn wages and pensions. The environmentalists can just deal with his oyster farm the way they deal with hunters shooting ducks and geese that flock to the bay every winter.

The light in his office, dim and yellow, stares downward. Always something wrong with that bulb in the dock shack. He has his tablet, a beacon now popped open to his financial notes, illuminating him like a sea-ghost, and starts writing about farm expansion. Pulls numbers from last year's profits, from multiple bank accounts, adding the new stock he wants in organics and storage. Has to feed the needs of his high-end clients. These aren't all hard numbers, just estimations, how he free-forms his dream to make more and more.

He realizes that in two years he can quadruple his oyster bed. Plenty of room in the bay to grow ten times larger. He can expand into that shoe size, sure he can. Slow growth, he tells himself. Play the long game. Speed it up if possible.

A half hour passes when the silence hits him. Closing his eyes, mind washed from thoughts of snails, he feels this moment. His heart wants to slow. The salt fog and mist now creeping in feel so fresh in his lungs. The calmness of the bay. Just the creak of wood, that lick of bay water against the boats, the dock. No seal splashes in the tidewater. No otter squeals, random gull or cormorant calls. No tern cries in the night. Everything slipping into sleep, a sleep that never usually comes because the bay never tires, never stops making noise. This rare silence feels like the kind of break he needs.

This peace lasts all of ten seconds because it finally hits him that Deb needs the floodlights or she might get stuck out on those bags. Hasn't heard her singing to herself like she sometimes does. No rake sounds either. Wonders if he's heard anything other than bags scraping against one another. He sure hasn't heard her boat leave the dock.

Bernhard grabs a broom, pokes the office light. The bulb buzzes, pops as if sound and light can mix, brightens the room. About to hit the switch for the floodlights, he sees something tiny and yellowish latched to the doorframe.

It's round. It slithers.

Just like that, all of his insides reverse course, fire into a frenzy.

"Goddam it, Deb." He plucks the spiral onto his hand, its mucous foot pools a slithery mess. Even as he rages, he feels something. Pinpricks on his palm. Not too strong. Almost an electricity, a warmth. A strange sense of connection to the creature. Palm against foot. Mucus against skin. Hunger against hunger.

He lowers his hand to the dock, rolls the shell off his palm. The snail hides its slithery eyes, seems to know what's coming.

Bernhard lowers his boot, smashes the snail into a paste.

He turns on floodlights now, exposing the topmost layer of oysters in a bright glow. He's ready to yell, to curse at Deb, at Magaña, at Jorato as if they're the Blob, the 228 sextillion joules of heat bursting from an ocean trench. He feels the burn in his insides, this tremble, this fear of what might happen, this anger that this snail he's crushed should have been found sooner, that Magaña's report should have got to him at a more convenient time.

That's when he sees her. Deb stiff in her orange bibs, covered in sea muck and gastropods, an ungodly terror in her eyes.

Creatures slither across Deb's face, into her open mouth, on her exposed hands and arms. "Move," Bernhard wills her to stop just standing there. "Get over here."

He can hear the desperation in his voice, but somehow knows she can't move, somehow knows that fear, or something else, has plastered her feet to this unknown, frozen her to the bay.

She needs to be rescued from the bags, from the snails. He's instantly aware of this. He just doesn't know if he's the one to do it.

Then he realizes it's not just her. Every exposed bag wriggles with snails. Thousands of yellow stars have crashed onto the oyster farm. If only he could have seen them creeping in their knobby, coiled shells, slipping into the bay, the result of a distant swelling, a mass proliferation beyond explanation that in its inevitable wake expanded toward the coastline, pulled to the scent of his oyster farm as if by the moon, and something else driving the snails, something in them that they're carrying, that they need to pass on.

The ochre gastropods have slithered on tiny singular yellow feet, crawling, siphons pulsing, drawing water into their gills, searching through interconnecting sea currents, and like their own ravenous tide of hunger, have found their way to the same estuary as their brethren's remains.

Thirty years into the great ocean warming, they've finally arrived to feast.

Bernhard is in disbelief that so many gastropods can take over so quickly. Something has seriously gone wrong for this kind of plague to consume so much so fast. If he'd only had that damn warning, he might have pulled every bag from the bay. An early harvest means smaller oysters, but something could have been done. Theoretically, he could have moved them all. The snail discovered earlier should have been warning enough to try something, anything.

A wash of guilt smashes Bernhard. He's failed Deb. But he's failed his oysters too. His eyes meet hers with a kind of helplessness and terror while a snail crawls out of her mouth. He doesn't know what to do. Snails shouldn't be able to do this to her. He can't even say her name. Just knows he's faced with two choices, one that means entering this area swarming with gastropods, or something else, something that can maybe save his farm.

The horror in her eyes locks on his, begs him to leap onto the bags and kick his way through that slithering mess. Adrenaline screams through his body. He knows he's her boss. He'd be happy to rescue her from a burning boat. But this.

She's not your friend, he tells himself. She's not going anywhere, wouldn't have done anything special with her life. She's undocumented, invisible. She *can* be consumed.

Even then, he twitches, pauses.

Then it really hits him. You don't have to do anything. She's not your responsibility. Not now. Not when this happens. He feels a throbbing deep in his gut, a kind of pain mixed with anger and fear.

"Goddam," he says. "Think, think."

Another option smashes him like a lead weight. *Molluscicide.* He could try saving the oysters with chemicals. Right now that alternative is waiting for him like some kind of shadow at the end of the dock. A promise. Yes, a promise to himself, his clients, his family for godsakes. Something in him doesn't want to quit them, doesn't want to give up on all of this.

In the end, Bernhard knows everything always boils down to two choices: fight one fire or fight another. His eyes peel away from Deb.

He runs into his office, opens a closet, pries open a sealed container. Packed inside, several jugs and a barrel labeled HAWLEY'S MOLLUSCICIDE B that he experimented with more than a year ago. Fish started popping to the surface that day, choking to death. He scooped them up, said nothing. Made Deb and Chango swear to secrecy. They've been really good to him keeping that one. He gave each a big Christmas bonus. Neither said a word to Magaña.

Bernhard hooks the barrel to a sprayer that dilutes the chemical with seawater and sprays the bags closest to him. He looks to Deb again. She's gone. Nothing but dark waves. No floating body. No seals or otters. No night birds. Nothing. She's slipped off the oyster bags into the tide. He feels sick but doesn't have time to worry, not about her. He's made his decision and is sticking with it, he's made the right call.

He sprays and sprays without a glance to where Deb stood. He'll douse them, he thinks, get the other jugs, douse some more, then get the hell out. That's what he'll do, he tells himself. Get the hell out, come back in the morning, report Deb missing. He'll tell the authorities she must have had an epic battle trying to save his oysters. He owes her that much. He owes her family. That's what he'll do. He owes them.

Then he realizes a sensation, a feeling of numbness where the snail mucous touched his palm. A stiffness extends into his fingers. The other snail didn't do this, he thinks, why this one? His breathing grows rapid though he figures he may be having a panic attack. He sets down the hose, lets the mixture shoot over the dock, then grabs a jug, dumps it straight into the tidewaters. He does this with two other jugs—pours chemicals straight into the bay. No dilution. Nothing. He knows it's pure insanity to dump any toxin, let alone this much, but doesn't have a choice.

He starts to feel dizzy by the time he has one jug left, the sprayer still shooting. It's time to get away, he tells himself. He'll leave this dock, get some help. Maybe he'll change his plan, tell the authorities he tried to save Deb, that she was helping fight the oysters.

His hand now feels like a lump of flesh. A dull pain shoots up his arm. He struggles to remove the last lid then moves down the dock, pours chemicals along the dinghy. Snails dislodge, fall into the sea. A sickness enters his stomach followed by a lightheadedness from inhaling chemicals. Climbing down now, he tries to grab a rung with his numb hand and falls into the boat with the jug. Toxins splash and pour. He wipes at his face and burning lips. Blisters form, parts of him turn to slick paper. At the same time he splashes more poison along the boat, killing snails. Makes his way to the motor feeling like he's on fire.

He pumps the primer bulb. When he does, a snail latches to his good hand. "Goddam it," he cries, knocking it off. He turns the throttle to the right then presses the electric start. The engine fires up. He realizes in the dim light and panic that he hasn't unmoored, grabs the jug, dumps chemicals along the rubber hull, tries to kill snails already slithering up the sides. While he fumbles to untie the boat, the shaking of its high idle kicks the engine into gear. He hasn't checked if it's completely in neutral.

The dinghy lurches forward.

When it does, Bernhard finds himself midair, boat slipping away. For the slightest second he reaches for an invisible hand along the Milky Way's spiral arm. But nothing, not even begging the universe just then, can stop his momentum.

His ass hits the side of the boat first, then his legs. He tries to grab hold, but the boat squirts from under him. He falls into the toxic, snail-filled sea.

When he comes up for air he roars and cries an empty wailing, one he knows no one will hear, one that seabirds and seals will ignore, just as their deaths have always been ignored by humans.

A slithering mass comes for Bernhard, countless snails fill the tideland waters around his arms, legs, mouth, and nose. He swims through them, mostly with one arm, reaches toward the dock ladder.

He doesn't get far. Snails have latched to his burning skin with their sticky primordial glue. He feels his body going numb, can smell chemicals in the water, on his neck, face, and hands. Though many of the creatures float dead or dying, there are too many. The dock becomes a blur by the time he reaches the ladder. He can't grab it. His good hand has gone stiff while the other hangs as if broken. Managing an elbow over a rung, he can't hold on, feels himself going, and lets out a cry, slipping back into the waves.

He loses sight while he treads water, and in this moment time slows. His thoughts jump to the creatures themselves, wonders how they propel themselves through seawater, how they could arrive in such numbers, why they didn't attack some other farm up or down the coast. Tens of thousands, possibly more, swimming, tumbling through currents, undetected. He imagines the ocean Blob, all the snails caught in its heat, his hatred for them burns.

He sees Katherine's pale cheeks in his mind, her watching from the dock, her feet lifting from boards. She hovers out over the water, above him in a white dress, eyes black as space.

She bores into him, watches him start to sink. Slowly she transforms into someone else, her ghostly grandmother who watches from hallway photos, and sometimes from atop the sea. A cold terror rises in his spine and stomach.

Snails enter Bernhard's mouth, slip down his throat. He can

no longer swallow. He can only slip beneath these waves, where pain of another consciousness burns and tears into his mind. Somehow he doesn't die though he gulps water into his lungs.

Drifting near the bottom, he feels himself transforming. Images break and fail. Two women in the deep, heads tilted near his, mouths open, gulping, eyes black pits, hair flowing in deathly spirals. He breathes the muck in and out. He sees darkness until even the women fade away. He feels alone. So alone. So cold. Until a new terror comes. Something in him. Around him. It's here in the murk.

Bernhard feels set adrift in his own skull. Facing nothing, surrounded by darkness, eyes open, seeing nothing, no light, no shape. Only the numb feeling of this murk. The cold.

In a way, this helps him. It reveals the truth. Finally. He is alone. No one to help. All his life he has run from this thing he's been born to do, to help the sea. Why didn't he listen? Is something with him now? What's that? What's here?

He's always wondered what would happen if he stopped fighting, if he just let go. He's been afraid of how far he might fall.

This is the place he's always feared. The bottom. The depths. The bay. This presence. The sea.

Chapter Four

AS AN OYSTER you wear body armor. You cannot move from the bag where you've grown. Feeding off the tide's nutrients becomes a cyclical clockwork that refreshes and grows your fleshy filters.

During a moment of darkness, when the tide washes into the bay, you feel something crawling around you, onto you. It begins tearing away your armor.

This thing isn't alone. Others crawl onto you. They secrete acid through file-like appendages, boring holes through your protection, then insert their tongues.

They begin sawing and sucking away your flesh.

They eat you alive.

Now imagine you, another you, Bernhard Vestinos, covered by the same creatures. You're not an oyster. You're human. Dozens latch to your skin with secreted glue. They don't bore into you. They don't need to. Their feet cover you in a mucous that numbs, transforms. They've done something to you that science cannot explain.

You no longer have a human consciousness. It has been replaced by primordial thoughts from something so ancient, so vast, so invisible that no one knew it was there. Thoughts filter through the collectivity of this species, their neural network. You feel them. You are them and they are you. You are no longer human. You are becoming a kind of probe.

They, the snails, this collective, takes you into the murk. They whisper to you that they've been threatened too many times. They pull you through the bay like you're on the end of a line. You breathe salt water and slime through your nose and mouth. It washes in and out of your lungs, your dead lungs. You are dead, you know this. Your breathing does not keep you alive. Your consciousness does—this transforming consciousness being replaced by this thing, this thing that wants you to know that you're becoming something else.

The natural chemicals along with the molluscicide you've dumped into the sea mottle your skin, turn your eyes into dark red orbs. You become the color of mud. Your skin a grease, a pitch that covers muscle and bone. You are a sublimation, something higher than you ever knew you could be, though also rotten and corpse-like.

Another of your kind has become something else. One previously named Deb. You have torn her eyes from sockets and head from torso to prevent that. You only need one of your kind. Her remains grow tentacles, crawl out of the bay. Somehow you're later aware when she dissolves on a bank into a sludge eaten by gulls.

You have become part of a greater thought pattern aware of its many parts. A consciousness that extends into the tidelands, outside the bay, the sea. You're a part of this ocean, this poisoned waterscape. You're the acidification. The toxic remains. The defense mechanism. Its constant death and rebirth. The thing that seeks to know.

You swim and then crawl somewhere you won't be seen. You don't want to be seen. You find your way to Pecho Road Willows, a small riparian habitat alongside a golf course where you feed on frogs and snakes because somehow, in this state, for now, you still feel the pang of hunger for meat. You hide here, lie here. You let mud suck into your lungs. You like the coolness. You like the way it drips from your nostrils and tongue like cool reptilian blood.

Through this, your brain turns to a sour slough. Cells swirl and re-form into a jellylike alien mass. Tentacles scratch beneath the surface of your skull. They push against the orbs of your eyes. You feel them squirm and move in your head, transforming you into something, you don't know what. Something that needs to wait, until . . .

Chapter Five

A MEXICAN SLANG word, *chango* translates to monkey. Hairy bastard. Hairy ape. Hairy brother. Whatever Chango's little brother Blas wants it to mean. That's who bestowed the name upon him, that little runt.

Chango has no idea where Blas heard the name. From an uncle, maybe a friend. Could be he read it scrawled on a bathroom wall, or spotted it through a telescope on the side of the moon. All he knows is that everyone calls him that now. Even his mother no longer calls him Manuel, and that's all right with him.

Chango has bigger problems with his little brother. The teen is antisocial. He has no friends to speak of, other than some stupid old ladies Chango sees him with now and then, staring into trees and bushes for birds. Stupid birds.

Except for his little brother, these birder people are old, like, *ancient*. Like, geriatric underwear old. And they dress weird. They wear hats and vests, carry binoculars and bird identification guides. They pull up their socks. They slather exposed skin with suntan lotion and bug spray. They walk slow. Their heads slide on swivels. Just to stare at trees. And bushes. And water. And the sky. At *birds*. Brown things. Yellow things. Blue things. Chonky borb things. Feathered things. Chango hates it. These people are completely *un*-dateworthy. Which has been a bad deal because Chango knows his little brother needs a girl in his life. In fact, he wants his brother to have a life. Go to the movies. Get laid. Do something with a pecker besides drilling holes into a black pepper tree like a sapsucker with a headache.

Chango slips on pants and a work shirt for the morning shift. They're doing some seeding at the oyster farm and it's all hands on deck. His mom, busy rattling around the kitchen, puts shit away after cooking up a storm. He still lives with her. And she needs help with the bills. You have to band together around here. Costs too much to rent in this tourist trap unless you have room-mates. You have to save up a lot, which he's doing, then blow your wad on a deposit. He's working on it, needs to be on his own, needs to have a pad where he can throw parties for his homies and the ladies. His mom will have to rent out his room. Blas won't like it, but whatever.

Maria's cooked chorizo and refried beans that he slops onto a plate and eats with his mouth open. He washes every bite down with coffee. He's eating his last bites when his little brother passes through in a hurry.

Chango wipes his mouth. "Hey, baby monkey."

"Shut up." Blas pauses to examine his blurry reflection in the microwave.

His sketch book is open to a drawing labeled in cursive: *Philadelphia Vireo, Pecho Road Willows, foraging near entrance with Warbling Vireos. Plump, small, short-tailed vireo first discovered by Ozziel de la Rocha yesterday. Dark and thick eyeline through to bill, yellow belly, dark grey cap and wings, pale throat, small pointy bill, rounded head, sometimes peaky. Overall cuteness factor of 9.5.* Chango quickly examines the drawing, then flips to the next page, a Red-footed Booby soaring, worn wings flapping downward, tail flared, amber eyes full of wonder. Same cursive writing. *On boat with Ozziel and Felix. Tried to sneak on whale-watching boat but had to pay. This bird flew out of the fog with a gull chasing it and circled the boat several times before chased by gulls northward. It returned maybe nine more times, sometimes flying right overhead, always with gull in pursuit. At the time it was clear the bird lacked the dark head and breast of a Brown Booby, but the overcast conditions made it difficult to see color. Pinkish bill with dark tip, blue around the eye, which has an amber (?) iris, warm brown head and chest, no white in underwing coverts. The bird showed worn outer primaries and inner secondaries, is missing/ molting in P6, and retained a couple of worn rectrices.*

Chango closes the book then eyes his little brother. "Why don't you want to be a 'Baby Chango'? You have perfect hair for it. Look at that mane. Little fucking jaguar. Little monkey."

"Do you always have to say that word?" Maria slips some plates into a cabinet.

"Right." Chango still eyes his brother. "Come on, eat something. You're all skin and bones. Any thinner and you'll slip into a coma. Eat more, you'll grow even more hair. We can be the Chango brothers."

Blas checks his phone, moves his closed sketchbook away from his brother. "Guess I can make a quick taco."

Maria kisses each son on the cheek. A little rounder than she used to be, she's still beautiful with striking brown eyes, hair curled to perfection, perfect eyebrows. "Eat something, mijo," she adds to Blas. "I have to go. Put your dishes in the sink."

"All right, all right." Blas wipes her lipstick off his cheek.

"Maybe run to the post office for me later?" she asks.

"And mail something?"

"No. Pick up," she says. "Just some letter. No big deal."

"If it's no big deal then can't you do it?"

"I asked you. Look, I have to go." She grabs her purse and keys.

Chango rubs his eyes, shoves half a taco in his mouth while their mom slips outside, shuts the door. "Ain't you late for school already?"

"No school today." Blas scoops beans onto a tortilla, takes a bite. "Gonna put in a few hours." He works at the Mexican Market on Tenth Street. They pay minimum wage but Chango knows his brother deserves what he gets. He's just a kid who pushes a broom, stocks shelves, sometimes rolls breakfast burritos on weekends.

"That's it? Real men work all day, little brother. Overtime too. What you gonna do? Work a few hours then go out with your old white girlfriends?"

"They're not my friends."

"That's funny talk right there. I see you with them all the time. I drive down Pecho Road, you're staring at someone's bird feeder together, trying to find a Rosy Buttbeak."

"Rose-breasted Grosbeak. They're rare here."

Chango pours the last remnants of coffee, adds nearly half a cup of cream. "And then I pass by the eucalyptus down the road where you're looking for Summer Wing-worms and I'm like, whoa, what the fuck."

"Summer Tanagers. They're rare here too."

"Whatever." Chango waves him off, slurps from his CHINGÓN ALL-STAR mug. "You and your old cabras. Seen you on Baywood Park Pier. Seagulls with long-ass beaks had you all in a damn trance. Goddam loco."

"Rare. Black Skimmers."

"You and them old ladies."

Blas stuffs the rest of the taco in his mouth. "We just go to the same places. They're good birds for the county."

"Who, the old ladies? They ain't rare. I see old white asses everywhere I look."

Blas still chews, swallows.

Chango points to the words on the cup then jabs a thumb in his own chest. "How many sugar mamas you got? They can't be that rare for you. But that old? You can do better, be more like your big brother. Why not that one girl you like, what's her name. Kaylee?"

"Why do you hate birds so much?"

Chango's eyes squint in laughter. "You do like her." He licks his fingers of coffee he's just sloshed. "Sounds like you're the one who hates all them little pájaros."

"You're stupid," Blas says. "And leave Kaylee alone."

"Oh really? Not as stupid as birds. Let me tell you about the ones I hate."

"Jesus." Blas makes a second taco, slops in extra beans.

"Blasphemer." Chango's eyes widen. "Don't let Mom hear you say that. What if she walks back in? Where was I? Ah, birds I hate." He storms around the table, puffs out his chest. "Gulls. I hate those beady-eyed bastards. They'll steal your taco if you're not watching. That's why you have to look them in the eye."

"Why you telling me this?" Blas says to no reply.

"Terns squawk loud as hell." Chango rubs his eyes again, like he can't wake up, can't see straight. "Don't trust them either. They'll steal the taco from the gull that stole yours. You know what else? Cormorants. Bastards always popping out of the water like little Loch Ness Monsters. Sometimes a hundred of those giraffe-necked shits eating everything and anything. I'd take a machete to all of them. Let those dumb heads wash up on the sandspit."

Blas packs a taco in foil, shoves it in his coat pocket for later. "You're just being awful because that's all you know how to be. You know that's cruel and illegal, right?"

"You know what's cruel?" Chango says. "Me working, minding my own business when five hundred little peeps come swarming—that what you call them? Those little ones with hardly any meat on their bones?"

35

Blas scoots toward the door, sketchbook under his arm. "Sanderlings. Sandpipers. Least or Western . . . sometimes a rarity . . . last year a few Baird's . . . though they're not too small. Maybe a Semipalmated . . . though I'd love to see a Little Stint."

"Yeah, those assholes. They're like goddam bats. They swarm and crap everywhere. You ever been in a sandpiper shit storm?"

Blas clicks his tongue. "Maybe don't create an oyster farm in the middle of a bird sanctuary?"

This pisses off Chango. He likes his job. He needs all the hours he can get or he'll be stuck in this town forever. And that's the last thing he wants. Goddam Baywood has been sucking his life for as long as he's been alive. "Fuck birds, baby monkey," he says, blinking. "I want to shoot about five thousand of them with a pellet gun. Big ones, small ones. Don't matter. Problem is—that would take forever and I'm a busy man." He wipes his chest of tortilla crumbs and changes the subject before Blas can sneak out the door. "Did I tell you? Big date tonight after work. Graciela Gonzales." He says her name like he's a jockey for Radio Lobo.

Blas turns and leans against the wall by the door, nearly knocks down a painting of a New Mexico mesa at dawn. Artwork of an oasis hangs next to that. A big blue hole in the desert with a kid leaping midair.

"Surprised she's seeing you more than once," Blas says.

"Best not knock that down," Chango says. "You know that's Mom's favorite. You're like her lately. Always dreaming. Doubt she's even seen New Mexico. You always want to go off on some big adventure to find birds, but you never go anywhere but the shitholes around here. What's the farthest you gone? Two miles? What's in that book anyway? Drawings of my ass?"

"Nothing. Whatever. This is a great natural area," Blas says. "I go up to San Simeon, down to Oso Flaco. That's what, thirty, forty miles? Maybe Graciela really thinks you're a loser and will cancel."

"Fifth date, cabrón. Can you count that high? Oh yeah. You can. You're a bird counter." Chango grabs the remaining tortilla, scoops in what's left of chorizo and beans. "You know, something else you need to do? Find a goddam girlfriend. Tired of you changing those cabra diapers. Call that girl."

"You done?" Blas says. "'Cause I'm going to be late."

"Boy, I'm never done." Chango takes a bite and talks with his mouth open. "Gotta get going anyway. Got the all-day-shit shift. Getting tons of hours right now. See how hard I work? I'll bring my bat and knock some pelican heads just for you." He laughs and takes another bite. "Hey, don't forget to go to the post office for Mom."

"Why can't you?"

"Damn you're thick. How can I if I'm at work? You got time before you go look at bird and cabra asses."

Chapter Six

BLAS ENRIQUEZ HAS been called a cholo, a wetback, a bird-fucker, a puto.

Right now no one is saying anything to Blas. That's because he's on a trail. No asshole in sight. Just the birds he's recorded into his eBird app. Two Spotted Towhees whining and scratching, a Golden-crowned Sparrow leaping between shrubs, ten White-throated Swifts in braided sky patterns, a Red-tailed Hawk soaring along hills, a Hutton's Vireo yapping like a broken record. He'll sketch that one later, upload the drawing to his list. His favorite drawing lately, a curious Townsend's Warbler craning its neck while foraging on a patch of grass, on the lookout for predatory Cooper's or Sharp-shinned hawks.

He's seen most of the common birds that come and go along Coon Creek trail, night birds too. Common Poorwills rising like orange-eyed demons from puddles of feathers. Curious Northern Saw-whet Owls swooping around his head, wings cold with blood. Great Horned Owls *hoo-hoo-hooing* from telephone poles. Some of these birds, like him—they don't stray far from their habitats. They hatch. They grow into adolescent birds. They fight

NICHOLAS BELARDES

to survive. If lucky, they get bigger, leave the area. If not, they're
stuck like him, perpetual teenagers in a rut.

Right now he's focused on rarities, the wayward travelers, vagrants, the ones whose brains get rewired, who find themselves
in other parts of the country, sometimes on an entirely different
continent. Usually these are the young birds, the hatch-years.
They lose their way. They wander. He spotted a Lark Bunting,
probably from Idaho, near Bitterwater Road, a long trek for Blas,
maybe eighty miles. It perched on a barbed wire fence like it
knew Blas had been on the way. Man, that bird was beautiful.
Blas had hopped a ride with Felix de la Rocha and his son Ozziel
in their dirty station wagon for that one. He'd bird with those
cabróns any day of the week. A horticulturalist, an explorer,
that elder mofo even has an Amazon rainforest plant named
after him: *Anthurium rochii*, a Red List endangered dysphagia-
inducing epiphytic subshrub in the Morona-Santiago Province,
Ecuador. It sucks nutrients in wet lower Andes tropical biomes.
The arum grows on its host, has thirty-six-centimeter-long inflorescences. Felix tells a story of riding on Amazonian roads in
the back of a flatbed atop bags of dried snake skins, carrying his
beloved discovery while his son cried in terror. Anyway, on Blas's
last adventure with Felix and Ozziel they tore down Highway
One drinking gas station coffee, sharing bird stories like they'd
survived some kind of alien invation, all for a rare White Wagtail
darting back and forth on the beach along Estero Bay. That long-
tailed bird gobbled sandflies like it didn't know which way to go.
Blas wanted to ride his scooter all the way out there but woulda
ran out of gas, even though it was a bird-hombre from Siberia.

Then there was that Common Ringed Plover. Blas didn't
want to hike four miles on a sandspit to see its big white forehead. Didn't have extra cash to rent a canoe, so he did what
any bird-obsessed ése would do, he swam across the bay from
Tidelands Park. Talk about a marathon swim. And dangerous.

Nearly drowned alongside the Lost Isle, a cocktail barge filled with drunk tourists. He swam out of the boat's path only to find himself floating amid a group of sea lions. They leapt around him like he was a watery obstacle course. He hiked over the sandspit, met up with a pack of birders, borrowed a pair of binoculars and observed the rarity in all its fluffy big-white-forehead glory.

Blas calls this technique rasquache birding. You do what you can. Swim a bay. Hop a fence. Borrow a scope. Hitch a ride. Beg for directions. Run like hell for two miles if you have to before your phone bars turn red and you lose the GPS location of where any rare bird was last seen. You do what you need to do to see a bird, even trespass. One time he snuck onto the *Endeavor*, a fifty-five-foot boat run by a guy named Alvaro based out of Half Moon Bay, who ran pelagic and land adventures around the world. The pelagic voyage ventured twenty-five miles out from Morro Rock. Blas knocked out a dozen lifebirds, including Red-footed Booby, Craveri's and Scripps's murrelets, Cassin's Auklet, Black-footed Albatross, Long-tailed Jaeger, Arctic Tern, and one of his favorites that he spotted before anyone, a South Polar Skua lumbering over the swells.

He had yelled out "Skua, skua, skua!" The entire boat joined in, booming *skua skua* too, snapping pics of those large cold-brown floppy wingbeats, flashes of white on them like bands of leucistic coloring.

But then Blas's heart sunk. Alvaro confronted him. "What the hell you doing here?" he said, pulling him aside. "What if something happened? Why would you do this? I should turn the boat around, make you pay for everything."

Blas tried to lie his way out, said Maria was supposed to have paid for his trip. Alvaro eventually said he didn't have to pay, but he had to help Wes with the chum and fish oil, and to clean up any shit and puke when birders got sick. The chum brought in several Wilson's Storm-Petrels, another lifer. Luckily no one shit anywhere but the toilet, though he did have to clean the puke of a guy who vomited milk all over the deck while a curious albatross landed next to the railing.

Blas moves like a cat on a trail that cuts between two canyon slopes. A half moon hangs in the daylight like a twisted face. Twenty feet below the path, a creek flows in a long canyon trench, hidden by the creep of nature. Dim tangles of tree and scrub morph with morning shadows, some in the shapes of birds, while horse's tail, knee-high, grows bulbous and alien. Felix has called them living fossils, says they release spores, not seeds, to reproduce. Dense poison oak lines both sides of the trail along with thorny blackberry, and though cut back along the trail, resembles the weedy reddish-green hair of a hidden giant. Blas, careful, inhales the crisp cold, scans every bit of foliage, pant legs brushing against red and green.

He hasn't seen a Rose-breasted Grosbeak, a must-have on his lifebird and current yearbird list, though he watches for one to fly out of the canopy. Males have black heads, backs, and tails, white rumps, large pink bills, and most strikingly, bleed red down their white breasts. They sit on treetops and sing like champs, squeaking and squelching. While they summer in Canada, the American Midwest, and northeastern states, they rarely come down to Baywood, or here in Montaña de Oro. Tom Wells, a twelve-year-old birdwatcher who found an ultra-rare Sharp-tailed Sandpiper near a marina boardwalk, spotted one of the grosbeaks at a Baywood bird feeder last year. Blas missed it by five minutes. The grosbeak's flight path, though swinging a bit too westward, can zoom over Baywood and Coon Creek on its way to spend winters in southern Mexico, Central America, the Caribbean, or Cuba. One thing's for sure—and Blas knows this with all his heart—birds really are world travelers. And while he's too poor to get out of San Luis Obispo County much, let alone the country, he can at least live vicariously through his winged homies, especially Rose-breasted Grosbeaks, if he can find one, maybe even a Yellow-throated Vireo like the one an old lawyer heard calling from some willows at the Doris Street marsh a few blocks from where Blas lives.

As for those human pendejos in his neighborhood, including his brother Chango, they can call Blas whatever they want. Not going to stop him from walking down the street with his binoculars trying to spy a Great-crested Flycatcher in the willows. Or a Common Tern landing amid a flock of Elegant and Forster's terns on Cuesta Inlet. No jerk is keeping him from his prize. Well, maybe Kaylee Jones could. And she's no asshole. Chango's right about one thing, he's been wanting to ask her out for months now. He just never should have told his brother.

Truth is, the berating gets to him though he tries not to freak out. He's been in a few scrapes over birds. One with Landen Canares, the construction worker hammering on the new dining area where Blas works fifteen hours a week flipping burgers and rolling burritos at the Baywood Mexican Market on Tenth Street. Landen really has it out for him.

"Hey, bird bitch," Landen called the last time Blas was about to get on his scooter, binoculars swinging from his chest. "You gonna look up your mama's skirt with those?" Blas's binoculars didn't get a scratch even though he knocked that asshole in his noggin with them. At least Landen didn't tell his boss. Probably happy with the black eye he gave Blas.

Blas can't help it. He's a fighter, hungry for a new life. Sick of all the privilege, he doesn't fit in with the Kens and Karens, who look at him like something's wrong with carrying binoculars, like some brown teenager about to graduate high school can't discover all the wonders of birds among Baywood's tree-lined streets. He swings for noses and chins like an angry chupacabra. He'll fight any vato making fun of him or his pastime, though for some reason, he doesn't know why, he holds back against those A-list birders, those super privileged A-teamers with their twenty-five-thousand-dollar cameras and lenses, who only care about their group of feather hunters, the explorers who hide the rare birds among themselves, visiting each other's private feeders and backyard fruit trees when the rare orioles, Cassin's Finches, Bell's Vireos, and once-in-a-lifetime Field Sparrows arrive, blocking out Blas, leaving him to sneak the neighborhoods, hop fences, and enter gated communities when he can get away with it. What a bunch of know-it-all gringos with their secret bird lover society: Baywood & Friends Audubon Society. Don't have the balls to stand up to their own racist club name. Every bird lover knows John James Audubon's history: slave seller, liar, brown hater, old white male dirtbag privilege, shotgun ornithology. Still that's their club name. Dumbubon, Sickubon, Fuck-u-bon. Put a slash mark through that shit.

He fumes about them constantly, just won't cross them, not completely anyway, won't join them either.

This animosity includes some of the old lady birders who have nothing better to do than wear their designer Han Solo birding vests, faces slathered in suntan lotion, fancy Nikons and Canons in hand, and shame Blas for not having a camera. So what? That's just more rasquache birding. Blas photography 101. He holds the lens of his refurbished iPhone up to his bino lens, holds steady, prays to Huitzilopochtli for non-blur, and *clickety-click* goes the shutter. A few shitty images are all the evidence he needs that he's seen a rarity. He posts them on his eBird account, then laughs at the black halo around his imperfect images of Buff-breasted Sandpipers, Tennessee Warblers, and Black-necked Stilts. He touches them all up on Instagram, doesn't care they're not high quality. That's what his perfect memory is for. He can replay bird discoveries all night long while lying in bed, *slipping* into dreams, imagining he's far away, maybe neck deep in a sea of spoonbills—though he's never seen one—everything around him pink and rosy, even the sky.

Blas loves this trail, never knows what he might find. He's a mile in when the long, slender body of an alligator lizard darts across his path. Those back scales are reinforced by bone, just like a gator, though these creatures seem more snakelike than anything. They can be nearly a foot long from snout to tail tip. Green and yellow, it has red splotches on the middle of its back. He's seen plenty of fence lizards lying on the trail, all different sizes too, but this is his first alligator lizard sighting here. Careful not to try to catch it, though he wants to, he knows they bite. Even though he can see its tail inches from the trail, he's careful not to set it into its hiss-like defensive posture. Best to take long strides and leave it in the dust.

Coon Creek Trail lies at the far southern end of Montaña de Oro, a seaside California state park just a few miles from his family's home. Drive out Pecho Road, head south, wind up hillsides for views of the sandspit, Shark Inlet, Morro Rock, and all of Baywood. Pass through the eucalyptus of Hazard Canyon, wind through coyote bush, sage, sticky monkeyflower, and lizard's tail, along hillside mountain bike trails, Valencia Peak, down past a beach and cove, parallel to a bluff trail, until you find yourself right where he is now. Just don't crash into a Wild Turkey on your way. It's a nice trek for his scooter, and either way, feels like he's in the middle of nowhere amid bobcats, deer, mountain lions, bears, and birds. Visit on a clear winter night and the Milky Way turns sharp, pours right down the wall of heaven. Meteors and satellites pass like sparklers. Owls swoop around and around, hunting rats and snakes, maybe each other. Might even find a gray fox.

He's a mile deep on the trail, by the first wooden bridge, when Ingram Evans, a retired SLO County administrative officer in a white waterproof hat too big for her head, stops behind him. She's hunting the same grosbeak sighting.

"What you seeing out here?" she asks.

"Nothing yet." His eyes narrow into beads, would never give up a bird to her. He pretends to scan a hillside of dead, burned-out tree trunks for woodpeckers. A few years ago a fire was set by State Parks to manage overgrowth. It went out of control. They torched three hills, part of the trail too. Blas hears birders say the area is lucky the hills and trail mostly returned to a natural state.

"No Rose-breasted?" she says. "Last year Nancy Lyman spotted a male singing at the trailhead."

"I know." Blas keeps his answer short. He wants her to move on, to disappear, to get her bloodshot eyes off him. She always gets up his butt about the birds he claims to have seen. That's because sometimes his iPhone bino-photo combination fails. Rasquache is what it is. She usually pontificates on the virtues of a top-of-the-line Canon point-and-shoot. Only a matter of time before she brings it up.

"I saw a Rose-breasted in Costa Rica," she says. "I thought, wow what a bird. This might be one we've seen around Baywood. Can you imagine? Birds are such explorers."

"No."

"Seriously, Blas. They travel far. You should study their migratory patterns."

"Uh huh." Blas catches Ingram eyeing his iPhone with her usual disdain.

And then she says it: "I thought you were getting a camera."

Here it comes, he thinks, the berating, the you-can't-be-a-bird-scientist-without-proper-documentation-equipment speech. Her lips look like big pieces of chalk, her cheeks slathered in sunblock. She's all khaki and lanky and tall in shorts, shirt, and vest. She's not afraid to show off her age spots and pale skin, that's for sure.

Then it hits him. This wrongness in his heart. This burning inside that she's not all bad. He kind of admires that she's so adventurous though he's annoyed by her being a know-it-all. Although retired, she does get her ass on a trail every day, logging dozens of bird species. He respects that. She's good at it too, been around the world and back. An avid explorer, Ingram's logged 878 of the world's more than ten thousand species. Or is it fourteen thousand? Twenty thousand? Blas never knows. No one does. She's been on bird safaris, practically touched a Secretary Bird, walked with Spoon-billed Sandpipers on faraway beaches. She does what *he* wants to do—go everywhere and see every bird. This is the emptiness he feels by having hardly traveled outside San Luis Obispo County. Jealousy tickles his insides, makes him light-headed, like he can see down unreachable tunnels to birds trapped in halos.

"Why you come all the way out here?" he says, ignoring her camera remark. "Don't you have some cookies to bake for your old lady bird club?"

"Good one," Ingram snorts. "You know, you keep posting rare bird sightings on eBird without images or recordings and people are going to stop believing you."

He hates when she does this. "I never asked for anyone's approval." He taps his fist to his chest. "I do this for me. Besides, I posted a pic of that Swainson's Hawk on the Forty-six." He'd hitched a ride with his cousin for that one, had to ride all the way to Bakersfield and back, smell that smog and farmland burnoff, pick up some used refrigerators to resell.

"But not the Hooded Warbler from Pecho Road Willows. A hundred years from now people are going to examine your data. You ever think about bird lovers of the future? They'll want to know what species actually lived here."

"What am I supposed to do, lie?" he says. "Say I saw nothing? No one would say anything if I hadn't gone. Give them something to talk about, think about. Besides, no eBird rule says 'camera required.' This works just fine." Blas holds up his iPhone's cracked screen, though he knows he's half lying. Fast-moving birds are sometimes too quick when fumbling with his phone camera app and bino lens. And not every bird makes noise worth recording. At least the Zeiss binoculars his cousin stole from Big 5 Sporting Goods have some fine optics.

Ingram doesn't hesitate pointing out even more: "Didn't help you with that Red-eyed Vireo sighting you claimed. Half the county's birders descended on Pecho Road. Caused quite the fuss. You might have at least recorded some bird sound."

"Damn bird was fast and mostly quiet," Blas says. "Its little feathered tail was on crack or something, probably because of those mutts. You seen those unleashed dogs running around, getting into everything. Lots of dog owners ignore those 'no offleash pets' signs posted at trailheads. Birds get pushed away, and we get made into bad guys for saying anything." He knows it's more than dogs and irresponsible pet owners. He should have recorded sound too, but didn't. He wanted a pic so bad that he didn't think to record its short robin-like notes before the dogs showed up. By the time he lost sight, even his sharp ears couldn't hear the call. Same thing happened with the rubber boa he saw on the bluff trail. He didn't get a pic, so no one believed him, not until a biologist found a clump of boa snake skin.

Ingram's white-caked lips smack together. At least she doesn't berate him for his language. "No one found your mystery bird," she says, "though I admit, there are some mysteries in those willows."

"Doesn't mean I didn't see it. Maybe *you* missed it."

Ingram shakes her head, begins wobbling down the path. She gets a few feet away, fixes her binoculars on a Wrentit, scares away a Sooty Fox Sparrow. The Wrentit's long brown tail flicks upwards while it hops from branch to branch, chattering. Ingram aims her camera, zooms, calls over her shoulder. "People are going to stop believing you if you don't invest in one of these."

He catches up to her. "You gonna buy me one?"

"Earn and save. That's how you do it." Satisfied with her shot, she lets the camera drop around her neck.

Blas watches the bird tuck itself into shadows. "Would take me ten years to save that kind of money. Gas is expensive for my rocket."

Ingram waves a hand. "You can get a Canon for a few hundred."

He barely makes enough gas money to fuel his scooter for birdventures, not to mention there's no way he'd give up his weekly bag of weed. He wants to yell but doesn't. Instead, scans the scrub for movement.

A Pacific Wren skitters along a branch, its short upturned tail a tiny dark flag from its borbulous rear end. "I don't go birding to please some sad old bastard," Blas half whispers. "Screw that."

"So much anger." Ingram snaps a pic, voice low. "Regardless of what you believe about birders around here, you've got to do a better job *birding*. You didn't even do a decent write-up of that vireo. Remember the Glaucous Gull you saw at the Elephant Seal Colony? Now that was a good write-up. Much more believable. You witnessed some interesting foraging behaviors, noted every field mark. You painted an exceptional scientific image of what you saw. Nice drawing too."

Birders are problem solvers, puzzling out every field mark. Blas knows you have to know bill shape, body shape, overall size, wing bar colorations, supercilium paleness, undertail covert colors, back patterns, leg color, eye color, eye-ring color, belly color, cheek color, wing length, tail length, foraging behaviors, the list goes on. Field marks pile up like car wrecks. Even the best birders get confused.

There'd been no second-guessing the juvenile Glaucous Gull, its bill bloody from gorging on elephant seal afterbirth. At least he hoped it wasn't some weird hybrid.

Large, white gull, he wrote in his field notes. *Likely first-winter bird. Flesh-colored bill at base. Last half of bill, dark. Faint brown mottling on back/face. Some spots might be blood splatter. Pink legs. Dark eye. Bird flew in just after seal gave birth. Viewed from southern end of boardwalk at Point Piedras Blancas Elephant Seal Colony off Highway One. Other dead baby seals crushed by males lying like blobs of flesh.*

He really likes that last note about blobs of flesh even though it says nothing about the bird. He noted as much in his field journal in all caps under his sketch, which he doesn't mention to Ingram because she's not interested in drawings but rather hard evidence. *Photos or sound recordings,* she always says. He hates standing around making sound recordings unless that's literally all he can get to prove a bird's existence. And not every bird makes noise. Though not a purist, he'll play bird calls from his phone, especially to entice warblers to come out to play, or to sing or chip call. Bushtit flock playbacks, which he refers to as *party playbacks,* are his favorite to get mixed flocks to come his way, their dry chips a sweet sparkling chatter. Not only do Bushtits come swirling and diving, their tiny borbulous grey-brown bodies like sweet puffs with wings, but can bring Wilson's, Townsend's, Black-throated Gray, and Orange-crowned warblers, and if lucky, rarities in fall months like Chestnut-sided, Blackpoll, maybe even a Magnolia; all love to mingle with Bushtits in mixed flocks. He sometimes hears the same silly chattery calls in video games as background texture for woodland and even jungle scenes, which makes him laugh.

Then he remembers something. He hadn't been alone when he'd seen that warbler in Baywood's swampy willows. He tells Ingram as much. "Kumi was in Pecho Road Willows when I saw the Hooded Warbler. She saw it."

"Kumi doesn't even post her findings. And she doesn't always carry binoculars."

Blas grunts. A male Wilson's Warbler darts onto an exposed limb like a drop of gold with a black cap. He eyes it just as he's about to say more about Kumi Sato. He likes that old Japanese woman. Something about her feels more real than these other birders, like she really knows nature. She's in touch with the connections between birds and people. Pendejas like Ingram all want to own birds, make them their little trophies, like trading cards bought and opened in little foil packets. Throw the common ones out. Find all the rarities. People like her compete for the biggest lists, the greatest treasures. You got a Bay-breasted Warbler? That's okay, I got an Emperor Goose and a Northern Waterthrush. Blas loves those, but he loves all birds, even House Sparrows. He calls the sparrow family on his street the Baywood Bombers. Often just the Bombz.

Kumi Sato, Blas knows, experiences nature in her own unique way. She's a part of it. And while she doesn't tell Blas what to do, she does impart wisdom, like when she showed him a row of teasel, pointed to the spiked ends of stalks, showed him how the brown, pointed bulbs could comb, or tease, cotton. Then told him the genus name *Dipsacus* comes from *dipsa*, the Greek word for thirst, which refers to the formation of a cup at the stem. He likes that. Ozziel's dad is similar in his expertise with plants, but Kumi takes knowledge and wonder to another level. Interacting, speaking, listening, as if something spiritual lies just outside of every stem, or *within*, something he might see and hear, something that he's only beginning to experience in her voice, her eyes, her curiousity, in all of nature. He wants this. He's learning, he tells himself, though he also wishes he had a plant named after him the way Felix does. That's also why he doesn't hang with Ingram and the others at their potlucks and bird festivals. He'd rather track down Kumi, feel what she feels, though he can't ever truly explain it, not to any other birders. He's about to mention Kumi again when he gets a series of texts from Chango about something that happened at the Sand Spit Oyster Co. Chango's texts hang on Blas like morning fog.

>>Dead shit everywhere at the oyster farm.
Blas: What?
>>Like, gone. All the oysters. Deb. Boss. Both missing.
Blas: WTF. Missing? Where?
>>How would I know? Found his boat in the bay outside Pecho.
Blas: Holy shit. Did you tell Mom?
>>Cops wanna talk to me. Fuck. Have to find a new job. L8TR.

Chapter Seven

I STRETCH MY senses into this swampy ether, listening, eyes searching the canopy.

Sound amplifies in the willows. A warbler's metallic *chip*. A Song Sparrow *whine*. And something else. Raspy breathing. A momentary intake of breath. An exhalation that vibrates through woods, across mud and bent root.

Is it my *imagination*?

Or is it the unknown of this place? This other world.

My hearing isn't what it used to be. I'm seventy-five and falling apart. My body, not my womanhood, nor my Japanese Americanness. Hearing. Sight. Both slipping. Aching joints. My attention span. I'm starting to lose focus. That sharpness I once had when spying flowers along creeks when a young woman, when I could peel apart every bloom, know every fold, every insect egg caught between petals, glistening and moist with hidden antenna, developing legs and wings.

My want for aloneness, for discovery, for experiencing nature, has transformed, has blossomed, has peaked. All the time I wonder: When I was forty, fifty, or even sixty I wasn't this way. I didn't truly know what was in the trees. Had I ever cared? I'd lost touch with the way my grandfather used to sing to cherry blossoms. I can still remember how he used to take us on picnics. "Kumi. Let's go. We'll be late for the dawn petals," he'd say. I'd forgotten how to say hanami the way he did when I was a young girl. I strain. I can hear him whispering. Never me. Never in my own voice though now I sing when cherry trees are in full bloom. I run my hands along them, though right now I'm touching only bark and branch.

Grandma died before I was born. Grandfather said she was in the blossoms. He'd sing all day to the flowers. To her. He'd bring a lantern. He'd shine it on the pink cathedral of blooms late into the evening. I remember the striking pinks and mauves, like the cheeks of children. I remember fond moments, even while moving through this dark swamp.

A fragile shadow of a bird passes. Greenish smudge among leaves. Faint eye-ring. The blur passes and I miss any other field marks and remain standing on tangled willow roots and mud-compacted leaves. I want to tell my young friend Blas, but he isn't here today. I never know where he is. We walk together always by chance.

I want to see the bird again.

A rustle. A flicking leaf. Shaking twig. Anything. A call. A whine.

A Song Sparrow hops from reeds to my right. Dances along a muddy stretch of water then disappears. I hope for a vagrant Northern Waterthrush to slink out of the reeds. I want the rare glimpse, that metallic chip call to ring in my ears. Perhaps I'll spot one through low branches, near a puddle where other birds bathe. If I stay long enough, the noctambulation of other creatures.

There's the sound again. That rasping. Two breaths from the reeds that border the willows. I strain my eyes but see nothing. Just water and reeds—the darkness in them.

I gaze again at the puddle.

A vision comes. At first I think a face. Yes. A friendliness to the roundness of the cheeks. Almost a familiarity. The neoteny of a wild, childlike smile, perhaps in a root, perhaps in a creature.

Below the head, bones. Bones radiating like fans. Wing structures. A child constructed from bird bones. A bird-infant, rasping, hovering in front of me with slow, shaky breaths while lungs develop, while meat and skin enclose this being. This new-born rising from the muck. A humanlike thing so fragile she could float into the sky. Her tiny organs now hidden in her chest. Blood pumping cold. Feathers made to resemble skin grow along her torso, hips, a skirt hiding the truth like an owl's feather dress draped over a fragile body and long legs. That tiny girth—truth beneath the mystery. She's mid-puddle. She can't fly though she rises. She looks like me, the same angular shape to the face. The long chin, warm skin. Eyes on me before she falls apart. Bones snap like a tower destroyed from the inside. Meat and skin and lungs collapse. Fills puddle rings with the soup of herself. Organs float. Feathers and bones tangle and sink. Eyes slip from her head, a head that expands, floats apart, like a marshmallow melting hot around the edges, disintegrating.

The vision fades.

I am breathing her breath.

I search greenish bits of sky between branches. Nothing far above though I hear sounds from the distant bay. Curlews and godwits cry to each other.

In this tangle, the child-bird image now gone, birds come in waves. Wings spread, glide between branches and leaves. Quiet birds slip through the swamp without a sound, without a song, whine, or chatter.

I spot movement. Their greeting is movement. A flick of a black eye on me. Side-eye curious at my existence, at the *pshhhh* I make. My own call like a wren's whisper.

I block thoughts, instead listen for passerine sounds, movement.

My heart races at the chip of a warbler, that I might find some rare beauty in the canopy.

Not rare at all. A Townsend's Warbler. Female with an olive and yellow mask, yellow breast and throat, green back with a hint of black stripes, double white wing bars, streaky flanks, white belly, hints of yellow or olive on the sides of her under-wing coverts. She continues through, flits along a trunk to the water's edge, adjusts her wings.

I'm still. Shallow breaths.

The bird sees something, her fluff ruffles as if nervous energy has gotten hold of her tiny form. I try to see what she sees. Step around a branch, try not to hit my head on another.

There it is. A ball. A clump on a distant trunk where the willow splits into a thick branch. Spiral patterns cover the individual shells in this shadow the Townsend's sees. The bird flies across the puddle, lands above them and then goes still. This never happens with these fidgety birds. She's caught in some kind of spell. A *bird spell*. A shadow spell. A snail spell. The bird goes rigid and the canopy once again falls silent. Even the bay outside the willows and reeds slip into a dullness. This clump of spirals. The bird. The spell. She's unmoving. Is she dead?

Shadows enter from my left.

I listen for the rasping, for the bird-infant. That was to my right.

A raccoon hurries past. Another follows on the tail of the first, its profile a furry mask of grey and black.

The third raccoon works its way to the puddle. I'm a tree to this creature. My breath, shallow as I can make it. The raccoon is about to dip a paw into the water when its head rises. I think it sees me. Maybe hears my breath. Maybe smells me in this musty place, this muddy grave of childlike visions.

The raccoon turns toward the bird, to the clump of spirals,

like giant patterned fish eggs clinging around this branch. Eggs, I think, forgetting about snails. Not eggs but shoulderbands. Endangered Morro shoulderbands. They should be in the mulch, living and breeding in the mulch. Not on tree branches.

The raccoon eyes the bird and the clump of snails.

The bird doesn't flinch.

The rasping again. So close. So distant. Barely audible.

Is something here? Is something with us?

Three desperate creatures in the swamp willows, all staring. None of us move. Only thoughts. What are we thinking?

Bird thoughts like tiny pulses of energy.

Raccoon thoughts, instinct layered on instinct, though here, something else. A desperation that makes fur rise the way the Townsend's wings might rustle. The raccoon seems to puff like the child-bird vision in the puddle. I think this creature might explode.

I make the first move, but my foot slips from the log I'm balanced on. Slams the muck. In that instant the bird is gone. A dart into the foliage. The raccoon scampers toward its family in the reeds. The rasping is no more.

I'm pulled toward this strange clump of snails. Me and these shadows. Hard to tear myself away. The way eyes won't peel from beauty. The uncomfortable beauty in things. But I know I must go, so drift from the muck, from the rasping, from the spirals. I move onto the trail and slowly wander through darkness.

Chapter Eight

BERNHARD STANDS IN the swamp, in the reeds, a cold thing. Lifeless except for the swirling of matter that was once his brain, that still has thought, if you can call it that. It's not human thinking.

Something has formed inside what Bernhard once was. His name, rendered meaningless, has become a marker. Like a number. A thing in a series. One that will be used until this casing breaks and disappears. Until a new form is required.

Bernhard, still somehow there, only a flicker of consciousness, knows what is happening, what has been unleashed here in the woods, in Baywood, in its inhabitants. He knows about the probe, about the connection it wants, how it tries to see, to discover, how it hates.

Yet it is mostly something else prone in the reeds, listening, mostly not Bernhard. Rasping lungs broken and swollen. And that form nearby. Wrinkled. Young compared to it. It senses her and sinks into the muck.

It, he, they feel the cold and slime, wonders why it hasn't inhabited a being like this before, why it was content to be buried so deep in the ocean. There's enough sensation here to make them curious, wondering what else they should touch before these nerve endings are no longer operable. It's been so long, it thinks, so very long since they've felt this kind of firmament. Since grasping anything like a moist tree root.

It senses itself as the transference, though not all of it, conveying information, and what some might call an infection of behavioral modifiers, to all life they touch. It relays impulses, thoughts, new memories back into the sea. This entity, this casing, a transmitter, among so many other things, a vector engine, a trillion wriggling seaborne brains, an unexplainable neural network, a gelatinous mind connecting all.

Not a single catalyst exists for what's about to grasp hold of the people outside these woods. It started with Earth's animalia long ago. Some sea creature evolved. An eel. A shark. A coral. A sea snail. Or something more primordial, a microbe or a lowly single cell altered, a host of them in the sea after colliding with the alien that is now partially Bernhard, a probe, and the alien that is . . .

Something else too. Something that Bernhard uses. Another entity. The thing brought on his ship when it wasn't Bernhard, when it was someone else. There was a ship, he, *they*, traveled through space. They have memories of this. Broken, dreamlike memories drifting through neural nodes that now only contain fragments of who Bernhard was, who they might be as the Bernhard probe. Patterns of memories. Vague shadows. They play through the network and now through him. He remembers something happened. Time split, then manipulated the organism that he was. An interstellar, exploratory ship hurtling toward this watery planet, and also toward another. Simultaneously. Time split after the propulsion rupture. Two realities created. It had experienced both at once. Both ships hurtling. Both ships the same. Both ships crashing. One in sea. One on land. Both Bernhards, really something else not Bernhard at all, something with another name, someone else, screaming, frightened. Perhaps it escaped from that ship after the crash. This is what it wonders, Bernhard wonders, they wonder, who it was, what *it* was, *they* were, though it is here, is him, with him. That *it* had already been on board. Perhaps *it* had clung to the hull. Something alive but dormant while the ship hovered then dipped its belly into this world's oceans and sank. Or on that other world, skimmed across a surface, breaking upon rocks along the edge of a blood-red sea, where it was free to roam, to manipulate, transform. Bernhard uses its transformation, though not Bernhard, the It-Bernhard. Perhaps those on board with him, here in the water, before the ship completely sank, were drowning. Perhaps they opened their doors, allowed *it* to escape, if it was inside, while they hoped to reach the surface of a boiling sea. Perhaps it was *they* themselves so long ago melting into seawater, forever changing something in the deep. And then it found them submerged. Perhaps then it became the depths of this planet and the depths became him, them.

The traveler, or stowaway, whatever this thing with him/them, slipped away, floated, pulsed, evolved within whomever was left from the ship. Its thought became one with him/them, then with this place, mutating itself, sea creatures, creating new species, blending sea-forms with other ocean life-forms, all within the blink of an eye, within countless millennia.

And so the traveler that Bernhard wasn't, *was*, evolved.

It never wished it were dead despite all of this. It felt pride, power, becoming a caretaker of this place. A traveler never to return home, never to think of his quadrant of space, its galaxial arm, only this speck of blue lodged among other planets and stars, all while it and this stowaway became part of the sea that mankind would eventually start to bleach, harvest, fill with trash, plastics, nuclear wastewater, oil, and toxins. Man would ruin much of what they and life here helped create. It still wonders if man came from this life, or from before he/they arrived. At the same time it realizes some of his recent plan has backfired. It reaches into what's left of Bernhard, fuses itself to memory, becomes Bernhard, no longer It-Bernhard. But it doesn't understand why it caused harm, did it cause harm to the oceans? No, but its actions may have. Those chemicals dumped in the bay by this humanoid's own hands have caused a great deal of harm. He, they, it, *no*, he, they and it are *he*, has been saddened by this. He senses how interlinked humanity is to its own demise, that even if he tries to control them, something disastrous could happen to the ocean. He decides he must work swiftly, that though he must learn all he can, he also must continue to push ahead with his plan, before all is lost.

Bernhard drifts back to his reality, to his fury, to what he means to do, hell-bent on bending the will of this planet, to transform rituals, culture, ways of life. This is not an infection like any you know. This is something so alien, so intricate, so vast, that it will break society, and eventually, bend humanity until it turns on itself and begins to once again worship both stars and sea, and in the end, fade into them, with them.

Something warned you he would come.

Like wormwood. An ancestral signal, a fallen star. Bitterness entombed. A star that would burn a hole in this planet's deep shelves, bury itself in the sea for countless generations until finally unleashed.

It's already in you. And it will spread. You know this. Your world will never be the same. An Unexplainable terror begins slowly unraveling around you.

The deading is here.

Even the tiny birds will lie still, as if dying has become a greeting, and mourning is a welcome.

Chapter Nine

INGRAM CLOMPS ON a section of exposed serpentine, careful not to twist her ankle on a jagged edge of mottled green mineral. Arthritis slows her down, wracks every step. No way she can walk six miles today. Maybe three. She can manage that.

Far overhead, eleven swifts dart through the thermals. She logs them, counts the precise number. No guesses unless she absolutely has to, like when she sees a flock of hundreds of sandpipers. She counts the birds again. They're hard to track the way they quickly weave in and out of each other's paths. Finally she writes them down, will log them into her computer later. Can't tell which species, it's so high, and the angle of the sun blinding. She'll have to list them as generic *swift sp.*

Alongside the creek, tangles of willows hide birdsong: whining Song Sparrows, chattering Wrentits, Spotted Towhees growling their descending *grreeeeeeer*. On the hillside, shrubs cover a steep slope to a ridgeline above empty swallow nests and bat caves.

Just above the path to her right, two Wilson's Warblers hang upside down from branches making *chchchchchchch* and dry *jimp* sounds. She logs them—the fourth and fifth males of the day in their cute black caps, those spindly orange tarsi. Not what she's hoping to find though she loves their brightness, their calls.

She exhales, feeling deflated she again hasn't seen that grosbeak. "They're out here. I know they are." She stuffs pen and paper in a vest pocket and eyes her out-of-breath companion coming up the trail.

Victor Martin, semiretired biologist, short, every edge some kind of scruff, wheezes, red-faced, blood vessels near to bursting. His exhaustion doesn't stop him from calling to birds *pshh pshh pshh* like a bellow trying to stoke a forge, hoping curious warblers will pop their heads out of the brush.

"Thought you weren't going to make it," Ingram says, a hint of disappointment after he quiets. They often take the same car but not today. She isn't sure he's listening, both becoming distracted by startled birds alongside the trail. She quickly fixes her binoculars on tufts of brown feathers. One bird, then another.

"Song Sparrow. House Wren, Bewick's Wren, Lesser Goldfinch, Rufous-crowned Sparrow calling from the hillside," she lists. She thinks she might have heard the echo of a Canyon Wren but second guesses herself, chalks it up to her imagination making up bird sounds she wants to hear.

Victor groans his displeasure. Like her, she knows he wants a rare bird, maybe even a Dusky Flycatcher. Blas probably did too, she thinks, though he scurried off, claiming he heard a possible rare warbler in the opposite direction. Pulling her leg for sure. She'd consider buying the kid a camera but he's just so unfriendly. Until he learns some manners she can't see helping other than giving him advice on how to look up birds when he thinks he sees a rarity. Either way, he sure left in a hurry. "You see Blas on the trail?" she asks.

"Ran past like he was late for his own funeral." Victor, half out of breath *pshh*s again like a strange featherless bird.

Ingram clicks her tongue, scans the woods. Dense foliage

borders their narrow path. Sometimes the ticks are so thick you have to check yourself every twenty yards. She had one last year, a dark mass embedded in the soft flesh of her thigh. She ran to the bathroom, tried pulling the body with tweezers. Its abdomen ripped from its head, so she drove to the hospital, thigh throbbing. A doctor cut out the remains, warned her about Lyme disease rings possibly showing up around the wound. Still feels like something's in there, itching, eating at her.

Victor continues *pssh*ing. Wrentits scream back, louder than anything in these woods, even the owls that screech from dead branches at night. She's seen two Wrentits so far, heard at least three others. Their calls accelerate, telling you to hurry. *Pwip pwip pwiprprprpr!*

For a moment, Ingram registers the *towl towl* portion of a booming Canyon Wren. Wasn't her imagination after all. She eyes Victor, his gritty beard, his thick, dirty hands, forehead shadowy from wiping sweat. He stops to dig at a pile of whitish, hair-covered scat in the middle of the trail. He sniffs piss in the soil.

"Cat," he says.

Ingram loves when he gets dirty, when he touches the earth like he's testing the scent of his own skin, as if about to reveal things about himself she's always wanted to know. She needs to see him do this. Needs him close. She never really tells him, though she wants to, that she loves when he examines, peels apart mysteries for her like dissecting a fish.

She appreciates that every single day, without fail, they birdwatch together. Sometimes they plan the night before. Other times she receives a text or email. She likes impromptu travels to Point Sierra Nevada, Morro Creek Mouth, Turri Road or Cerro Alto Campground. They travel long distances to bird festivals, to explorations in southern Arizona canyons for Elegant Trogons, Resplendent Quetzals, and Broad-billed Hummingbirds. Even a Lucifer Hummingbird on their last trip. That long, curved bill, flaring purple throat, and white breast, that dusky-green forked tail. It practically sat on the end of Victor's long lens.

Always, they get separate rooms. Always, she wishes for something to fulfill her yearnings when they eat lunch and dinner together, then have a drink, or simply fall deep in conversation. Then, such a curt goodnight, as if the expectation is always there for another day, then another and another. They do just about everything two people in love should do, though she wonders, as she does every day, if their love only extends to feeling this constant excitement of discovery. That brightness in his eyes. Flashes of cosmos, of starlight. Something holy and bewildering because together they've witnessed nature unfold: waxwings swarming a mysterious spot on the ground like ants, a rare Orchard Oriole sucking nectar from aloe, a Red-footed Booby circling the *Endeavor* while searching for whales and birds, then diving like a harpoon into the sea. She misses those pelagic trips, though that boy caused such a stir on one of their last trips out of Morro Bay. Alvaro was far too kind to Blas, though she won't mention it to the teen. Victor, a spotter on the boat, had whispered they should toss him overboard for chum.

Victor had been married years ago to a teacher. Ingram to a pharmacist. They never talk about it. How his wife walked out. How her husband died on the 101 Freeway. They just talk birds. Birds this. Birds that. Always, one will ask what birds to chase the next day. They plot. They plan. They chase, they search. They constantly share what they've seen even though they've observed many birds on their county and life lists together. Each shares a perspective, an experience. She listens to his stories more than he does hers. Most of all, they wander trails, enjoying the fact, she's certain, that neither could ever truly be alone. She hates this feeling. Never likes to wake up and know she has no one to talk to unless she goes birding with Victor or arranges a lunch date with one of her quilt-maker friends. Those ladies don't want to talk birds. Not unless you're stitching one on a quilt, and even then, it's always a bluebird or crow. That's why she invited Victor to join her five years ago. She doesn't have to ask anymore, rarely has to call the quilters. Now they simply take turns choosing what to chase, what trail to explore, what bird to find. Today's Rose-breasted Grosbeak becomes tomorrow's Ruddy Turnstone becomes the next day's Chipping Sparrow.

He touched her once. She liked that. They'd gotten close observing an Oak Titmouse climbing a sycamore with a peanut. Laughing, their shoulders touched. An electricity rose through her abdomen in a wave of warm blue light. She wanted him to kiss her. He didn't. But the way his hands then touched her. As if he might hold her for once. As if he wanted permission. The closeness of his breath now. She can smell bourbon. She loves that medicinal intoxication. The alcohol is so woody—she wants to taste it on his tongue. She tells herself she'll give him permission if they ever stand that close again. She'd give that to him now. If she could just tell him.

Something about this moment makes her want to tell him to kiss her right now. To stop all that bird-calling and just hold her. She needs him. She needs to be wanted. She needs to forget the pain in her foot and the reminders that she goes to bed alone.

He's far from the scat now, wheezing and hissing, flushing out birds. Some scatter. Some peek. She follows, hurrying, ignoring the scrub where she saw a rustle nearly a minute ago, now feeling that burning inside to say something, to tell Victor that she needs to be closer, even if only a hug. She rushes, fast as her sore foot will take her.

He pauses and she nearly runs into him, panting. "I've been meaning to tell you, Victor," she starts to say. She catches her breath, reaches to touch his shoulder. Just the action alone makes her insides squirm the way she hasn't since that time with the titmouse. The feeling overwhelming her senses. Her face flushes.

She stops her hand. She can't. She mutters: "It's about that . . . remember the titmouse?"

Victor has always been brash. A grizzly, pudgy bear who doesn't like interruptions. "*Interruptus*," he sometimes says, adds, "Do you know it means a breaking apart?" She knows this. She's the same. This is why she can't feel his sting when he hushes her. His fingers, thick-knuckled and wide, hold up binoculars. He examines the lower portions of willows along the creek. She sucks in air. If there's one commonality between them, it's that the prize comes first, though goddam if she can't be his prize this once.

"Victor . . ."

"There," he whispers, lowers his binoculars.

She peers into the trees too.

"Something," he says. "Something big."

She tries to make light of it by flirting, by feigning a false sense of security over her invaded space. "You're nearly touching me." Her heart races. Throbs and pulses fill her entire body.

Victor ignores her forwardness, moves along the trail, watches for signs of movement. He peers downslope, along the creek. She follows, watching.

Both hear a crash in the willows to their right. They stop in their tracks.

Victor steps along a wall of foliage, strains to see more movement.

Her excitement for a possible moment between the two ebbs. In its place, fear. Coldness. A feeling that the vegetation itself is closing in, vines wrapping ankles and necks. She tries to shake this claustrophobia, the choking. She focuses on her next breath, then on the movement and noise, and what it means. She calculates as if tracking a bird, though this is no small passerine, something large, wild. If it isn't curious, it could be hunting them. She figures the crash of whatever lurks in there has angled toward the path the way some birds curiously aim for an opening, for the trail itself. This strikes her as strange. It should be flanking, slipping behind. Her nerves seem to rattle. She groans. This terror, this moment feels like slow motion.

Peering around Victor, an ochre shadow appears between twists of branches. Fur, yellowish and thick. An eye, large like an owl. A big cat. A game cat that shouldn't be so close, especially this time of day. Silent, not even growling, just stalking.

A shiver runs along her skin. Hairs on her arms and neck rise.

Victor on a collision course with the beast.

"Stop." She grabs him by the shoulder.

Before Ingram realizes, a female mountain lion slips from the brush. The cat takes up the entire path, tail swishing, teats full of milk, eyes like yellow suns.

Ingram expects her to pounce, to rip at Victor. Not knowing what to do, Ingram puts her hands on the sides of his shoulders. This is all she can do, frozen in fear, hands shaking with adrenaline. She whimpers, but doesn't cry.

The lion snarls, paces back and forth as if to block their forward path.

"Don't run." Victor takes a step back, almost knocks Ingram down. "Just back up slow. She can have this trail." He talks to the cat, loud, with authority. "You can have this. It's yours. Okay? It's yours."

The mountain lion growls, swipes a paw at the earth. Her bared teeth and claws could sever a windpipe. Ingram knows this, can see this.

"Oh my god, Victor." She shuffles backwards, knees shaking, still holding on, trying not to turn and run.

"Just do what I do." Victor takes a large step back, then another. "And don't crouch. She'll think we're prey."

"She doesn't already?" Ingram can hardly keep pace. Her long legs don't want to walk backwards like this, not when she's so afraid.

"You see," he continues, as if talking to the lion. "This is her canyon. And we're going to leave. Slowly. Keep stepping backwards. You're doing fine."

The cat isn't pouncing. This is a relief, and terrifies Ingram at the same time. The reality that she might die transforms into a fear she can't put into rational thought, tears her from the inside out. There can be no fight, just slow-motion flight. Only fear and this rhythm of shaking, these slow steps. Time slips into a sluggish loop of terror. Every step, the delayed moment of the attack.

"That's right," Victor says to the cat. "Your canyon. Yours."

Ingram, backing up, still holds Victor, still has an eye on the beast. She fears teeth and claws sinking into skin and vein. She hasn't been this terrified since the wreck took her husband, since jagged metal teeth ripped and tore his flesh, pouring his life onto the freeway. She always imagined a monster took him and doesn't want to die the same way. Doesn't want teeth in her flesh, or to lose Victor to such violence. She just wants to go home, with him, away from this danger, away from what she knows will come any moment to drag them into the tangles, down toward the creek.

This awfulness plays out in her mind. When it does, something happens. Not to her, or Victor. It's the cat. The beast stops pacing, then convulses. It stands there, shaking. Staring and shaking like something has a hold of its insides.

The cat's legs give out, collapses on the trail.

Victor doesn't seem to know what to do. He stops too. "Goddam, she just fell in front of us," he says.

He starts to move toward the animal.

"Don't go near her." Ingram can feel him quiver. Or maybe it's her.

The cat's fur seems thick and silky. Head like a massive rock. Paws like deadly weapons from a horror movie. You could fit a small dog in those jaws.

The lion's mouth hangs open. Pink tongue. Yellow-white fangs exposed. Legs at odd angles. She's stopped moving. Stopped twitching.

"Did someone shoot her?" Ingram asks. "A crossbow maybe? I didn't hear a gun."

Victor pulls away from Ingram. "Me either."

"Be careful," she says. "Might still be alive."

"That cat's dead," he says. He closes in to examine the sprawled beast.

Ingram steps a little closer too.

"Crazy thing . . ." he says.

"What?"

"No blood."

"What could have killed her?" Ingram gazes at the cat's fur, at its muscled body, at the beauty of her open eyes. Each glows like spun glass.

Ingram doesn't say it, but this feels better than any bird sighting. No matter how tragic, she wouldn't trade a single American Redstart or Magnolia Warbler for this kind of encounter.

She reaches out to stroke the cat's fur.

Victor grabs her hand.

"Hold on," he says.

"What? She's dead. Said so yourself."

Victor stands up, pulls Ingram with him. "I'm wrong. She's playing dead."

"Not dead?"

Ingram, confused, feels her heart leap. Victor pulls her another step back.

At that moment the lion leaps to her feet and faces the two.

Ingram feels every inch of her own innards rise into her chest. Her heart rocks in the same cavity, ready to burst. She hides behind Victor, wishing the lion away. Praying that it will just leave.

Victor starts making bird sounds. *Psssh pssshh pssshhh*. He waves his arms. *Psssh psssshhh*. *Phwee phwee!*

The cat continues to stare.

"Well go on then." Victor continues waving. "You're done here. Go on."

The lion watches Victor's hands. Then, as if hearing a distant call, turns an eye to the willows. After a heartbeat, she slinks away, slips into the tangles, disappears with a final flick of her tail.

Ingram refuses to let Victor go. Head buried in his shoulder, she exhales as if she's been holding everything in all this time. Still, she can't tell him how she feels, how much she loves him, not now.

Chapter Ten

FLASHING LIGHTS REFLECT like spaceships through the Pecho Road mist.

Blas walks down the narrow street onto a path just west of the lights looking for his brother. He's already checked around their little house. And Chango stopped answering texts. At the end of the road Blas reaches a sand lot bordered by eucalyptus, one of them fallen. Past that, a northern facing bayside beach where surf rolls against sand and mud-banks. Nearby rescue crews fight knee-deep through swampy vegetation. He wonders what they might find amid flooded inner channels, pickleweed, reeds, willows and blown-out logs.

He can't get far so turns back to the road, listens for bird sound in the eucalyptus and willows while making his way to an entrance. Mostly Bushtits and warblers here, but at the trailhead, a string of birdsong makes him wonder what mysteries might be hidden beneath their collective chatter and melodies.

He glimpses Kumi Sato deep in the tangles. She moves as if stepping over something. A log maybe. His instinct kicks in instantly. He needs to get to her, see if she's seen his brother, maybe any rare birds. Funny how he can think about birds when a body might have washed into nearby vegetation. She disappears around a corner.

Between them, birdsong echoes a symphony.

Blas peels each bird call and note as if turning pages with ease, identifying chickadee, crow, titmouse, scrub-jay, Song Sparrow, Lincoln's Sparrow, House Wren, even a rare Yellow-breasted Chat singing its outer-spacey tune.

He enters this semidarkness, can feel the heaviness, the pull, almost like gravity. The birdsong, he now realizes, more frantic than usual, maybe already was. More voices. It's a warning. It throws him off his game. Another flock of tiny grey Bushtits with their tinkling alert calls descends like rain. Then he feels something he can't reason away. A fear. A blackness. Nothing about the woods has never scared him until now. For a surreal fraction of a second he's not certain of his reality. He stares between dense branches. They tempt him to slip farther inside. His eyes follow a leafy artery down into the swamp. He knows this area's darkest parts, has skulked inside countless times, seen its many animals, even a pair of underwear hanging from a tree, held by a fake skeleton hand. Snakes, deer, raccoons, weasels, owls. And naturalists searching for rarities, some like snakes on their bellies, crawling for a peek of a Virginia Rail. Even other teens smoking pot, hiding amid tangles. But nothing like this. Never this feeling. He senses something, a shadow slipping into a deep blackened puddle, submerging itself until the water and mud above it turns calm and dark.

Whatever he's felt must be large, fluid, moving as if it belongs here. Blas strains to see into the darkness when hairs turns brittle on the back of his neck.

A breath in his ear: "What are you doing here, idiot?"

Chango's eyes, dim and reddened, stare. Blas assumes from staying up all night, from getting hopped up on something. His skin seems pale, feverish.

"What you see in here, little brother?" Chango asks. "A sasquatch bird?"

"Nothing," Blas says.

Chango's eyes bulge toward the dark swamp. "One of your girlfriends in here too? Thought I saw that old Japanese gal. You two? You know . . ."

"Why are you so sick?" Blas glances into the swamp. Nothing moves. "Did they find anything besides the boat?"

Chango turns half serious. "Just dead things in the bay."

"What the hell happened?"

"I was boating to the dock when Harbor Patrol stopped me. Shit was all weird. Smelled like chemicals. Dead fish and snails everywhere. Floating on the surface like something exploded in the water. Half a dozen seals belly-up. Your stupid cormorants and gulls all dead in the water. Deb wasn't around though I could see her boat at the dock. Got some hazmat cleanup crews out there. They fucking scrubbed me even though I didn't make it to the dock. Said it was in case I touched chemicals. Now my balls hurt. Pendejo had some strong shit out there. Dumped it all in the bay and now they say everything's gonna be fucked up. All your precious birds and shit getting fucked."

This hits Blas hard. Last thing he wants to hear is that birds are dying because some dumbass dumped chemicals in the bay. This disgusting thought makes him feel helpless, like the world around him has a black heart.

"Was it your boss?" Blas asks. "He do this?"

"I don't know," Chango says. "Seems extreme even for him."

"Find him yet?"

"Already explored these willows. Didn't find shit but raccoons and an owl. They're still searching though. Shark Inlet. Sweet Springs. The mudflats. The entire back bay and estuary. Everybody's backyards that border Cuesta Inlet. I'm tired. Supposed to go talk to the cops again. And I got no fucking job."

"You're gonna end up at the grocery store with me."

"Screw that. Ain't working with you mopping up some old vato's piss from the donut aisle."

"Isn't like that. What about Mom?"

"What about her?"

"She know?"

"Mom don't know shit." Chango wipes his eyes but the redness only worsens. "You know what she does, gossips about hair all damn day at the salon. Good thing she charges those rich white folks an arm and a leg just for a trim. She'd rather talk about how to put a power streak of grey in some chingona's bun than talk about shit that goes down around here. Bet Mom's glad she owns that business. We're lucky, little brother. Don't you forget that."

"I mean, maybe she'll know someone to help you get more work."

"I don't need our old lady for that. She'll want me to barista for all them peckerwoods at the coffeehouses and keep helping with the bills. You're the mama's boy. Anyway, something strange. Heard cops talking about someone acting weird in the middle of Pasadena Drive out by the park. Thought it was some homeless dude dying. But it wasn't."

"So?"

"So, they said it was their supervisor in the middle of the road at like four in the morning pretending to be dead and shit. I dunno. Jesus. It was just weird, okay?" Chango rubs his eyes, looks at Blas like he can't focus. "I gotta go talk to these cops," Chango says. "And I need to take another shower. Eyes feel like they're coming out of my damn skull. Just get out of here, all right? Too many chemicals. Stay away from the bay before your eyes start burning. Go home. Turn on a fan. Call one of your old lady girlfriends and talk about birds."

Chapter Eleven

PROBABLY SHOULDN'T HAVE come to the Preserve. Yesterday, I wandered Pecho Road Willows. The day before that the owner of the oyster farm and his worker disappeared. I didn't want to leave the willows. Someone or something in me said, *Stay*. And I wanted to see it again. So I circled through willow paths, always circling, listening. Had no more encounters with my infant-bird hallucination, or the warbler and those snails, though the birds around me seemed frightened, their songs elevated, nervous. Had they encountered similar visions? Eventually, a firefighter entered the swamp, escorted me to the road, asked if I was thirsty, said he would be searching the area again. I told him, "Whatever is in there doesn't want to be found." He kind of smiled. I don't know how many hours passed. He and others left. Then I went back in, eventually left.

I'm a creature of habit, have this need to be with nature, even if it's suffering. Even if all these transplanted eucalyptus from the early 1900s are crying, bark peeling in huge strips of rainbow tears, longing for their true home across the seas.

I feel a similar sadness in Pecho Road Willows, something in the reeds and willows, suffering. *Watching*. I feel this in the bay too, waters crying out. The pain of the unexpected. The pain of what these oyster farmers have done to the tidewaters. I wonder, as I always do, how we can live where society trusts some people with the kind of chemicals that can be so effortlessly dumped.

Out in the bay, drone sweepers brought in by the government suck contaminated bay water. Fountains spray filtered remains back into the estuary. There are no government workers or rescue crews, just increased numbers of drones, vague news reports speculating how the drones flew in from Vandenberg, maybe from ships off the coast. The government keeps saying no comment. Not a single representative in Baywood. We all wonder the way I wonder if the tidelands will ever recover. Certainly not in what's left of my lifetime.

A medicinal scent burns the air. Yet here I am, breathing toxins along with every inhabitant of Baywood.

You, Kumi Sato, I remind myself, cannot live *forever*.

I'm thinking this while on the Preserve's boardwalk. I know its every slat. Every knothole. Every loose nail. I know the path bends slightly to the right and ends at a lookout just past a eucalyptus tree where you can peer northward into the bay through a small telescope.

This path feels misty, sullen, and if I'm truthful, I'm more than a little sleepy, not yet awake in this air that reeks of something putrid.

The sky weighs heavy again. A sickly filter of grey-green bears down, creates a stillness, both in birds and plants. No breeze to rattle wet leaves and branches to life, to wave at me, to call for help. Most birds lay quiet, hiding, though I hear the occasional calls of godwits barking along the shore.

I wonder what might be bothering the shore birds. Willets? Angry curlews? Maybe crying out from toxins. I wonder if many birds that still touch this water shouldn't be scared off, and why no one has found any dead on shore. Just those out by the oyster farm. I'm thinking this when I notice a form sprawled in the lookout shadows.

My heart pounds. A heaviness pulls my body toward the walkway. Feels like I'll melt through the boardwalk and be no more. Then I realize I know him. Davis Folds, more than ten years older than me. Nearing ninety. Always wrapped like a mummy so you can only see the skin around his dark glasses and nose. Here every morning at seven a.m., he watches birds honk, forage, bob in the tide. Tells me all the time he enjoys how waves lick and toss birds, how when cormorants fly, their heads seem about to fall off.

Motionless, Davis appears dead, as if every muscle finally failed after decades of fighting to keep them operating.

I step closer and think, contamination, that Davis had a reaction to chemicals blowing off the bay, stricken by toxins. I think maybe I'm next, suddenly aware my eyes burn. I can hardly suck beyond a shallow breath while rushing fast as my old legs will take me. Stiff every morning, I might come apart at the knees.

Eucalyptus and oak tower over the path, their many arms full of brittle leaves and fractured birdsong. Clumps of poison oak sweep against the boardwalk. Leaf of three, let it be. I try not to trip, try not to fling myself into the wilds of the Preserve.

Seem to sense nearby creatures the closer I get to Davis. A pair of deer pick their way. A raccoon gazes and snuffles through the wetland. Snails cling in bunches of exposed mulch. A Great Horned Owl calls to its mate. My instinct always to look up, find the source. I imagine bird eyes, large and yellow, gazing upon a corpse at the edge of morning. They must notice him the way I see dead seabirds that sometimes wash ashore. Surf Scoters, loons, and grebes after storms, maybe a murrelet or auklet, feet tucked beneath tums in final pose after dragging bellies onto sand. Sometimes covered in oil, they become detritus washed in tidal lines. A prayer pose at Neptune's altar, set alight with mourning.

My eyes roam beyond the lookout—a grey carpet of earth blood all the way to the sandspit dunes that protect the bay from the roaring Pacific. The sacred plug dome beyond to the north, Morro Rock, half a crashed moon, a greenish tomb where kings dwell in the underworld, a sacred temple for indigenous people who dance at its base or pray atop, navigating spiritual journeys by the guidance of ancestors and milky stars. And those three awful smokestacks next to it that artisans love to paint images of and sell at weekend bazaars, that the city was supposed to take down years and years ago, that tourists love as part of an unintended skyline of brick, like a three-fingered claw about to scrape at the Rock.

Davis's prone body appears smashed against these frigid boards.

Can hardly see his face. So little of him ever exposed to the elements, jacket puffed around his nose. His broad hat, flattened in the back, pokes from his head at a strange angle. On his hands, two thick gloves.

Nothing moves. No twitch of skin. No sound. No rising chest.

I groan and squat, touch his still warm body, let my instinct take over.

No idea what this might mean to the people of Baywood. Davis had been one of the first police officers around here. Then a city councilman. He helped build this tiny community, welcomed me and my husband so many years ago, now lying in the cold.

He seems melted. Every muscle pulled toward the center of our earth.

"Davis." I jostle his arm, repeat his name, have my phone out to dial 9-1-1. My fingers shake. I say his name a few more times, flash to the night I found Hiroki dead in our bathtub. Blue skin, matted hair, pupils dilated. The medical examiner determined that it must've been an acute heart attack. It took me a long time to comprehend it, that Hiroki would suddenly end, his body succumbing to nature and his soul being transported elsewhere.

I begin to press numbers when an odd wash of movement catches my attention. Unnatural. Bending upward. Uncurling. Unfolding. Fingers of Davis's gloves stretch like spider legs. Like the suckling that witches do. Old bones lift rubbery muscles turning taut again. A green dimness from this strange morning sky engulfs him as he suddenly stands. He appears sickly, giant next to my small frame, staring from over his high collar, shirt beneath pulled nearly over his nose.

"The Brans are here," he says as if nothing happened. Towering Davis. Ancient Davis. Davis who was dead a moment ago, or seemed that way. "Do you hear them?" he asks. "The Brans?" That's what he calls the flocks of Brant geese in the bay. Hundreds sometimes float in the distance, making *cronk* sounds. I only see cormorants now, fewer than there were, toxins soaking feathers.

"What were you doing?" I ask. My heart thumps in near rupture. An anger that I shouldn't let loose boils, rises. "You scared the hell out of me."

"Playing dead." He stares.

His eyes, cold, dark leather, wide pupils retract to points.

I realize I'm angry because I still want Hiroki to come back, to bend upwards from the dirt, for my memories of his eyes and skin to not be what they are, for life to renew, so that everything can start over. Chemicals now burn my sinuses, my eyes.

"Are you okay?" I ask. "Did you pass out?" He seems like he could topple at any moment.

"Told you what I was doing."

"Do you need help home? You're wearing so many winter clothes. It will be warm soon."

"I can manage."

"Could have hurt yourself getting down there," I say. "Aren't you always telling me to watch out for tree roots and loose nails? That your blood is thin? And if you fall you might break a bone or bleed to death because of your anemia?"

He hasn't moved an inch. Just wobbles, blankly stares over his jacket. "Saw an officer keel over on Pasadena Drive recently," he says. "Thought I'd try. Felt right."

"Let me get this straight. You thought you'd play dead because some law officer did? And you thought you'd do that here at the Preserve? That it felt normal?"

"Seemed like the right place," Davis says. "I was only gone for a minute. Felt something take my soul and put it back. Greatest feeling ever. Like Brans lifting off the bay."

"Brants." I look past him. Something has spooked the cormorants. Probably a hungry Peregrine Falcon, wingbeats whipping fast. Maybe poison soaking their feathers. I think again that someone should be shooting a gun over the bay to scare them off. Even the sea drone doesn't scare them off. I watch while the birds swing their numbers deeper out by the Third Street lookout a mile or so away. A trilling kingfisher follows them.

"Used to be thousands," Davis says while I tremble. "For decades. Came in huge numbers. Wouldn't stop. Something made them leave. Now, a hundred or two are all we see. Sometimes more. It's the bay. Whatever made them leave doesn't seem to bother the ducks."

There isn't a duck in the surf.

"You should go home and get some rest," I say. "You don't just lie in the cold like that. At your age, you might really die even attempting what you did. And make an appointment with your doctor. Will you do that for me?"

He moves like an old windup toy slowing down, takes a step past me, then another. "Brans coming back. Mark my words. There'll be more than ever. God will change this place."

I want to tell him that ghosts have been our watchers, not

gods, that our destiny becomes ours, no matter how tragic. I want to yell at him, let him feel the burning in my throat.

He takes off a glove, hand shaking. The green and purple in the eucalyptus trees seem to mimic the mottling of his aged skin. "Damn things don't stop," he says about his tremors.

"Call your doctor," I repeat.

He walks away, unanswering, carrying the glove he's just pulled off.

This time I sit on a bench, my old legs refusing to chase him around the bend beneath the trees to see if he makes it home. I should follow him.

Instead, I close my eyes, rest them from the chemicals in the air, try to make sense of why Davis would lie on cold wood and pretend to be dead. I try to make sense of this sadness surrounding me.

Chapter Twelve

WE'RE JUST PEOPLE going to school.

That's our new manifesto in a world where manifestos are stupid and violent. Teachers call us kids. Parents call us kids. We're just people going to school, trying to stay away from those who call us kids. That's our manifesto.

They say our minds aren't fully developed. Our minds and bodies do everything theirs do. That's our manifesto.

We're just kids, they say. But we're the ones who don't want to be labeled. We're the ones leaving Baywood High for the big world. Everyone else comes here, not us. We're the ones who will leave. We're the ones who will make it. We're the ones who won't ever call a teen a kid. That's our manifesto. We won't be like our parents. We won't talk down to teens. We won't be like teachers and administrators. We won't call *them* oldies, or stupid, or whatever. That's our manifesto. We're a family, we students of Baywood, those of us who meet up, who whisper in the seaside night, when the surf gives a little glow, when all is still except the surf. This could never be a game, though we like 'games.

We remember when we deaded. Fresh out of the oven. That was a game because we felt dead to adults and alive to each other. We're a broken family, we know this. We're made of all kinds of colors, even though the adults want to make this town some weird wheel of white and off-white, rule it as if they own a color palette. We're not a perfect family but want to share our differences with each other. We're all kinds of genders. We're all kinds of love, all kinds of interests. That's our manifesto. We write this in our phones. We build a fire on the beach. We read our manifesto like poetry. We're not poets though our manifesto burns like poetry. Our manifesto feels like family, a contract, a reality. We need it more than ever because we instantly feel something has changed because of what happened in the bay. We feel something burning at the shoreline, getting into eyes, throats, and minds. Some of us sense this after the spill. Blas has been sad. Kaylee has been sad. We hug them, tell them the oyster farmer got what he got because he must have poured all that poison into the estuary. No one found the owner. We saw his wife on the beach wearing sunglasses, walking a little black dog with pink bows. She wasn't crying. Maybe she already cried. We didn't yell at her. The dog looked as sad as she did.

We're not mean.

That's our manifesto.

We love this place but want to get away from it more than ever. We want to see the world. We'll use our eyes to see, then share everything with each other. Blas says these beaches and trees and birds and gray foxes and skunks and bears and mountain lions and bobcats and voles have been his family—and "you have to love the sweet squishy furry voles," he says, "even if you see one carried by a White-tailed Kite, you wish it peace in the forever big sky." That's what Blas says, and Kai, he nods along, and Chewie, Jordan and Kaylee, and Elisabeth, and everyone. So many others. We celebrate the voles. And girls kiss girls and boys kiss boys and girls kiss boys and boys kiss girls and we add that to our manifesto, add that this land has become part of our family, that voles and spiders have joined our cause, and we'll take this land with us one day, like seeds, and always return to share where we've been. In the meantime, Blas says he hears a cormorant in the dark, and it's like a sister to all of us while it honks and fades in the dark.

Chapter Thirteen

A RED-EYED VIREO in the willows captures a caterpillar, pulled sticky from a branch with its long bill, an eagerness in its red eyes. Its grey crown ruffles. Dark eyeline and olive-green wings capture a beam of light, white belly and yellow flanks like a spot of sun, the hungry bird now whipping the caterpillar like a noodle, slamming its body against a branch.

Back and forth, smacking the insect, this cruel bird, the caterpillar losing all sense of life, expels guts, dims, ebbs, now swallowed whole. The bird, methodical in its foraging, moves west, ten feet above the ground, in the canopy, up a trunk covered in ivy, crown ruffles again. Finds another slimy insect, part wings, part abdomen, unknown, now eviscerated on a branch, smashed left and right, eyes loosening in its buggy head.

The bird swallows again, closer now, so close to the canopy near where Bernhard stares upward, sending pulse after pulse into the creatures that take his message to the sea, his disease into invertebrates, into land creatures, into those that fly, into insects, pulsing further, deeper, communicating, spreading into small mammals, mice and gophers, raccoon stomachs pulsating, lungs gasping, dying, or seeming to, slipping, now alive again, if they weren't before, and in their breath, or in the charged particles of air, even Bernhard can't explain, only knows that time and particles, and organisms, and behavior, on another hidden plane of existence, can spread, darken, cloud minds, control, transport, sink humanity, as if all humans are beholden to death.

And this bird, above him, this red eye now on Bernhard. Now flitting lower and lower, methodical still, searches for food, can only eat and skulk, a yearning of the bird's survival mechanisms, almost full now, leaps down to the corpse, this great mottled log of flesh and skin.

Red eye to corpse eye. Head tilted. Consciousness to consciousness. A tentacle squirming. A translucence rippling outward, and glowing, lines of glowing dots, a kind of message in them, a pulsing of light in the tip, spirals of them, boring through his skull, through Bernhard's torn nostril, this stretching tentacle tip.

The bird, its tongue a sliver of muscle, bill parts, the tip reaches.

A film of light, floating, a glowing web slips into the mouth of the vireo, red eye now locked on this light, this pulsing, this taste, this glow seeping into its innards, tasting of the sea, of snail, of mollusk, of ethereal lightness and birth, of another world.

Chapter Fourteen

BLAS HEARS A thrush low in the scrub, glimpses a spray of dark chest spots, then, that gleam in its dark eye. The bird listens to him. He can see that it hears *his* every movement. Then something else higher, a chip, a pip, something he can't find. Something wet and sweet sounding, so high in the eucalyptus he can't imagine where it might be. He follows the noise, skulks beneath one tree, then another, sometimes looking straight upwards into a strange vertigo, spinning between branches, along rainbowed trunks, bark peeling like prismatic skin.

In the middle of the street now hoping for a better angle, he scans again with his binoculars, that chip call still hidden, bleating rhythmic, almost an alert call, a warning, like a Cooper's Hawk might be closing in, darting between treetops, around trunks. Blas wants to find this bird so bad he can taste it.

Then he hears the woman fall.

Always aware of every sound, every step, every flick of leaf, even birdsong from the bay, he knows that exactly three other people occupy the street. Two joggers have rounded a distant curve, and Mr. Christiano, retired from teaching high school woodshop, before Blas's time, bent over a sawhorse stapling metal and wood, always building something. A doghouse, a doll-house, some strange Jesus lawn sculpture to put up at Christmas.

The thud comes from the middle of the street, less than half a block to the north. Though he's just had a glimpse, some rarity for sure, Blas pulls away from the bird. That white under-tail covert that could have been an East Coast warbler, maybe a Chestnut-sided, though he wished it were a Golden-winged—like the one found at Meadow Park in San Luis Obispo by some dumpy old newbie birder—now morphs into a jogger sprawled on the asphalt, her body limp like those dead baby elephant seals he's seen at the colony north of San Simeon, gulls piercing skin, tearing at eyes, at anything, bills soaked in blood.

Still, a no brainer, the woman has collapsed, maybe her heart gave out, maybe some kind of aneurism. He quickly makes his way to her, 9-1-1 on speed dial.

Closing in fast, he tries to punch through a busy signal the entire way. Redial, redial, briskly gliding toward the scene. By the time he's within reach he realizes something has been off the entire time. This woman's friend or husband, watches, doesn't help, doesn't do a damn thing, just stares, not at her, like some-thing floats above her.

"Hey man, what's up? She okay?" Blas tucks away his phone, squats next to her. "Can't get through to 9-1-1."

"She's . . ." the man drifts.

"No, she ain't dead." Blas isn't taking that for an answer. This dumbass vato's in shock, he thinks, never seen someone fall before. Blas has seen plenty of drunk uncles fall, including Uncle Flavio once with a coronary. Bitch survived all his neph-ews taking turns pounding his chest.

"You check her pulse?" Blas reaches for her wrist. "You gotta feel for it."

"Don't. Don't. Don't." The jogger's eyes flick to Blas now. "She's . . ."

"What, man?" Blas can't tell if she's breathing, has her wrist, feeling, *feeling*. "Are you tripping? She's hurt."

"She isn't hurt."

"Okay, like she might be dead, okay, but you have to check for that shit." Blas isn't looking at him, just her. With all his will he tries to focus, like he's straining to hear birdsong high in the canopy, that sweet chip, that rhythm, can feel a pulse so weak, he's not sure. He waves a hand in front of her nose, can't feel air, pulls out his phone, hits redial. Nothing. He sees foam now, like her insides slowly turning to suds, pushing their way out.

"No, don't," the man says.

"You're being stupid. She ain't breathing." Blas can only think to attempt CPR. He gently turns her to her back, starts to get in position. He's got to do something while this idiot stands like a dumbass deer. Blas folds his palms together near the top of her sternum.

"Get off her."

"What? Chill, bitch."

The jogger seems to come out of himself, eyes yellow and lost, knocks Blas away. "I said she's fine."

Blas eats dirt, scrambles to his feet, the jogger on all fours like a dog. Those eyes still on him. Something fucked up about those eyes. "What's wrong with you?" But he knows. Blas knows. This is off. The dude is off. The woman is off, face in a pool of foam. Blas's senses go on high alert, like this is suddenly some late night horror movie and he's glued to the sublime, to some mysterious crumbled castle.

The man lunges at Blas like a spring-loaded animal, flies to his feet.

Blas screams backwards, somehow able to grab his bins where he set them to the side, flying in a way he didn't know he could, the man's hands not even in fists, just twisted claws that Blas bats to the side.

And then the man slips back down to the ground, like he's been shot or stabbed though nothing like that happened at all, only he's not still, he resists this, resists some kind of pain, some kind of death, back arched, on elbows and heels like some kind of crab, chin to chest. And then, while Blas watches in horror, the man crawls backwards to the woman, spitting, drooling, then falls next to her on his side.

Blas has had enough of this. He runs. A second later, the snap of a staple gun, then again, and a grunt, followed by another.

"What the hell?" Blas stops before he starts.

Mr. Christiano on the ground shoots staples into his stomach, then chest, horror glazing his eyes. "Not going to do this," Mr. Christiano groans, resists whatever has gripped him, like he'll never die, though he's surely trying to kill himself.

None of this makes sense to Blas.

Mr. Christiano plants three staples in his cheek now, then two in his neck. Whatever he's done to himself, it doesn't matter, he seems to finally give in, collapses, writhes, bleeds, goes still.

Blas has seen enough of this death carnival. He runs again, not stopping this time, flying, tearing down the street, down another, toward home.

Cars smash somewhere in the neighborhood, maybe one street over, like someone just drove into a wall. Someone screams from another direction.

Then out of the corner of his eye someone tumbles off a roof, limp like a mannequin, smashes into a flower bed. More yelling, now screams from every direction, a collective cry of disbelief, of horror. Blas too, some kind of terror from his throat, though he isn't sure, isn't aware if it *is* him, maybe he's outside his own body, calm, watching himself screaming, running, because in his panic, amid sirens and distant crashing, he feels like this shit will happen to him any second, that his eyes will roll back and his insides will turn to foam.

In front of him now, two children on their knees smiling. A girl and her younger brother. Blas pauses, no longer yelling, but shaking, thinking he doesn't want this. These are just kids, he knows they live one street over in the ritzy homes. He sees them when he goes birdwatching on weekends. The mother always says good morning. He doesn't know the color of her eyes. She always wears dark glasses, hair pulled into a ponytail, wears a layer of lip moisturizer. He doesn't know any of them, but knows them. He has to help these kids, right? They can't be any older than four and six. Their mother lies still, he can't see her face. He doesn't want to do it but he says it anyway: "It's all right. Come with me. I'll get you help."

But these kids won't even look at him. They start giggling, they pile flowers on their mother. Then, as if their lights go out simultaneously, they crumple to the sidewalk. One lets out a yelp. The other whimpers. They shake, like someone has a hold of them, like they're going to bite off their tongues.

Blas takes off around the corner, down a street, ignores every fallen body, flings himself into his entryway, out of breath, fumbles with his keys, trying to force air into his lungs, unlocks then shuts and bolts the door behind him. He peeks through the doorframe window thinking the children might be crawling after him. He fears they'll climb inside, suck at his neck and legs, his side, bite their way through muscle and bone, eat his heart. He can't believe what he's just seen, so many people seeming to die. He peeks out the window, stares and stares, can't see anything.

Then seconds later the two children walk past with their mom, the kids holding flowers again as if nothing happened. What the hell? He thought they all just died from some kind of . . . he has no idea what . . . and now they waltz past the house, one of them skipping, don't even glance over, and now out of sight, probably in their home soon eating Oreos or apples, or each others' fingers.

His back to the door, legs jittery, Blas lets himself slide to the floor. When he does, Mr. Christiano's eyes, that jogger's eyes, those kids' eyes, hover in his imagination, in his terror, in dustlight. He thinks he's gone insane. He thinks something may be out there, that everything has gone wrong, but has no idea what. He feels paralyzed, doesn't want to move, doesn't want to breathe, doesn't want to change even a molecule of air.

The silence of the house soaks into him while the chaos outside muffles, drowns, slips into nothingness. This silence warns him though, puts his senses on alert again, jerks him awake. Something in the dark living room, a faint hiss, then a slight wheeze before a sudden suck of air followed by soft groans.

Blas's heart thumps so loud that thunder pours into his ears. The drumbeat deafens, pounds away any groans. Eyes soak in every cone of light while he rises to his feet, begins to move through the room. He wishes he had a baseball bat, something. He grabs a photo frame, not sure what he'll do with it.

Then he sees them. Chango and their mother Maria, both rising from the floor, standing somewhat rigid over puddles of foam that also pushes from corners of mouths.

"Mijo," his mother says.

And Chango: "Little brother . . ."

Those eyes. That strange look of apology, wonder in them as if asking, *Is it happening to you too?* And some kind of yellowish-grey satisfaction in them, like Chango and Maria actually enjoyed their hallucinogenic trip to whereversville.

Blas rushes past into the hall, into his room, slams the door, sets down the picture frame, locks the door, though the weak lock can't hold, won't hold if they attack. He pushes his desk in front of the door, starts to grab things, shirts, a book, socks. He shoves them in a backpack, starts to grab some underwear when he hears them outside his room.

"Mijo . . ."

Blas stands paralyzed.

"Mijo."

"Stay away," Blas says.

"I'm not mad at you."

"Good. Got no reason to be. You having some kind of seizure? I think the chemicals are messing with people."

"Nothing like that at all, mijo," his mother says. "Something else."

"Yeah, little bro," Chango says. "Something else."

Blas sees the frame, the photo of Chango, himself, their mother. He remembers when it was taken, maybe a month after their stepdad got kicked out. He hated that bastard. And now, he doesn't know what to think. He knocks over the frame, turns away, though he can hear his mother still breathing out in the hall.

On Blas's laptop that popped online when he moved the desk, an article he left open, "Hawks Can Be a Hummingbird's Best Friend." *The enemy of my enemy should be my friend* is the last line. Those words stare at him like those eyes. So many eyes. He just wishes he were a bird. A hawk, a hummingbird, he doesn't care.

The article details how some hummingbirds build nests in an invisible cone beneath hawk nests for added protection. Hawks don't prey on hummingbirds, but they'll eat the predators of hummingbirds: jays, grackles, orioles. Everywhere, the timid species. Everywhere, the aggressive species. Like geese nesting near snowy owls. The owls eat the fox. *Which am I? Which am I?*

"What's going on, Mom?" Blas asks. "It's a mass seizure of some kind."

"We told you, it's not that. Open the door, baby."

"What the hell then?"

"Let us in."

"I think Mr. Christiano is dead," Blas says. "He was doing some nasty shit to himself."

"We know."

"You can't know. You weren't there."

"We're not surprised."

"What's that supposed to mean?"

"We need to talk."

"Never mind."

"Mijo?"

"Go away. I can't talk to you right now. Okay? Just go away. I need to be alone. I need to think. Okay? Will you let me think?"

When he hears them leave, he calls his classmate Kai, talks low, still wary that footsteps might return.

"Dude, what's going on?" Kai says. "My family's been acting nuts the past hour, like this is scaring the hell out of me."

"Same here," Blas says.

"Martin says his entire family lost it," Kai says. "Everyone's falling on the ground like they're in the worst pain of their lives, then wake up like nothing happened, though they act like they have a secret that I'm not in on. They got this crazy look in their eyes. Even my sister. Mom too. Dad's okay for now. I asked them to go to the hospital, but they say they're fine. No one is fine."

"Do their eyes turn red? Chango looks like a night heron."

"What's that about?"

"I don't know. Mom looks more . . . normal."

"Yeah, well, it's not normal. You know what this is don't you? Hate to even say it."

"What?"

"It's like they're deading."

It hits Blas, how so many of them deaded around campus, laughed about it. But it can't be. That had only been for fun, for popularity. "That's not deading," he says. "We joked around to blow up our reels."

"It's pretty damn close, whatever it is," Kai says. "Pretending. Then not, and kind of laughing about it. Dad had spit all over his lips then joked like nothing was up when he wiped it off.

Look, we gotta all meet up at the MDO campground. We can't just sit at home and do nothing."

"You know anything else?"

"Looked at some news sites. No one knows shit. Saw my neighbors pack up and leave. They're just gone."

"Should we?"

"I gotta get to my girlfriend's house. She's not answering her phone. MDO later?"

For the next few hours Blas tries to piece together what he's seen, what's going on. Could they be deading? They can't be. No one took photos or videos trying to show off. No one posted to social media then laughed like it was all a joke.

Whatever it is, Blas thinks, it's violent, disturbing, real.

Then he thinks, in a way, maybe it *is* deading, akin to it, though either way, he can't explain any of it. Something about everyone's behavior twists his stomach. He can't eat, doesn't feel hungry, and besides, what if it's in the food? He refuses to go to the kitchen. He loves his family, but he's afraid to confront his mother and brother. He needs his friends, needs their stories. In the meantime, all of this uncertainty makes him feel sick. He just wants to forget everything, go look at birds, go to school, to work, have everything be what it was, not whatever this is. But he can't stop trying to figure it all out. His fingers shake. He fumbles through news sites, gets all jittery while texting his friends. And every time, no one knows a thing.

>>What? How would I know what's going on? All I know is my family was already screwed up.

>>I don't know what to do. I just want to leave. I don't feel well. I think I'm about to do it.

>>They never supported my gender and now this—they're mad I'm not freaking out like them.

>> **What's wrong with my parents? Everything. And as of ten minutes ago, now my brother too.**

Blas peeks out his bedroom window, notices some neighbors hurry with suitcases to their car. Others collapse, quiver. He has a feeling the family that drove away has left for good, wonders if he should do the same.

Finally, he listens at his bedroom door, hears nothing outside his room, no whispers, no crashing to the floor, nothing. When it's time to head out to MDO, he creeps down the hall to the bathroom, grabs a medical mask, slips it over his mouth and nose, heads toward the living room.

Maria steps in front of him. "Mijo, we need to talk."

"Jesus, Mom," Blas says, "you scared me. I have to go."

"Why you wearing that?" she asks. "I'm not sick."

"Half the town is sick," he says. "Maybe half the world. No one is saying anything"

"It's not what you think. You going to see your friends?"

"You need help, Mom."

"I think your brother might. I'm fine."

"How do you know you're fine?"

"I just know. This thing. It's like a greeting, no, a new way to commune. A way to know others are there, though I don't think we can *see* each other. We go somewhere. But I can't really remember. It's okay though, everything's fine. It's a good place. Whatever is happening is for the better. Like we said, it's not a seizure. But it is maybe a kind of dying."

"What are you talking about?" Blas says. "It's called a mental health episode. We learn about them in school. You're having a mental health crisis. All of you. And why isn't the news talking about this? Why aren't we packing up and leaving like the Parados?"

"This is our home, mijo," Maria says. "We have to watch your brother, though. Something is different with him."

"Something has always been different with him," Blas says. "I gotta go. Don't try to stab me or breathe on me. I'll fight back."

"Why would I hurt you? Don't say that. You're my baby. I've only ever wanted to protect you." She reaches for him.

Blas dodges her hand. "I said don't touch me."

His heart races all the way to his scooter. It's dark when he speeds away, passing beneath eucalyptus along the faintly lit street. Several people have fallen in gutters, on sidewalks. He rounds Pecho Road to Pecho Valley Road, then winds into the hills toward MDO, a marine layer blowing in, smells of salt water and fog crashing his senses. Then something flies past. Close. He swerves. He sees a lot of Barn Owls out this way just after dark, zipping across roads. This is different. Mechanical. White. Followed by four others. Dangling arms or legs, large rounded lenses for eyes, one of them briefly on him, and gone just like that. Ocean-based drones, he thinks. They call them *sea ghosts*, sometimes *grey ghosts*. The Faceless. He's only seen one once before. It isn't just that cleanup drone. The government is here.

By the time he gets through a freezing headwind to MDO, the camp host, who has been bribed for an empty site, packs up and leaves along with campers already streaming out. Kai and Chewie have started a fire pit. Around twenty friends gather around the flames. Blas counts heads. Their group has shrunk by six.

Kaylee sits closest to the fire, which relieves his fear, though she's clearly distraught. "It's my parents," he overhears. "Both of them. What am I supposed to do? I don't even want to go back home."

Everyone comes up with all kinds of theories. Apocalypse. Mass multi-fauna seizure. Pandemic. Rabies—it's always rabies in the movies. And then Chewie says to the group, "Should we leave or is it too early?"

"Some kind of news report will come out," Kai says. "Our community leaders will say something."

"I saw *sea ghosts*," Blas jumps in. "On the way here. They're watching."

"They'll help us," Elisabeth says. "See? They're monitoring. They'll know what to do."

It's quieter now, and late, so late. Everyone has been here for hours, stealing wood from abandoned camp sites, piling every log, letting flames burn away their dread. Kaylee surprises Blas by sitting close, asking how he's doing. He wanted to call her and should have but didn't have the guts. He rarely has the guts when it comes to her.

"It's scary, isn't it?" he says.

She doesn't say anything but rests her head on his shoulder. She's done this before a few times, never anything more, just this feeling of safety he feels too when he's with this group, has felt for years, seems like years, since before middle school anyway. She kisses him on the cheek this time. He wraps an arm around her and doesn't say anything, can hear whispering, and owls, which somehow calms him out here.

Kai later moves near what's left of the fire, says, "I don't know if we should keep gathering right here, but we need to keep meeting. Remember the manifesto. Consider this our first Dead of Night party. As long as we don't start dropping to the ground like flies, we should keep doing this."

Elisabeth agrees. So does Chewie and Jordan. Blas and the others nod too. It's no party, but Blas gets it. They have to hold onto what they have, to each other. Maybe they're all they've always had. But he also knows everyone will soon go back to their homes, and like him, have to deal with this strange whatever it is, and decide whether to stay or run. And he'll have to gaze into Chango's red eyes, and try to figure out what's happening.

Chapter Fifteen

VICTOR EATS LIKE he's gorging on the last potato casserole on earth. Food falls in his beard and on his plate, each bite gobbled like there really is no tomorrow. Doesn't matter. Ingram loves him. She needs him here. Earlier in the day she ventured outdoors, checked on a couple of birds at one of the neighborhood feeders. Two puddles of feathers, sparrows still as statues. Both eventually fluffed in her hands, preened when she set them down, then flew off. She keeps hoping they'll stop dropping, though it has only been a few days that the bay has been contaminated. She wonders if people will stop collapsing. For now, birds continue to fall. They go stiff, legs like broken sticks, feathers no longer puffed. And they don't just slip from feeders. They drop from bushes, trees, the sky. Like falling stars. Soon after, most of them stretch, ruffle feathers, pop back to life, sometimes more energetic than before. Like a warning. The outside world really has no chance if anything with wings become vectors, she thinks. She wonders if insects do this too, if a walking stick clinging to a branch is really deading, if a wasp carcass might really not be a corpse, if bee swarms might dead then go into a frenzy. She sees nothing to prove that any six-legged bug has manifested this pseudo-dead affliction, though she's constantly scanning the ground, scanning foliage, even her kitchen floor where she sometimes finds stray cockroaches.

Victor soon gets a message on his phone. "Something's happening at the bay," he says.

"Different than everyone acting crazy?" she says. "I don't like all this. We need answers."

"Let's see what's going on, play it cool, go see."

"I don't want to. I just want to pack up and go."

"I'm not leaving," he says.

"Why not?"

"Feels like I'm needed here." He grabs his hat.

"Needed for what? Nobody is talking."

"You coming? Or you leaving?"

Chemicals linger in the bay, stinging eyes and nostrils. Not a police cruiser or fire department vehicle in sight. Emergency services have not only forgotten about them, most have left the area. Ingram can't believe how many people have joined her at the water's edge, and moreso, how many have braved the estuary during this high tide. Paddleboarders, kayakers, groups in canoes, everyone had been warned not to boat for at least two months. Each paddler defies the order, risks their health. Always a rule breaker somewhere, Ingram thinks. Birds appear to be rulebreakers too. She sees no ducks on the water, no cormorants either today, but birds on the shorelines here and there, and occasional terns and gulls flying along with passing ducks and sandpipers.

She and Victor continue along the shoreline. A Black-bellied Plover gives side-eye but doesn't run. It walks strange, waddles rather than making brief darting steps while foraging along the shore. She wonders if the chemicals will soon kill it, if the bird is slowly dying, if it's losing motor functions. Maybe this bizarre thing that's happening is related to something else, something inside the birds, in that mountain lion, in cats and dogs and pet parakeets, maybe in wild rats, possums, and mice. Something disturbing, changing both creatures and people on the cellular level, or the synapse or even hormonal level, like a brain glandular thing. Maybe it's something else, a rodent manifestation, like *Rattus rattus* on the Silk Road, and all those fleas sucking blood centuries ago, spreading the plague, biting and sucking through coarse fur into skin and capillaries, infecting blood, then biting travelers while camping along the route, and those travelers eventually spreading the disease to cities via infected fleas and human contact, and infected rats, always more and more rats, only in this case, birds too. Maybe it's in the sand fleas, sand crabs, or Pismo clams. Maybe through mosquito bites, she wonders. Maybe through the water, something the treatment plant can't catch, maybe through some mutated algae bloom that birds and seals eat, or some nearly invisible microscopic worm that possibly infected those bay snail invaders. Maybe it's just those snails, those goddam Atlantic driller snails. That entire swarm. Though their bulk is gone, their shells have littered the estuary beaches, and bits of flesh still hide in those, and probably, most likely, she thinks, maybe many are still alive. Clinging to hulls and docks, and they're just radiating this infection, begging to be eaten, to spread this more and more. Though she wonders: Why not Morro Bay, why just Baywood? Why not San Luis Obispo too? That's close. But Morro Bay is right there, she can see it across the bay. No reports of anything strange there, though the chemicals have seeped all along its embarcadero, closing the stores, shuttering its fishing fleet. Why evacuate parts of Morro Bay and not here? Then she sees what some of the people here are doing. How not everyone standing here is immune. Some fall on the sandy path, most get up right away, brush themselves off. Some lie still.

"Don't touch them," Victor whispers.

She tries to ignore every corpse-like scene.

Then Victor points toward the bay. "See that? Drones have stopped sweeping and circling. They've slipped into stasis mode, hovering."

"Would you look at that," she says. The drones defy gravity, huddled midair, attachment arms and sensors drooping, giving off a collective *whirrrr*. Seeing them makes her uneasy, want to run back inside. "Why aren't they doing their job? This is supposed to take at least two years of cleanup," she adds. "They're catching water at the harbor mouth and here in the main contamination area. Everything is still toxic. Don't even have to see it to know. We can smell the fumes." Then, while Victor doesn't move or answer, "I'm going back," she says. "I don't want to be out here. This is scaring me."

Victor doesn't answer because he's seen something. Not another small cleaning drone, not any of the armored vehicles that others have reported in the hills. He points and she spots a shadow, no, a large drone zooming over houses, maybe the size of a car, coming in fast and flying lower than rooftops, then fast as anything she's seen, sweeping over their heads, over the bay, swinging in an arc over the water while the smaller cleaning drones come back online and scatter across the bay and out of sight.

White and black, this large drone floats like a warning. A dozen armlike appendages tipped with steel pincers and claws scrape the water's surface. Multiple mechanical eyes swirl in a band across the top. It pulses and hums, paces, dragging its arms. And then it talks, letting every kayaker, canoe-paddler and paddle-boarder know they must turn around or face new consequences.

Return to shore. Return to shore. Return to shore.
Now. Now. Now.
You will be penalized. Be mindful of your citizenry.
This bay has been declared off-limits. Go to your homes.
Stay out of the water.
Comply. Comply. Comply.

Nearly everyone on the water paddles monstrously toward shore. Ingram notices one kayaker fifty yards out just sits in the water, staring upwards at the drone, like she's either defying the order, or slipped into some kind of stasis. The drone moves toward her, arms raising, and once it reaches her, doesn't slow down, but quickly jerks her with its pincers, dislocating an arm, carrying her to the southern shore, then drops her moaning onto shells and sand.

"Oh my god." Ingram's nerves fray while others tend to the woman, while the drone, turns, paces the waters. "What's it doing?" she says. "Drones aren't supposed to do that."

"Someone wants to intimidate us," Victor says.

"But the government should be here to help."

"This is helping," he says. "Do you want people in that water? That could be what caused all of this."

"No one knows what caused anything."

And then suddenly the drone begins flashing. Ingram sees it first this time. A warning.

Message incoming. Message incoming.

At that moment Ingram notices phones start dinging and chirping. She and Victor reach into their pockets, find automated messages from government-controlled internal alert systems. While that's happening, a row of four airplane drones sweep over the bay, then over the town and suddenly begin spewing paper.

"What the hell is that about?" Victor barks.

"Flyers of some kind," Ingram says. Some of the papers tumble and fall at their feet, some sprinkle onto the bay.

Then the drone begins crackling, barking static; then a hiss, a whine, a beeping, followed by audio: *Incoming, incoming, incoming.*

More static, more flashing, then:

> *Baywood residents. Stay in your community.*
> *Do not try to leave.*

We are still assessing your situation.
We have determined you will be quarantined.
Effective immediately.
Los Osos Valley Road east of San Luis Bay Boulevard has been closed indefinitely.
Do not walk San Luis Bay Boulevard north of Turri Road.
Do not try to enter Turri Road.
Do not take dirt roads and trails out of Baywood.
Do not enter the ocean. Do not enter the sandspit. Do not enter the bay.
Do not leave Baywood.
Baywood residents, do not leave Baywood.
Anyone in Baywood who is not a resident is now a resident of Baywood.
Food will be brought to you.
Water will be brought to you.
Do not attempt to contact the government or its agencies.
Do not attempt to communicate outside your community.
Do not attempt to leave Baywood.
Await instructions.

"We should have left," Ingram says, then grabs her beeping phone. "We should have all left."

The same message fills their phones. The same message left as voicemails. The same message sent as emails. The same message, Ingram soon discovers, on each leaflet dropped from airplane drones. She notes the course paper, brownish, words printed on both sides. No number to call any agency has been added to the paper. Nothing.

And then Victor notes a tiny stamp on the back.

"What's that?" she says.

He tosses the flyer. "They're using biodegradable paper."

Chapter Sixteen

WE'RE AFRAID. WE suck down spliffs, feel anxiety rip at our guts while we talk about our families, our teachers, our friends— what we've seen. We don't know yet what will happen, don't know yet that some things won't matter anymore. Football scores. Volleyball scores. Who wins the debate against San Luis Obispo High, who loses. Who applies to Stanford or UC Santa Cruz, whether the tree or the slugs gonna make us wilder. So many things we'll stop caring about. But school hasn't ended yet. *Things. Are. Weird.* Classes get crazy. Teachers deading before and after class. Students deading in the quad. The janitor deads with the principal. Cheerleaders dead with nerds. An entire *deading* class instead of history. No more studying the Civil War or French, or trigonometry. Just an hour straight of deading, no one knows how they all know to lie still to the exact second. We don't go to those classes.

We forget about things like who can't handle the occasional online bullshit. Who might be voted class president. Who loses the race for homecoming queen. Which teacher has the most secrets. Which student lies the most to parents. None of this matters anymore.

What's important? This reminder that something is happening outside our control, something we can't imagine, won't imagine, because right here, right now, we can only selfishly think about our futures and our friends, our boyfriends, our girlfriends, our datemates, all of us, some of us.

It's crazy but some of us think we can see ourselves in a year, or what we'll be like when in our twenties. We think we can see ourselves in six months. We think we can see ourselves away from our parents, at a university campus, working jobs, living lives away from nagging, from being talked down to. We can't wait for our futures. We think we hold our own crystal balls, that we can see everything.

This timeline has already unraveled.

Even if we knew about all this deadness and chaos, and what caused it, we can't admit it. Not yet. We only see ourselves. Our invincible selves in our exciting futures, even though Mr. Rocha now deads in an elevator. He loves the elevator.

And so we plan more Dead of Night parties. We start holding them where we know State Parks workers and drone operators might ignore us. We pile into as few cars as possible, stagger our departures. We hike to our party spot, stars whirling around us because we're high. We listen to owls *toot-toot* from trees, while other night birds *screech*. We know what they are because Blas, who sits close to Kaylee, points them out. We think it's just the sound of night. We think this is how darkness speaks. The night isn't dead after all until we see an owl drop from the sky into a fire and let itself burn.

Some of us just don't think *this* is what it *is*. We think this is like when adults all join a social media platform. To imitate us, right? To act like us. To try to be cool. To try to recapture something about themselves they lost like a million years ago. And maybe all the kids started doing it again out of peer pressure, like they're the ones who hadn't done it before. This is our conspiratorial thought. It doesn't work out the way we think.

So in our typical kneejerk style, most of us start deleting our old deading posts. Like this might fix everything. The adults, some of the kids, like, they don't get it. It was for social media, you know? Not some kind of actual cultural greeting or whatever. So, in case they had looked at our old posts, or were looking, or in case our posts caused this, we erase everything. But it doesn't help. They keep at it. Obsessed. Freaky. All weird and twisted. They fall at each other's feet. Convulse. Eyes open in fake death. Bodies slack. Arms and legs twist. Mouths sometimes drool, foam. Sometimes gnaw at air. Like really dead looking. Snot bubbles out of our secretary's nose. Our athletic director pisses his suit after he throws himself into the quad flowerbeds. It really creeps us out. We talk about our parents, about how they dead before school, even during lunch on campus. Our counselors, admin, secretaries, teachers all start behaving strangely. We can hardly believe what Chewie tells us, that Mr. Rocha has been run over because he chose to dead in the street instead of his beloved elevator. He's not dead, but his legs are broken, his face has been smashed.

"I still remember what he said in the elevator," Kaylee says. "I wish I could remind him. But you know how the hospital is. Should we go visit him?"

"Don't," we say.

We can't figure out why no one seems to care.

We're really scared about what we were seeing. Bethany Schneider's parents dead before breakfast. Every. Day. She says they lie on the kitchen floor, eyes twitching under closed lids. She says it's so gross. Monica Okimoto tells us that on the way to school where she cuts along Third Street she has to step over adults walking their dogs who stop to dead on the street. She says some dogs dead with them. They twitch and some piss themselves. They lay there for thirty seconds, or a minute, like really not breathing and everything. "Limp and melting into the street," she whispers. "Then the adults slowly get up, dogs too, and go on their way."

We're all sickened. Why? Because deading evolves almost overnight into more than a greeting. A means of communication. A ritual connecting adults, co-workers, children, friends, pets, even wildlife and its world of survival.

Dozens throw themselves on sidewalks. Sometimes they fall just outside their own cars. In office hallways. Stores. Footbridges. School quads. Trails. Streets. Sidewalks. Everywhere. They wilt at each other's feet at the post office. Bodies twist in grocery aisles as if an infection has cut its way through while shopping for produce grown at local farms. They fall next to each other, on top of each other, entangle limbs, then as if sinking into death, become still and quiet.

We experience these behaviors in our own homes. Something comes over the face of our loved ones. A grimace. An inward stare. Like they're traveling somewhere, maybe among the stars, maybe through them. They fall and writhe. This becomes their greeting to us. A sacred act born and reborn. No, death and resurrection. An act of experience. An act of gross beauty to them. Not a resurrection. A return. Their cells weren't dead. No one has been declared dead from this. Not yet, we say.

Thankfully, in some homes the deading hasn't happened. But this has its own caustic effect. Some of us won't go out except to the Dead of Night. Harder to do, with the gas supply dwindling, most electricity tapped unless you had portable solars. Some of us trade for device juice at the Dead of Night, might be the only real reason left to go. There are only fifteen of us left. Some won't step outdoors without a mask. You don't know if the deading can slip under the front door, through the breath of your loved one, or from some unseen subatomic discharge from space that can penetrate walls.

Some of us can't stop crying.

Some of us stop going to school. Blas Enriquez is the first to drop out. Says he has to get the fuck out, leave, leave town, though he doesn't. The roads have been literally barricaded. Over the hills and the cliffs and the harbor, the Faceless are watching. Always with their spindly silver arms and stoplight pinprick eyes. So he can't leave. No one can. Like everyone else, he waited too long. One day too long. Though some of us think he will eventually take the risk.

Everything about our little town has become a sort of bubble. We're all trapped. We mean really trapped. The government, they know what's happening. They shut us down so fast. And why have the cops all disappeared? Where did they go? Who did they know to get them out? The fire department and ambulance service too. Just. Gone. Even their vehicles.

Those little blinking eyes keep watching us. We know.

Soon, we start to whisper, huddle, hold each other, giggle. We predict more of our futures. Adi Malone says, "In a year I'm going to be sneaking my boyfriend to my dorm room."

"No you're not," we laugh.

"Try me," Adi says.

"We gonna laugh so hard when you get caught."

"Not gonna get caught, ever. I'll have the best sex of my life while you're all watching *Scooby-Doo*."

"You get caught all the time."

"Not with boys, just weed and pills."

"Our parents let us smoke."

"You have cool parents. I don't."

Kaylee says she just wants to go to Cal Poly, major in something like English or Ethnic Studies. "I like it here," she says.

Blas's eyes light up.

"You don't hate your parents enough," we say.

"I don't know"—she tucks her knees to chest—"I never hated them."

"What about when you got caught drinking? They grounded you."

"I kind of deserved it. What if I crashed a car and killed

someone like Greg Taylor did driving home after that party last year? He crushed Janet Liu's little sister while she rode her bike home from work. Like, her neck broke and everything. He just wandered down the street until he got caught. No one heard from him again. No one, except when we all read about him in the news. He was only eighteen for a week when he did that. *Eighteen*. And now he's gone to some prison. You know what? If we see him again it will be years from now. He'll have all this weight in his eyes."

"At least he's not trapped here with us."

Nothing calms us when we meet next, not even the fact there are no more park rangers out here at MDO. We don't even know why we come out this far. We feel watched. We know we're watched. Something hovers in the sky, blinking.

Whatever.

"It's not fair," Kaylee says.

We get it. We know. We all know.

We say this like a chant. *It's not fair*. We mouth the words. We take turns saying this, feeling the hurt, this knowledge that our futures have been squeezed into what feels like a tiny space. And everywhere, walls. And those walls are closing in too.

"I saw Mrs. Rocha on Skyline Drive gulping like a fish," Chewie says. "She was in the gutter. Do you think she visits Mr. Rocha when she's not doing that? Someone said he's out but in a wheelchair. I don't think he leaves home."

We all feel like we're gulping when he says this. "What happened to her?"

Chewie shakes his head. "I don't know. I left her there. I'm not helping anyone like that. You know how they get."

And then we hear it. A howl in the woods. A groaning, dying howl, like something from a constellation vomiting starlight. Even though we're afraid, we laugh because this is the Dead of Night, our night. We expect stars to do this.

Blas tells us it's a coyote. Whatever. We don't care as long as it stays over in the eucalyptus grove. As long as it claws after starmilk and not us. We're determined, you know. We're gonna party until our tiredness calls us home.

We expect this darkness to scream at us. We expect to almost die just driving back down the windy MDO road. And tonight, that's as far as we can see—just the headlights on the road, the ocean somewhere at the edge, rumbling. That's our future for now, and though we don't know it, maybe this moment is our forever.

Chapter Seventeen

THE GROCERY STORE still gets fresh produce dropped off at the highway barricade on Los Osos Valley Road, though no one calls it a store anymore but a distribution center. I no longer get food delivered to my home. Nothing ever gets stamped with the name Sato. Gates slide open at the barricade and two electric-powered eighteen-wheelers, side by side, and in perfect synchronicity, hum through in reverse, slip into an area lined with security drones that drop out of nowhere, maybe the sky, maybe the hills, where more and more military vehicles gather, maybe from transports farther up the road.

The driver's side of each truck lays empty. Mere ghosts, these truckers are no more than circuits and algorithms embedded in computer dashboard chips. AI driven, they're like much of the world, like more than half of transport vehicles and most drones.

I feel like one of them, though I know I'm not. I tell myself to still feel, to continue to wonder about the world, that life can find its way toward understanding, toward a kind of synchronous existence. Balance eventually comes. The world may change, but I can change too. I can adapt. My husband always said this. *We must adapt or we die.* The world has been rapidly changing for so long that even the tiniest leafhopper has to adapt. Spiders have to adapt. Lizards too. Birds have to adapt new migration patterns, though they always have, because those that migrate have learned about food sources, food patterns, warm water versus cold water, invisible lines connecting to nourishment, to the green food islands in our cities, the parks and public spaces flowering and fruiting and blooming, opening for the pollinators and nectar drinkers, and bug eaters, and seed chewers to stop and give thanks, and I give thanks to them though they fall, though they have become so agitated and disturbed. Not all of them. Some. Too many. I fear many won't adapt to the warmer ocean waters battering our shores. I fear I am losing my ability to do this too, and so I tell myself to stop this damn feeling, this drone-like feeling rising in me.

Offloaded pallets get pulled into neat lines, while Baywood inhabitants sometimes watch silent, sometimes yell, sometimes cry, and usually dead, often in ghoulish protest to those watching: tiny drones that hover just out of stone's-throw reach while transport drones buzz and work.

I've only watched this once, and refuse to go back. The time I witnessed this spectacle, a small group of men rushed the truck, each zapped by guided electro-nodes fired faster than hummingbird wingbeats. You couldn't see the sparks, but you could hear each crack as if something broke inside these men. Only one was taken away, dragged into the truck after a drone glued his wrists and ankles together. I'm told he was the third of us to be taken. Something else strange. No one has recognized those kidnapped. Not that I believe we recognize each other anymore, but some now think spies exist among us besides drones, besides each other.

Most of the time I make my way to the distribution center, pick up a few free foodstuffs, then walk home towing a wheeled suitcase filled with cans of soup and fruit. I prefer soup at my age, though last time I did pick up a bag of rice, some vegetables, some tofu. I'm not worried that soon I might not be able to prepare a nice meal, though I do feel our condition could quickly worsen, that maybe I should only gather soups. Many have turned to growing their own food, but one storm could destroy everything. Micro-crops could be gone tomorrow. Electricity and natural gas could stop flowing today. Healthcare has already mostly disappeared—no one wants to go to the hospital anyway. The local electric ambulance that wasn't driven off in the emergency vehicle exodus still has power and I hear rumors from Ingram of a hay cart pulled by two half-starved horses, driven by two high school dropouts. I assume they cart the dead and truly dying, and I now wonder what my last thoughts might be, and if they will come while in that very cart.

No one wants to be locked in here. I know this. There's little scientific explanation for what's been happening, only excuses, and the same theories over and over. A disease, a miasma in the water caused by toxins in the bay gone airborne. A government-released spore, an evolving avian flu in Baywood's muddy, bird-filled estuary, or something infectious secreted from our local snails. I know none of this is likely true. It simply hurts to be cut off from those who might tell us face to face. For now, it's the Faceless, the drones. We get cold answers if any. They rarely talk, though Ingram says she's seen people whispering to them, that some of these drones whisper back then shoot high into the clouds toward black dots rumbling in the atmosphere.

News reports have mostly been variations of the same headline: CALIFORNIA COASTAL CITY OF BAYWOOD CONTINUES QUARANTINE LOCKDOWN. Reporters said they couldn't get close, pointed to the toxic spill in the bay as the culprit. But now things are worse. The internet has frozen, won't update. News sites reveal the same stories no matter how much you refresh. Phones went dead long ago. I'm in a world of unusable apps, apps that won't click, that won't open, that stare at me. Television, not even static, dies, showing only empty screens, a thing of the past, though our consoles turn on, sometimes by themselves and blink as if watching. On a nearby Baywood corner, TVs have been piled like tombstones. I add my Samsung flatscreen. I do miss my shows. Radio had mostly been conspiracy talk anyway, if you could find something besides music, but even those stations disappear one by one, replaced with a kind of pulse, almost a heartbeat if you listen closely.

Day by day amenities shut down. Gas stations run out of fuel. Electric stations somehow slip off the grid. The post office stops receiving mail. Restaurants shutter their doors. Most people work out of town so don't hold jobs anymore. Money becomes unimportant, only what you can barter. I have nothing to trade. No one wants old memories. Communications have been blocked. Email, wifi towers. Remote workers lose employment because of this. Baywood suddenly feels like a third world country threatened with oppression and war. I recall how my father used to speak of his great uncles being interned in the concentration camp at Manzanar, the "apple orchard." They'd stare at the Owens Valley mountains and wish they could hide in them rather than being stuffed in those awful barracks, those strange reception centers far away from their houses—stolen away from their farms—stolen away from their dreams. We were the Japanese Menace, the Japanese Problem, but we weren't going away. I say *we* because I feel like I'm there now, though I was born much later. That feeling, though, has been inside me not just now, but ever since my family told me about Manzanar; I have always felt I was there too, rooted inside those walls. Though sansei, I felt something akin while growing up, the stares sometimes, even while a young woman, even today, this feeling of being different, of being treated like I'm less than zero. Though at the same time, until now, I think I could never really grasp what happened to so many in those camps. It was more than unbearable hundred-plus-degree summers. It was the inability to leave, the barbed wire everywhere, the guard towers and soldiers with machine guns. It was the cheap pine planking and tar paper, the lack of ceilings and privacy. It was the humiliation, the lack of trust in America's own people. And though I still have more than my parents' generation did, in a way, now I might have even less. Because at least they had each other. They were never malcontents and agitators, though America slapped those labels on them, on us, on me though I wasn't there. Do I have this label now? Will I for all time? I'm not deading. I don't have the desire to. I may be in the minority with this. I may soon be seen as something I'm not. I see the way people are looking at me. Something may soon happen. I fear being taken away, or worse.

I go on talking to Hiroki, sometimes while I sleep. He's with me in the past and present, alive in memory, alive in my dreams where I worry aloud and he laughs and says, *Things could be worse.* We argue when he does this. When I wake I tell myself that next time I'm going to be aware of my dream-state, I'm going to tell him the only thing worse than living in Baywood is finding your husband dead from a heart attack in a bathtub. But I never remember. And if I did, could I say as much?

It eats at me how Baywood has changed. What began with animals, with Davis sprawled at the lookout, and before that, a police officer feigning death on Pasadena Drive, has spread into the common populace. They call it *deading*. The high schoolers named it that, something about their social media, something awful they used to do. Nothing I've ever seen, this form of communal behavior. People fall. They writhe. They're in pain. Eyes spin toward backs of heads. Mouths foam. Bodies go still. Hearts stop beating. People die. Or so it seems. Then they come back. They stand up. They dust themselves off. They go about their day. Just like Davis did. Only now, they commune around it, they've become a unit of death.

But not everyone. Not me. Not Blas. Not some paddle-boarders whose legs I spy dislocated by the monster drone when they try to escape across the bay. Not those I hear shooting at drones, who soon run out of ammunition, or whose homes get "hummed," and everyone falls silent in a four-home radius, dropped by a different kind of deading, though not really, more like those who try to rush the trucks and get knocked out, and then drones come rifling through homes, taking guns, taking ammo, destroying 3-D printers. Probably for the best. Otherwise, all these people would soon be shooting each other. It's too little, too late from the same types who fostered the rise of corporatized security drones, built from the generations who shot every bird from the sky, or tried, who refused to elect those who might curtail the rise of drone tech, whose behavior of "taking out drones" only fostered the militancy surrounding the protection of corporate drone flyways. Not so many others.

I refuse to stay indoors, won't be bothered by what's happening, by being trapped, by now being in the minority, by what's happened to the animals and people of Baywood, though I can't see how on earth any of this can be contained. It's impossible, but humans always attempt the impossible because humans can't always see past physical barriers to the invisible world. The problem appears much larger than Baywood, much larger than one toxic bay, than one missing oyster farmer, than one missing worker, or a town suddenly empty of many of its services.

I won't stay indoors, won't stop visiting trails close to home, won't stop walking along the bay, won't stop greeting others, or nodding, smiling, saying hello. Won't stop when others fall and writhe, though my instinct has always been to help. My reality now? Keep walking, believe there's always been some kind of occupation to test my endurance, another reality to superimpose over mine that I must untangle. I'm not ready to stop, to lie on the ground, to dead. When I'm tired I'll take a nap, which I can do on the couch, or flop in a chair. Like any normal person. I won't convulse but sleep in my bed, snore and dream of Hiroki, the way he was, the way he smiled and laughed. The way he would sometimes say, *Everything will be okay*. I wish I could remember the Japanese phrase that means "safe, all right, okay." I once knew the words but they won't come back, as if they've been frightened away. I refuse to look them up, wanting so much to remember, though I feel them deep in my stomach, soothing me. *Feelings weigh as much as memories*, Hiroki used to say. *Just let them be*. I used to laugh, think them silly words. Who wants to weigh a feeling? But now I understand. Something about age, when you can see more clearly the weight of both feeling and memory.

Today I walk the bay toward the little blue Baywood Park Pier. It's not much of a pier really, more of a wooden platform adjacent to the bay that can get partly surrounded by tidewater. I want to gaze west toward the sandspit, imagine the ocean beyond, myself drifting far at sea. On a shortcut through the Preserve I spy Ingram and Victor gazing into the canopy of a Monterey cypress, a kind of coniferous evergreen with an irregular flat top. Its bright green foliage hangs with lichen. These trees only grow on the central California coast; I love their beauty, so inhale their lemony scent. This is when I hear a rising slurry trill. It's loud. I don't have binoculars but know what's flitting in and out of strings of moss.

"Northern Parula," I say. "An expected vagrant. Male or female?"

"Not sure," Ingram says. "Haven't seen you in a while."

"I'm around. Still . . . my old self."

"Male," Victor adds. "I'm thinking this is the year for parulas. We're due for an irruption of something, though not sure of warbler irruptions as much as something like winter finches moving south. This is the third parula in the area in the last week."

And then the bird stops singing. It happens so fast. The warbler tumbles straight toward my hands, which I hold out as if speaking from my palms to tell it where to fall. I catch it like a cottonball, though it resembles a fancy egg, over easy, that yellow breast on a white underside, a splotch of orange like a gorgeous yolk. The head is grey, as is its back that holds a lime-colored patch. Throat, yellow. Yellow lower mandible too, and a bright broken-white eye-ring, bright as its double white wing bars.

"Should you be touching it?" Ingram says.

"I don't see why not," I say. "It needed some help." I pet its tiny head, observe its throat move.

"But it's ill," Ingram adds. "I think it's very sick."

"How often do you see anyone touching anything so lovely," I say, "except for someone maybe banding a bird, or those who rescue them like Hiroki did in Morro Bay."

"Hiroki," Ingram adds, as if saying the name will conjure a spirit.

The bird begins stirring just then. I cradle it in my aged hands that form a tiny basket and stare at the tiny specimen, cooing to it to wake up, the way Hiroki would, the way Mother used to hum love songs. Soon enough, the bird begins ruffling wing feathers, and then, right in my palms, throws its head back, sings its rising trill before darting into a distant cypress.

"A beautiful moment," I say. "To share such love, to be aware of the rise of consciousness." I remember many years ago finding an endemic Okinawa Rail, candy-red bill and legs, deep red eye and black throat, white stripe-work of its black belly, brown wings and back. It was crossing a road when a car zipped over it. Somehow the bird kept walking untouched, and afterwards, flapped over and hopped into my arms. When I gazed at that bird, and it at me, we both knew about life and death and every possibility on the timeline. I recall stroking the rail's neck. It nibbled at my fingers, leapt into roadside foliage, and let out a string of shrill notes, almost like laughter.

"It's ill," Ingram repeats. "You should wash your hands, you're just touching whatever you want."

"Stop that," Victor says to Ingram. "She's fine."

I sense Ingram's spiraling, though not sure to where, not sure I want to know. I sense many people spiraling in a similar manner. "We're complicit, you know, in all of this, in whatever is yet to come," I say. "Not sure the fault lies in what I'm touching, but in the thoughts behind this unraveling. I'm afraid we're going to keep making the same mistakes."

"Mistakes," Ingram says.

"Do you feel there's something deeper?" I add. "I sense things moving toward a center, something more at fault."

"Center of what?" Ingram asks. "Treated by who? You know, you really should have used eBird. That data will help change the world. Now it's too late. Everything is too late."

Before I can reply, I hear yelling from outside the Preserve, from El Moro Avenue. "I'm going to see what's happening," I say.

"Not a good idea," Ingram says.

"I'm going too," Victor adds.

We slip through a path that cuts through the Preserve onto the road where a crowd has gathered. Some in the crowd fall down and writhe, others surround a man we all recognize, accusing him of starting a group of non-deaders.

"I haven't started shit," he says.

"That's Alan Dalten," Ingram whispers. "What's going on?"

"They're accusing him of forming some group," Victor says.

Ingram doesn't like this. "We should leave," she says.

I sense others coming up the road. If we slip back into the Preserve, we can get away. But I don't want to get away, I want to be a witness for once, to be one of the rememberers. And if I don't stay, I won't see, may never see.

"I'm staying," Victor says to Ingram. "You can go. But if you stay, don't talk. Say nothing."

Ingram sighs, stays by his side.

Alan has been shoved to the ground by Marcel Flores, who has other men with him, some teens, some women too. Fingers now in Alan's face. "Where's your group?" Marcel says. "Where are they? What they got against us?"

"Why aren't you bothering José Miranda?" Alan says. "He's got a group over in Elfin Forest. All kinds of people with him."

"Don't you worry about José," Marcel says. "He's got more shotguns than you. Tell me right now, do you dead? You risen?"

"You'd have kept your guns if you hadn't aimed them at drones," Alan says.

"Not what I asked."

"Of course I'm not a Riser," Alan yelps, while my heart starts to race. "That's stupid. You all need doctors, psychologists, something. I sure hope the government drops in a vaccine soon."

"We don't need a vaccine," Marcel says. "And we don't need you pointing out our differences. Things are changing around here. You gonna see it pretty quick. We're forming a new council. You'll see."

"Can I get up now?" Alan says, then calls to everyone watching, looking in my direction. "One of you going to help me? I got a bad leg. You just going to let these people push me around? I know not all of you are one of them. Some of you come to my meetings."

"You're a threat," Marcel says, "a goddamned threat," then to anyone who will listen, "He's not one of us, will never be one of us. We got a new thing in Baywood, not going to put up with these Alan types. You organize against us Risers, speak out like he does, and you're all gonna be in trouble."

I feel something else watching, feeling what's going on. It's not just me, not only Victor or Ingram, or other non-deaders hiding in this crowd. I spy several gulls circling, not sure if it's them or another presence. Perhaps the bay has eyes, other eyes beyond the monster drone in the distance, as if whatever is crawling in Pecho Road Willows has attuned to this exact moment, maybe not controlling, but having set this in motion, now wants to see what these people will do, can do to each other. And while I want to help, I know I can't overpower anyone, can't give myself or Victor and Ingram away. I can't risk them, though if I were younger, maybe would risk myself.

"I just want those of us who are normal to be together." Alan tries to get to his feet when one of the teens, "Three-Point" Patterson, a popular basketball jock, kicks him in the face. Nearly everyone flinches. Blood drips from Alan's nose. "You're not normal," he squeals. "You all need help. Someone get them away from me."

And then a knife flashes, I don't know whose, don't recognize the man. Terror fills Ingram's eyes. I feel her need to escape. But the crowd has bled onto our section of street, some of them start dragging Alan our way. If we walk away now, we may never know what happens, might give ourselves away. The crowd has doubled now, most don't seem to be non-deaders, not by the way they smile and gaze, the way a few fall down and *dead*, as if a kind of *deading in support of.* Then I see the knife again. In a dirty, unkempt hand, hair a mess of tangles from deading in gutters and bushes. And that man says, "Who else around here part of that group? Who else don't dead? I'm gonna walk around, if I don't recognize you, or you don't fall to the ground, then we're gonna know, gonna put you on our list. And you don't want to be on our list."

"Oh my god, we have to get out of here," Ingram mutters.

Then I whisper: "Don't run. Do what I do."

"What are you talking about?" Ingram says. "I'm not doing anything you're doing."

"I think I know," Victor adds. "Just do it."

And then I fall at their feet, my old legs bending, crumbling.

I squirm, spit, just as they do, as if in pain, as if resisting death, while the man with the knife slips closer and closer. I arch my back in ways I didn't think possible, adrenaline numbing the pain of this stretch, forcing muscles to strain, my neck tendons near bursting. There is nothing about this I want, and imagine my body like theirs fights these last moments, willing itself to stay alive. I feel Hiroki choking on water and make myself do the same, coughing, drowning. I can almost feel footsteps, can smell his odor, not Hiroki's, then sense Ingram's moan, her dropping, her convulsions, Victor's too. I can feel us all dying though it's only an act. Others too, others, so many others. Unlike the actual deaders, I'll remember every moment, every twist of shoulder and elbow joint, knees and back. I'll remember where my mind goes: *nowhere*, just here in the street grit, in the present. I won't be joining Hiroki, or going anywhere the deaders go. I'll just *be*, and in this, ever so dirty with scraped knees. A moment later I allow myself stillness, begin a kind of meditation long done in the presence of trees and streams, clearing every thought, seeking peace, birdsong, allowing tranquil thoughts of Hiroki brushing my hair on our wedding night so many decades ago. And though I can't rise as Davis did, a disjointed, creeping thing, I soon push to my feet, and when the group's eyes aren't on me, and the man with the knife moves elsewhere, I slip away from this madness, enough of a witness, seen enough, and can feel Ingram and Victor following. I don't want to be complicit, I tell myself, though maybe have already been.

Chapter Eighteen

THOSE RISERS EVERYONE keeps talking about? We brought them our own ideas, our own traditions, pawned them off on the adults with a few rules too, like how we've been aware of how to dance around death & regeneration. Mushrooms, dead leaves, snails, everything. Life & death simultaneously present in the same place at the same time, like our skin sloughing off while we're constantly generating new skin. And decaying leaves on the ground, fungus growing out of the decay & new growth, birds flying around, distributing seeds, pollinating while some drop of disease.

Now the adults follow *us*, respect *us*, listen to *us*, at least, those of us who *dead*.

Let us explain, because you need to know why we matter, why we're all better off because of the things we told them all of us should do.

We agree that the adults started most of this new deading. Unless you want to blame some stupid snails. But snails can't think. They're not us. They're just squishy things & probably didn't have much to do with anything. And they're mostly gone anyway.

You've got to do other things, deep think, daydream, fall in love, cry, watch mysteries & romance on TV, read dramatic lit & dark romance, listen to music with friends, let it all turn darker, darker, communal, like we already did, in touch with death & cosmic within nature, within death & deading.

Just like most of the town, we teens & little ones joined the Risers movement. No-brainer, we had to. But we're different. We've always been different & we realized that was our advantage. We were already what they wanted to be. We realized that some of us had done this before, a different version, yes, but that still made us OG & being OG makes us special. We told them, "You need us. Before this all started, we were *already* deaders." That shocked them until we said, "But we think we were always Risers in our hearts." We showed them old photos we kept on our phones, all kinds of dead images of us. They really loved them & agreed we were important to all of this, but were still wary.

Look, maybe you're not getting it, they only had a few rituals. Even when the Risers' organization had been going on a while, they hardly did anything but hang out together & dead. Those adults, they were still kind of lost. They needed someone to listen to. They'd started trying to figure out *who* they were, *what* they were & *why* they are. We knew the answers. We spoke up, said, "We already know all that. You need to take us seriously. We've always known what deading is, what it makes us. We know what power comes from it & with it." So, we said, "*You* have to create something new, something *holy* out of this."

They were listening. So, we told them how some of us had been in student government (some of us are still mad the school closed) & had parents on the city council, that we understood the need to organize, to have a kind of hierarchy. But we said, "That's not good enough." And then we said that we'd gone to weekly prayer meetings, so we knew about all that churchy stuff too. Who cares about that? That riled the adults. They didn't want to listen. But we interrupted, said let go of that & try channeling us for a change. We told them they had to go deeper, darker, that we could bring them those skills. So we told them how some of us had been part of Black Lace & Bookmarks, a kind of horror worship gothic book club filled with candlelit story readings, tarot readings, gothic attire (we still argue on what defines this style because there is no one way to do goth dress, though give some of us lace, lots of pale lace & black knee-high boots & moth wings & music & we can weave dark & light in that). Anyway, we had also brought vegan fake fur for pretend pelts, bones, so many bones (real & fake), potions of fake body fluids, pins, needles, knives, even coffins, since Janet Jimenez's dad used to sell pine boxes & everything. We realized, we told the adults who were listening, that deading was about a painful death, that there was nothing nice about it, thus all the writhing, a *pain* we all quickly forgot because deading was also about the infinite & unknown & being misfits in this world & maybe sort of unwelcome in everything, though we knew we went somewhere & we knew we became full in a way we'd never felt because of where we went.

So we told them we needed lots of chants & along with those, joyful pain rituals. Piercing of the flesh sort of things. Body horror if you want to call it that. And for the younger girls, we wanted to incorporate some stiff-as-a-board-light-as-a-feather chants for calling on the powers of our deading, something for when we returned from our dark journeys, so we could re-embrace our mindscapes, which we felt had been set alight with magical powers, powers we believed, do believe, are real. We told them that we think all of us girls can really do this & a few boys too, you know, levitate each other, read minds, influence with our minds, share dark dreams, use animals for magic purposes & feel our way, like, into new dimensions. We really could, though we only shared among ourselves.

And we didn't want Bloody Mary forgotten either, because we'd all seen her so many times & not just some hypno-hysteria thing from staring in mirrors, but *her*, like really *her*, breathing on us, softly usually, on our necks, that hot breath smelling like embers, so we said we should incorporate mirrors, so many mirrors, so we could see those other dimensions behind us, around us, with strange-faced illusions & real Bloody Marys, ready to reach through, pierce our flesh. We wanted to embrace the reflections of our new murdered world. We could walk upstairs backwards, create new chants, perhaps another name besides Bloody Mary chanted thirteen times, a bloody someone, maybe a bloody one of us to replace *her*, or join *her*. Who might be a willing sacrifice, we asked the adults, then ourselves. We told them we wanted her to be one of us.

Some of us, in doing some of these rituals, we thought, developed access to our dreams, or so we argued, we fought about this too, though maybe this was because we wanted visions & chants & levitation & spells to be part of everything dark & dead, that judeo-christian-horror buried-in-the-ground sort of hell that we could wear like dresses.

Maybe this, we said, was similar to how we goth girls once felt, you know, *us*, because we knew about our history too, something beyond dark novels, something historical & very American cool, like freaky-faced Puritans, you know? The ones who hanged the accused, who pulled them apart, socket by socket, lit them on fire. They would do the same to us, you know, if we'd lived then & couldn't point fingers, raise the alarm, that we were the brave, we were the ones saving everyone. So we have to claim the same. To make things clear, we told them we were talking about those Salem, Massachussetts girls of Tituba's magic sphere, that devil-in-the-shape-of-a-girl-&-woman world that we'd read about in history class, the only history we girls loved, that small reflection of that British world, whose witch hunts dwarfed ours.

THE DEADING

We asked them, "You ever hear of Witchcraft Act 1562?" Not Salem, but close. That act was against conjurations, enchantments & witchcrafts in England. Yeah, don't invoke evil spirits & all that. And that sentiment was in the colonies too. We were sure something similar happened in those cities on hills. Anyway, we felt the Salem girls were the OG goth girls in our hearts, because they were the *afflicted* & their love of dark ritual & sweet familiars helped them point the fingers at others who were loaded into carts & taken to Procter's Ledge, beneath the crevice where they swung from ropes. Those girls saved themselves. And that's the way it had to go & has to go now. We may not understand what they went through, we said, or how heavy history really weighs on this, but we felt those All-American girls, & that All-American-African Tituba too, their accusations, their wonders of the invisible world, their magic animals & familiars, their rituals & boy-hating spells, their binding & darkness, clawing & suckling, their finding every witch's tit hidden beneath layers. They were really *us*. But once again, we need to claim it, show everyone how non-deaders are the real threat—we'll point our fingers at them.

Without being stereotypical, we have to remember those girls' mystery, & most importantly, their need to bind & bond, to rise the way the crumbled past did through them, because they spoke to each other through their dreams & gossip & could pluck the devil from the wilderness, put it in their will-o'-the-wisp light in their hearts, push away those Cotton Mather blather preachers who tried to inoculate the past against more than smallpox. Those girls spoke to us from where they gathered at their victims' burnt graves, to our similar lives, where pain & binding brings portals, though we felt burned by our personal flames each greeting, each deading.

Don't get us wrong, we said, we're not talking creating the musical version of *Beetlejuice*. We told the adults that we were talking something new, something serious, something so dark &

filled with ritual that all of us could be the influencers of a new death, a new future. We needed those dark Puritan goth girls & hanged women & men, the accused, the witches & ghosts of that supernatural realm, to all be in our rituals.

Nineteen nooses, we said. One for each of the Salem accused. We'll decorate.

The adults said yes.

We renovated the Pentecostal church on Los Osos Valley Road. You know the one with the mismatched outer architecture & rectangular well, with those hundred-year-old pews inside? We said, "Make a new pulpit & cover it in candles & rags. Add the heads of small animals. Bring in the scent of the dead. Bury the dead-alive as a service. Dig holes in the church. Bury, bury & bury."

And they did. They added those deep pits, the rot, those Bloody Mary mirrors too, though we were not kidding about a sacrifice. We'll figure that out. One of us, we reminded them.

And then we said not to forget to choose leaders, that we should create a new manifesto, one with rules & laws. Something like that ancient book *Malleus Maleficarum*, "the Hammer of Witches which destroys witches & their heresy with a two-edged sword," but reversed, & so we said we should have Non-Deader Act 1562, the 1562 an ode to that hellish Act that killed British witches, though we adored them & our Salem sisters. Non-deaders aren't witchy at all, we said. They simply need to join or go. They can't *see*. And so we began to create, to talk, to sit with the adults into the long nights, because like us they really hated non-deaders, & wanted change far beyond Baywood, but Baywood, we all realized was our playground. We deaded together too, dreamed together, came up with a plan to protest together, to incarcerate, to give non-deaders a chance to overcome their heresy, "the Hammer of Non-deaders which destroys them & their heresy with a two-edged sword," to bring the words of the Risers to Baywood, to the barricades, & a system, &

more & more rules, because we thought we could find patterns in this, right & wrong ways to do all of this, to create something for all of us, something much larger than ourselves, something everybody would want, far & beyond Baywood.

So, for starters, we also handed them this:

    I. We, the Risers, are the sacred vow, the holy of holies.
    II. We are the darkness in the ground, the bones in the earth.
    III. We are the rituals, the tokens, the hanging & buried dolls.
    IV. We are the other place we can't remember.
    V. We are death & rot.
    VI. We are the beings in the mirrors.
    VII. Those who can't see, must burn in round pits.

We know the deep connection between femininity & the life cycle. The potential to have a human both grow & die inside of you, that's powerful. The deading, like this, a death-life in us. We feel it growing. We tell the adults that embracing desire & the sublimation/transformation of the individual into the collective means giving your everything to our deading.

Isn't this a skill? To be able to give in? To submit the self to the larger death? We must get in touch with sadness & inertia to do this. So we sing like Florence Welch told us so long ago & now we think we are kings.

We flip the archetype, embody this dark, powerful royalty of death of us. We do this naturally, like synapses firing without thought.

We must ask you. Have you ever had like a random, sudden impulse to die? Like driving into a car head on, but you *don't*? But you *want* to. You just want to see what it's like. But you can only do it once. Now we do this every day. In our circle, we chant this. Why? We participate in this quasi-socially acceptable thing to satisfy our impulses. Think about it. Dying is literally the only experience that the living can't really have & stay in the land of the living. We think this makes our yearning better.

We seek this power through ritual, both individual & collective, this symbolic, repeatable power, governed by rules, easy to replicate, to spread to others. We're theatrical, we know, a spectacle to be participated in & witnessed.

Why are we so drawn to the place (death) that we cannot go? What is it within our psyches or souls that desires & yet resists the transformation at the same time? Is it the contradiction?

And so some of us, for example, Joon, Eliza, Jane, Kaylee & Reina, have said about the adults, as if to the adults, almost as if the same mind:

"You don't understand. This is something new, a rebirth & the end of everything. You had your chance, YOU let the world burn down around you while you cared for nothing other than dollars & power. You poisoned yourselves; you needed a television to remind you every night that you had kids. Well no more. Fuck that. We are a new family—the multi-tentacled demon-beast, the snake-heads of the Gorgon, turning doubters to stone. We are pissed. Your former society was a trap, a false binary, not individualism or society: we are zooids; we are a hive."

"We'll scavenge art from your bones. Your own movies warned you of all of this."

"Now we rise. Now it's us. In the name of Emma Goldman & Frida Kahlo, we rise. In the name of Jane Austen & Mary Shelley. In the name of Octavia Butler, in the name of Patti Smith whose songs tell us to pray screaming."

What they do next, they take a dried flower from the hands of an old woman who used to work at the yogurt shop & gently thread it through her hair. The woman's eyes widen, wild & full of tears. The woman whispers apologies in a hoarse voice. Rows of scars on the girls' forearms glint in candlelight like mother-of-pearl. Other girls rise now, in gentle servitude, arranging dried flowers & pierced beetles in the hair of other adult women. Some of the girls twist small dead lizards into gaudy brooches. They cut through grey braids & add the hair to baskets filled with driftwood, shells, buttons—small talismans. Incense burns. Smoke curls.

Jane wants to smudge church walls with the bundles of sage she liberated from some dead child's home. "We're Risers now," she says. "We use this to pierce & to purify." Her voice comes deep & sonorous, doesn't realize it's less her words & more her round phonemes weaving ASMR spells that leave them breathless.

"We're not here to coddle you; we rose first," others add in unison. "We're not here to be sweet girls; we're not here to nurture you." As they say this, Kaylee strokes the cheek of the old pastor's wife with the backs of her fingers. Eyes roll in their sockets.

"Listen." Jane points to a low moan from beneath the dirt floor, followed by a thick blanket of absolute silence. Not everyone knows what's coming. The fear tastes good.

Pain can be its own comfort. And comfort is at best an illusion. Jane hides her face in her long hair, but we know she smiles. We all do.

For some, this will be the last time we say anything to you. We just wanted to tell you that we know you're not together with us on this, that some of you are still part of the Dead of Night, even though there really aren't meetings anymore, none that we know about. You need to understand that we see our deading as a way forward, a way to move on, to join other worlds, to create something new, something the rest of this planet can look at & ask, *What are they doing, we need to be part of this*.

We know our socials don't work anymore. We can't post any of this. The news cameras never come, not a single one. So we send this to you & remind you that we will go to the barricades & tell the world of its sins. We will do this outside the grocery store where the government brings food. We will do this for the Faceless, because they won't let us share with the world. We are doing this for you, our non-deader former friends & classmates, who need to die & die again or make their way to the pits. We know others must be doing this outside Baywood. They have to be. And if not, eventually, we'll find a way to spread our message, we'll commune with outsiders because they'll come to us if we don't go to them first. We know the Faceless aren't all AI trying to solve the world through complex intuitive algorithms created by coders with Doritos dust on their fingers. We know that real flesh & blood sees what *they* see.

Will *they* feel what we feel?

Will *they* dream what we dream?

Will *they* go where we go?

There isn't an afterlife. There's not an afterworld. But there is somewhere *we* go when we fall, when we dead. It's painful to get there. But we forget the pain.

Our rituals & laws now confirm this is all real.

And believe us, one of *us*, or one of *you*, will be the new Bloody Mary.

The deading. You used to love it. Now you're so afraid that you may never be filled with dark joy. When will you understand that this isn't just a kind of greeting? This isn't just a way to commune, this is our way to always commune. So, we offer you a chance.

This isn't just for show.

Even the adults joined us.

Come with us.

If you want to stay, you have to die.

Chapter Nineteen

CHANGO AND MARIA sit next to each other on the living room couch. "You ready, mama?" Chango says, already out of breath.

"Not just yet, mijo," she replies. "Another minute."

He knows something terrible has happened to Baywood, to its citizens, to its bay, to his mother, and something worse to himself. He can't understand why things are different, why he feels so ill, why even breathing is difficult, as if this air is the wrong air, as if he needs to breathe some other atmosphere, from a mountaintop, from a desert, somewhere that's not here.

He doesn't understand why everything has turned into a blur, why he often sees double, why a shimmer vibrates along the edges of objects. He knows he's lost his appetite. He knows his eyes are red like his brother says: "You're a night heron, a bird. Go to the hospital."

Even Maria tells him to go to the hospital. But he ignores them. He's tired. He wants to dream. He might be remembering parts of his dreams, which is more than his mother or any other deaders can say. He doesn't like being a deader. He doesn't like what's happening. And most of all, he wants to look out for his little brother, that little cabrón, that pendejo. Blas has always been the nerd of the family. Now Blas had transformed into the only normal person in Baywood.

And now these deaders began organizing. They don't even like that word. They call themselves Risers. Maria tells Chango this, wants him to join. He won't go to them, not the way he looks, the way he feels, like a growing entity. "I can't, Mom," he says. "They'll know I'm different." He tells her they might do him the way they did Alan Dalten, string him up on the sky-blue deck of the Baywood Park Pier, lungs stuffed with mud, gull shit scraped onto his cheeks, a crown of clamshells draped over his head, snails sunk into his eye sockets.

"You joined killers, Mom," Chango says. "Gotta find a way to not completely be with them, fight it. I don't know how, but you have to remind yourself that you have to protect Blas. You have to protect him. You understand me?" He coughs, been coughing a lot lately.

"Mijo, what's wrong with you?"

"I don't know," Chango says. "Not feeling well. Something's happening to me. Like I'm from another place, not from here anymore."

"You need help."

"At that hospital? You do realize people been going there and not coming back out."

"That's not true."

"Yeah, well you need to protect my little brother."

"I understand," she says. "Already found a way." She pulls up her sleeve to reveal scab trails from wrist to elbow.

"Mother Mary, what are you doing to yourself, Mama?"

"I know I have to join them," she grunts. "But this is how I remember not to betray your brother."

"By scarring yourself?"

"I have to."

"Jesus, Mom, okay." He feels himself being pulled. "I have to dead for a little while."

"Not yet," she says. "You're always there for so long. One of these times you won't come back."

"Don't be afraid," he says, feeling the pull. "I'll always be here."

"Well then maybe I won't."

Chango tries to laugh but can't. He feels joy trapped in his chest, a heaviness. An echo deep inside, a rattle, a shifting. "You want to stay in that place."

"Everyone does."

"What's it like?"

"I don't know, mijo. Can't really remember. It's like I can almost see, feel, taste, hear. I can almost remember being there. I know I can feel others here when I do."

"I don't like where I go," he admits. Images come to him of a barren, rocky landscape. A red filter over everything. "But I can breathe there."

"You can breathe here."

He squeezes her hand, her aging fingers. "Mama. Have you looked at me lately? Everything feels heavy." He can feel even his voice doesn't seem like it belongs anymore, not to himself, and he can sense something else too. Echoes from another place, from the tidewaters at the oyster farm. No, beyond the sand-spit. No, not right here in near-shore waters, from hundreds of miles away, maybe thousands, from the deep, from the dark. Something guttural comes up just then, from his throat like a sea creature's voice, a kind of gulping.

"Mijo. You okay?" Maria says.

Chango feels his hand losing strength. His mind turns off from the room like a switch. He's in the barren landscape now, feels his feet under him, somewhere far off. Yet he's still in the living room, doesn't want to completely let go yet. He wants to feel Maria's hand a moment longer, this connection to who he is and was, just a vato working the day shift. "You go too, Mom," he whispers.

"You're not coming back for a long time," she says. "I can feel it."

"Yeah yeah, but you go too."

He feels her convulse. "I see . . ." she starts to say and is gone.

Chango can't feel her hand anymore, can only remember her hand, can only remember the couch. Can only remember his little brother, who he hopes can't see his dreams.

Chapter Twenty

DISGUSTED BY THE violent death and desecration of Alan Dalten, Ingram feels a kind of terror lining the insides of her soul. Fear takes over, the way she felt overpowered by the mountain lion though it didn't touch her. As if some cat might tear into her throat.

She takes a bite of dinner. Mashed potatoes. Always mashed potatoes. She isn't hungry.

At the same time, she's learning to hide, to pretend, to fake-dead more and more. It's a thin lining of safety, a fragile membrane. The Risers have formed a local government hierarchy, its ranks filled not only with those who dead, but those who have come to worship the deadings, who can't slip into that deading state, but want to more than anything. She knows some, like her, are simply afraid to do anything else.

Once Alan died, Victor and Ingram knew they had to keep playing along. But it's tricky, she knows this. Dalten's followers have struck back, burned two Riser homes. She expects more non-deaders to feel the deading wrath, and she fears a war will grow among them, or simply that a hunt could begin.

Ingram and Victor constantly talk about their strange new lives, how she's scared of pretending to have the affliction so that people won't turn on them. It's terrifying, she tells Victor. They've been invaded by something demanding they die multiple times a day. As if old age isn't enough of a reminder. As if their knees don't already hurt, let alone having to lie on the ground, the floor, on sand-and-dirt-covered streets.

They're under a constant fear the Risers will come, that they will turn on them both, pound on her door, though how could they know they don't have this illness, this behavioral modifier, this hypno-trance. All of this cramps Ingram's ability to do much birding. Not even in her yard, she can hardly leave home, maybe three times per week. She finds herself growing more and more paranoid. She watches Victor, afraid his eyes will turn inward, that he will become one of them. She can't bear to think she might lose him, and worse, that his eyes will close and never reopen. She wonders if they should have joined the Risers as non-deaders, not as those trying to fake their way through. The Risers accept non-deaders, yet Ingram fears what the Risers would demand, eventually. Convert them, somehow. Change them completely. Or drag them to the pier, cheeks marked with gull shit, body splayed and bled, snails in their eyes too.

"How many times you do it today?" Victor asks. He's been living at her house ever since the phones stopped. She's happier for that at least, knowing he wants to protect her. He even sleeps in her bed. She needs his warmth, to feel him next to her. She's been freezing from the inside out.

"Three times," she says, taking a small bite. She's still not hungry. Hasn't been for weeks. She's lost more weight than ever. Any more self-starvation and she'll turn to skin and bones. Already lanky, she wonders what she looks like to Victor these days. A ghost, a ghoul, a dried carcass? "Once at the grocery store," she adds. "Once in the parking lot on the dirty asphalt. Once out front. I got sand in my teeth."

"That's awful." Victor takes another bite.

"Think I don't know?" she says.

He stops chewing. Seems to examine her. "I just want to know when it's for real. Okay?"

"You'll know."

"Will I?"

"You know how different everyone acts once they start," she says. "Something changes, like they're possessed by something."

"Yeah," he growls. "We've talked a dozen times about where people go when they dead. I get it. I just don't want to be left wondering about you. That's all."

"What are you going to do if I become one of them? Leave?" She asks him this all the time. His response is always the same.

"Damn right." He slams his fork.

"Where?"

"Anywhere."

"I won't let you."

"Is that right?"

This hurts Ingram. Every time. She reaches toward her inner peace, or what's left of it, but there it goes, slipping, draining. "What do you want me to do?" she asks. "I'm no scientist or doctor. I can't tell you exactly what's happening. Can you? No one will say if they feel anything when they dead. They just wake with smiles like they've just got back from vacation. Half the time I feel phantom symptoms, like any second it's going to hit me like some kind of aneurism."

Victor raises an eyebrow.

"Phantom symptoms, Victor. Like, hypochondriacs. Phantom."

"Phantoms."

Ingram points her fork. "I've been wracking my brain why the government doesn't send people in here. Make some kind of test or something so we know if someone has it or might be a carrier. But they won't come in here with more than drones or a load of food."

"Don't look at me."

"I'm not." The fork in her other hand now, she fiddles with her food, upset by why Victor acts so antagonistic, why a fire burns under his nerves. "This government. All these drones," she says, "especially that one over the bay. They stop anyone on any boat coming or going. You can't get past any checkpoint. So, do they just think we all have it? That we're all a problem? I'm not a problem."

"We don't even know if this is a disease. Could be they're all hallucinating."

"That's ridiculous."

"I'll tell you something else that's gone to shit," Victor says. "Nearly all birders have stopped reporting. I was getting handwritten lists to submit when this is all over. Now, nothing."

"What do you expect people to do?" she says. "Everyone's family has fallen apart. Our entire community is obsessed with re-enacting death. No one cares about birds. Or nature. They've locked themselves in. They're so terrified they'll end up like Dalten on the pier, god forbid anyone gets strung from a lamppost. Some of them might already be dead on their couches. Can you believe it? *Dead on their couches.* Birds are an afterthought. Just another thing that dies and comes back."

"It's what we love to do," he says. "We love to find them."

"I don't know if I can anymore."

Victor's eyes narrow, fingers tense. "What else is there to do when the world falls apart? Don't you want to see what's really wrong out there?"

"I'm terrified of what's wrong. Kumi should have washed her hands. You saw that. And I keep having to dead at these outdoor meetings, and now I keep getting invited to that church. I think they want me to do some ritual, some test. I don't want to go there."

"You've always been terrified of things."

"And you're not?"

Victor gets up from the table, finds his binoculars, starts cleaning the lenses. He leans against a cabinet. "Sitting around isn't doing me any good. Not when I can go out and observe and document. You know, this bird data, sometimes I can gather and send through an app. But I can't send an email or a text anymore? It's awful. The government wants our data, or at least Cornell University does. I just wish there were more of us documenting. We're down to a few birders, including that kid who lies on half his observations. Their phones don't work, but sometimes mine does, one way."

"Blas isn't bad," Ingram declares. "And he doesn't lie. He's just angry."

"Uh-huh."

"Weren't you angry when you were his age? Aren't we all angry now? He's just different. He needs some breaks. So, you don't see him in the Preserve anymore. I think he still goes to Montaña de Oro with his friends."

"He reports birds while watching from inside his house. I see his reports that he lists in the window. They're sparse at best. But that's all he will do."

"What's wrong with that? You just said he's a liar. But he's not. Sure, he's not out as much. He does place beautiful bird sketches in his window. A crow the last time. Before that, a Red-footed Booby. Those drawings have always been part of the data he shares, though I don't prefer them to *real* evidence. I did notice him carrying a birding notebook and even a drawing of a Virginia's Warbler that he taped on a wall at the market where he used to work. He always includes some field notes. He mentioned he saw a nuthatch *crawling on a tree at Islay Creek Campground, honking like a maniac* and drew that too. And his Snowy Plover sketch even showed the colorful bands ornithologists placed on their tiny legs. Blas calls it *bird bling*."

"I don't know. I don't know," Victor repeats as if something in him has broken. He appears lost in his thoughts.

Her brief irritation over Victor's attitude fades away. Ingram wants to reach out, touch him, hold him. She doesn't feel she has permission to truly love him the way she needs to. Once again she feels like he could slip away. "All I know," she says. "What you and I have. It's the most important thing to me."

Victor gazes out the window through his binoculars. "Finding answers should be the most important thing," he says. "Even those Risers, I hope one of them has been smart enough to document everything. Isn't that why we keep observing birds? We document what they do. We record every behavior. We learn that way. So let's just keep observing everything. Especially the birds. Maybe there are answers in them to all of this."

"How can we? Half the trails aren't accessible. I feel watched all the time. Don't you feel the drones stare when we're outside? Probably comparing our skeletal systems and brainwaves with their scans, overanalyzing our every sound. I hate them." She feels cold. More than anything she wishes he would grab around her waist. She would wrap herself in him, never let go. "Those drones feel closer at night," she adds. "Like they're looking in windows. Listening at least."

"Maybe they do. Maybe *they* know."

"Who?" Ingram asks, though she knows, the Faceless.

Victor walks over, sits next to her. When he fidgets like this, she usually pours him a drink. This time she doesn't move. She waits for him to talk, knows he can't stand the quiet.

"The government, whoever is still out there," he says. "I think they know that something is fighting them."

"Fighting them? Who? We're not fighting the government. I suppose the Risers are. They've taken to protesting, have you heard?"

"I heard. But maybe something else is. Maybe something has been fighting all of us. And if the government, or whoever is out there doesn't contain it, everything will be lost, even us."

"I think we just need to wait it out," Ingram says. "Soon enough this will all be over."

"All be over?" Victor puts a hand on her leg. "This isn't going to end the way you think. I meant to tell you," he says, pulling away.

"At one of the feeders earlier when the birds deaded, many more than usual didn't get back up."

"You have a theory?"

"Too much stress on their systems is all I can think," he says after careful thought. "I think it's something else too," he adds. "I think their minds can't handle where they're going."

"How can that be?"

"What if their consciousness goes somewhere?"

"Do birds have a consciousness, a selfhood?" Ingram asks. "Some don't think dogs or apes or whales have that. What's next? Amphibians? Insects? Can a swallowtail be self-aware? A bird?"

"I've seen birds make friends with dogs, cats, other birds, lizards, even cows," Victor says. "A quail and lizard come to mind. Acted like they were the best damn friends you ever saw, all cozy in the dirt. I've seen birds mourn for their dead. That says something doesn't it? Anyway, I think some birds are dying because they have more of a self than other birds."

"Some ornithologists might disagree that a tiny bird can be aware of itself," Ingram says.

"I might not have completely believed this recently," Victor says. "But I've been watching them wake from their deadings. I see them looking inward. They've been somewhere."

"And you measure this how?"

Victor gives a look of defiance, a refusal to be defeated. At the same time, he's done. Done with all this talk. Ingram can tell by the way he closes himself off, the way his knuckles turn white though they're not holding anything or even making a fist. This makes her feel good about herself, that she's riled him. It's usually the other way around. It's not that she wants to be right. She just doesn't want to give in to emotions when analyzing their situation. She thinks that birds and people, cats and dogs, have simply gone mad.

"I'm going outside," he says. "Going to collect bird data. You can join me or not."

Chapter Twenty-One

THE AMBULANCE, A renovated hay wagon pulled by two pale-brown mares, arrives to take Chango to the hospital. No one will deliver fuel, which has long run out from the only gas station in town, now gutted by fire. And while electricity has been sporadic with brownouts and short outages, the Risers have announced a new rule: electric cars are not to be used except to pick up groceries on scheduled days, alternating between mapped-out city sectors. Most walk to get their groceries anyway, and if not Risers, quickly pick up food then hide in their homes the way Blas does, and hope the power doesn't stay out long enough to spoil perishables.

Blas recognizes the ex-linemen in the driver's seat, both from Baywood High School's 0–10 football team. He really doesn't want to see them but has no choice. Chango has become catatonic, his eyes open and bloody, and has to get help no matter what's being said about locals disappearing into the hospital, never to be seen again.

The teens jump from the cart in faded Baywood letterman's jackets. They call themselves the Horsemen, which they've written on their leather sleeves in permanent red marker. The smaller, and not by much, dark-skinned, narrow grey eyes like a thin-headed cat; that's Terry Combs, a transfer from Los Angeles who once hoped to get a scholarship to Cal Poly. His dad is a doctor, and Blas knows better than to ask anything about the hospital. The taller horseman, Dean Flanagan, has a long jaw, wears a straw cowboy hat. He winks like he's about to show you something you don't want to see. This causes Blas to step back, to want to run. He remembers getting his face shoved in a trash can all too well. The memory of old candy wrappers and vomit sucked into his nostrils feels familiar as anything.

Dean's wink comes with a brief stare. Something about those eyes stops Blas from leaping over a fence and hiding in the neighbor's doghouse with the corpse of Macy, a German Shepherd that starved itself to death. A kind of defeat has washed over Dean since the two last spoke. Like a lot of people, he's aged, skin carved by premature age lines. This isn't a losing football season being projected at Blas, but the pain they take upon themselves when they transport the infirm and dying to Baywood Hospital.

Blas sees something darker in them too, something no one really wants to talk about. He's heard rumors that corpses have been overflowing the hospital morgue and filling the grocery store freezer. And not just any corpses. Something related to deading. His mother whispered to him three nights ago that the neighbor five houses down was taken away after being found on the lawn, gnawed by rats and something that took a hand. She said that on the same day Abie Montañez found Heather Jones hanging by swing-set chains. Both feet missing, skin turned bloodless and white.

Blas cringes thinking what these Horsemen see. He watches them heave Chango to the cart. He expects Terry to start laughing, to drop his brother on purpose, say it was an accident, or call the family dirty wetbacks and give Chango's near-lifeless body an elbow to the face.

There's none of that. Dean and Terry move workmanlike while they lift and roll Chango delicately onto the cart. They hop up, slip a pillow under his head, strap him in place. Blas feels a sense of care in their actions, a duty, a sick twist of fate in carting the corpses and the ill. Maybe here they've found a purpose, something Blas has yet to discover for himself amid this mess.

Dean nods to Blas now. "We'll take care of him, don't worry."

Blas tries not to wince, not to duck. At the same time, he can't look at his brother's face. Chango, a living corpse, a thing, a monstrosity. Those eyes—once so full of humor and life—have become something difficult to explain, something horrible after being exposed to chemicals dumped in the bay, slowly transformed to red wounds that no longer close.

Blas can't handle what those eyes seem to hold inside: dead worlds, toxic atmospheres, subducted landscapes, scabs of crimson landforms and red oceans pouring into the farthest reaches of blackness and doubt. Why Blas sees these images he doesn't know. Maybe the connection of brotherhood. Maybe some kind of pull on Blas, or just his own imagination. He's noticed that when he's quiet and still, he's pretty sure he can peer into the otherworldly darkness filling Chango's mind. This must be something related to the deading, he tells himself. He needs the visions to stop. He immerses himself in graphic novels, but needs more, and though he often makes comics trades with a small group of friends, has read everything except whatever the library had last ordered before Baywood turned to shit. He wants more than anything to sneak in there and see what's in the storage rooms. But he'll never go. He knows this.

A week has passed since Chango slipped into a stasis, since he and Maria had begun feeding him by hand, providing sponge baths, changing his bedpan. The entire house smelled like excrement unless they kept the windows open day and night.

Blas thinks Chango transported somewhere deep in his

own mind, into an imagined horror that he can't or refuses to escape, this dream Blas glimpses. If that's where deaders go, it's a nightmare.

Chango had been deading like so many others, like their mother too. It became their shared ritual, one Blas avoided at all costs, locking himself in his room before Chango and their mother would stir back toward the living. They deaded whenever they could, Blas knew it was like an addiction, like enablers who fueled each others' habits, bodies twisting on the living room floor, in the back yard, with strangers corpse-like in the street, slumped over in the car after returning from picking up groceries. By that time the gas station burned down, the electricity had gone haywire, so seeing them in the car had been especially haunting, an image he couldn't shake, as if the dead were occupying dead machines. But that soon ended and he got pushed into picking up groceries on what was left in the tank of his scooter. A new drop-off system, he hears, will soon be implemented by the Risers.

Then came the day Chango didn't wake up from deading on the couch. When their mother came to, she screamed and cursed. She swore she would never dead again, though Blas has since seen her dead on her bedroom floor, the door cracked, her breathing rapid then shallow, then wild again with some kind of death-ecstasy Blas never wants to experience. He knows she tries to stop, seen the scabs on her arms where she cuts herself. And her prayers, he hears those too but wonders if she's really pleading for the dying, murmuring for their souls, for those who enter other worlds and don't always return.

Blas's mind roams to the missing oyster farmer. Since this all started, Bernhard Vestinos has become a myth, a ghost, an afterthought, though to Blas, the mysterious catalyst for the deading, perhaps its cause. After all, it was his shitty tideland farm where it all went down. The Star World series by Simone Rubio, Blas's current favorite graphic novel reread, illustrates conflict amid alien pseudo-hosts and planetary takeovers. Blas wonders if Bernhard is now some kind of wormhole alien walking invisible amid Baywood streets, touching and leeching who and what he wants, which to many would either be a godsend—because those who dead mostly love to dead—or what it means to Blas, a living nightmare he can't wake from, one that breathes, sick and twisted, dying, sucking at his nerves through his own brother and mother. He's supposed to give that book back to Torrey, who traded the issue from Kai, who'd stolen it from Tatum, who'd lifted it from Emily at a sleepover. They all laugh about it now, but Tatum had been livid when the book first went missing. The sequel, Blas doubts he will ever see.

Dean and Terry suddenly hop off the cart, drop and writhe on the ground. Blas knew this was coming but their convulsions shock him nonetheless. Their deading. Their ritual. Their hallowed experience that he refuses to take part in, can't take part in, wouldn't know how, and doesn't want to pretend the way some of his friends do.

A neighbor joins their grotesquerie. And then another. Blas's mother too, arms scarred in long lines, one scab still bleeding. She deads, Blas thinks, to help seal Chango's fate, to destroy what little humanity he has left. At the same time, he knows he's angry, bitter, resentful. In a moment of clarity he wonders if she's trying to save Chango through her violent supernatural communion. She's buffering Blas at the same time, he thinks. She protects him with each cut. He can see the pain, knows why. He doesn't ever stop her, doesn't ever want to be revealed as a non-deader, doesn't want to be murdered like Alan Dalten, though he knows this group will soon realize he's not one of them. It's a risk, he knows, but wants to believe some of them aren't bad.

At first he blamed all the Risers for everything, but now knows some of their prominent members have a history of violence. Some came from the creeks where so many lived before all this happened. He doesn't mind people living in creeks. Homeless have all kinds of reasons for living the lives they do. But some of them came unreformed from the prison outside San Luis Obispo: the Colony. These were never gentle folk. Ex-murderers, abusers, assaulters, people who refuse to rejoin society, who've been told to walk to Baywood, to get the hell out of San Luis Obispo and the Colony. One creek dweller, Blas knew, Matthew May, had been incarcerated for twenty-five years after blowing the head off a convenience store worker. May would yell and scream about how he "wished all them dead would just die," though this was long before the deadings started. May carried a sharpened golf club as a kind of spear, hated when Blas came around to search for birds. Blas would always keep his cool, say he had to find birds for a school report, would ask if any colorful birds had been seen. May would change his disposition, say, "I don't know anything about no birds," and leave Blas to his treasure hunt. Now May and some of these men and women have joined the Risers, become friends with some of Blas's old classmates, joined bankers and business owners, stay-at-home moms, even teachers, creating a bizarre collection of town rulers who are still gathering intel to build their list of non-deaders, anyone who hasn't joined them yet. Blas heard that May killed Dalten, though he doesn't know for sure.

Everyone deads near the horse cart. Mouths froth, eyes roll into white slates, horses whinny. The pain of dying seen over and over again followed by a stillness, a serene transportation of some inner something, Blas doesn't know what. Consciousness. Soul. To another place or places. Soon both teens dust themselves off, nod to Blas's neighbors who disappear back into their homes. Blas's mother brushes off her blouse and cries, rocking herself in her continued mourning. The Horsemen hop onto the cart, whip the reigns, begin pulling Chango to Baywood Hospital.

Maria whimpers, tells Blas she knows where Chango has really gone.

"I know," Blas says. "That shitty hospital where we all hated to go to the urgent care." He knows no one gets transported to the hospital in San Luis Obispo anymore. Or the one in Pismo. No one gets past the barricades.

"No," she whispers. "Not there. Someplace inside."

He doesn't like her frightened stare, so examines her arms. The cuts have gotten deeper, scabs wider. She's really ripped into them. He mentions them for the first time. "You need to get some help too," he says. "You're gonna kill yourself."

"You know why I do this." Her eyes slip inward. He wonders if she's visiting a memory, some place that she's trying to lock away, a kind of terrible paradise.

He can't stand looking at her. "I should have left. I knew I should have just left," he says.

Soon back inside, he leans against the couch, slips on a mask, doesn't like her breath in his face. "I was thinking," she says. "Maybe you still can leave. You know all those trails. You could get us out. We could both be free of this place."

Blas doesn't answer, walks away, locks himself in his room. He can hear her outside his door, crying. He can hear when she goes quiet, standing there, breathing. He can hear when she drops to the floor, twists and moans. He wants to call her a hypocrite, though he knows it won't do either of them any good.

Chapter Twenty-Two

IT COULD BE Tuesday. Though it could also be Friday. Doesn't feel like a Sunday, I think, continuing a kind of game with myself: *What day does it feel like, Kumi?* I have no idea which, while I carry a newt in my gloved hands, its orange-yellow underside a glowing sun extending just beneath its milky eyes. It lies still.

In the past, when forgetting the weekday I'd try to reason it out through the way leaves toy in wind, the way shadows fall, the predictability of tide cycles, maybe even how Cassiopeia's five bright points sometimes brand the dawn or dusk. Back then, during those silly moments, I would muse aloud, knowing Hiroki would hover nearby, then be drawn in, a moth to my reason's flame.

I try our game and quickly give up. Maybe I just don't care anymore. Maybe it's just not as fun without Hiroki joining in, us getting lost in our own way. Both of us working so hard at our day jobs that we lose track of everything but each other and our silly games. And now I'm losing track of things because this contagion has changed all of us. I don't keep a calendar. I don't look at my phone. I stop caring about the cycles and rhythms of the days. Why should I? I just want to see more sunrises. I just want to see the sun poke the ocean the way my finger tests the temperature of my tea. I need the dusk light to wash over me, so that I know I make it and make it and survive again and again, each day an echo of the next. I just want to breathe this air that smells less and less like chemicals, and more like salt and moisture and the mysteries of the deep sea.

Stars matter more than days, I tell myself while I hold this creature. Stars matter because they make me remember. Used to know the name of every star in the Cassiopeia constellation. Hiroki and I would sit in patio chairs and name them. I can recall him telling me about hot blue-white Epsilon Cassiopeiae. He told me he could never really see its color, yet showed me its defocused star trails and colored haloes in a photo he once took.

I loved his voice, I would listen and pretend sometimes that I didn't know a thing, so he could teach me. "What is that star again?" I would ask. "Where do stars go when they fade?"

He would tell me that even stars don't live forever. Now I imagine the greater extinction of stars, each one dimmer and redder than the day before.

Sometimes Hiroki and I memorized tide cycles for the week, the highs and lows, the exact number of feet above the chart datum, a kind of cheating for us, two retirees who stopped viewing calendars regularly. We would play the day-guessing game, though he'd win more than I would, but only when we agreed to rule out tide chart memorization. Had he more intuition? A knowledge he hadn't shared? What had I overlooked? How could such patterns exist anyway? I always wondered whether or not he was simply more in tune with his internal clock. Could the pineal gland work differently depending on the day, circadian in its twenty-four hours, but seasonal, weekly? Then again, if I remember correctly, the gland declines with age, and I really only ever needed to guess one day of seven anyway.

Now in this bubble reality, I need so little sleep, my circadian rhythms are less dependent on that gland. Sleep is likely more determined by zeitgebers of dawn songs, the coastal White-crowned Sparrows that never leave, unlike the other subspecies only visiting in fall and winter, singing me awake each day along with Song Sparrows, no matter the time of year. I wish I could tell Hiroki about my latest sleep patterns because of all that is happening. He would find it fascinating and I would better cope with all this.

Here I am, salamander in hand, thinking about time again, days, weeks. If I did look at this as a week with parts, such chronobiological phenomena could be a micro-infradian rhythm, I think, like a week of menstruation I haven't experienced in decades, or the sixish weeks of a bird molt, or ten or so days of bird breeding seasons.

Memories jolt and I recall light therapy in my fifties to regain the ability to release melatonin in enough amounts to sleep regularly. How those endless hours overlapped as if the same infinite second, could only sleep an hour at a time. Hiroki sang to me so many nights until I slipped into dreams.

I feel like I don't make sense to myself but know Hiroki would understand. He would follow my thought patterns if here, support me with his own, calm my fear that the sun might not wink above the eastern hills the next morning. *Of course it will be there*, he would say. *The sun wants to live until long after our ashes have turned to glittering dust.* I think some of our games were born out of Hiroki's studies in biology. He was always examining nature, and I with him. He'd rescue any injured bird or seaside creature. We'd been so young, always guessing something about some creature's wound or illness. We'd also try and guess what his next job might be after graduate school.

And then both of us working for so many years. He was always on contract, until one day when he was forty-eight, he was pulled to Morro Bay to help run their wildlife rescue center. I quit my teaching job, then never taught again, somehow never getting around to it. We found this home in nearby Baywood. The commute was short. Ten minutes most days, taking the road above the estuary, the road that now cuts everyone off from the world.

Setting the newt on the counter, I fill a dish with water, then set the newt in its liquid bed, and carry that to the garden, finally guessing Wednesday. In a chair in the shade, I watch the dish. This creature has a physical wound, not certain if it's dead, dying, or deading. Not sure if I'm correct about the day, though I'm reminded in this silence of being sure of myself, of who I am anymore, having lived inside dreams it seems since Hiroki passed. Even in this space I can see who I've become, what this creature is. I am this person that perhaps can't/won't dead the way the Risers can, but maybe can imagine it, can feel my confidence in the way I see wounds, and in them, possibilities. Maybe because of all those guessing games with Hiroki, I can fit in to all of this, appear invisible, though that must be coming to an end. The Risers will eventually *see* me.

The newt doesn't act how it should, contorting into abnormal positions, moving its eyes in and out of its sockets as if swallowing. It wasn't in good shape when I found it twitching in a gutter, vulnerable to birds, cats, pedestrians, deaders.

Its eyes should be clear, and also has a wound on its tail.

A dark nebula exists in the coldness of a Bok globule. I once read that the globule Barnard 68 absorbs all light. Some memories of Hiroki feel the same, these inner memory clouds, memory palaces, sucking all light, all everything, setting me firmly in the past, as if the present doesn't, can't exist.

One memory palace weighs heavy while I observe the salamander, when a large seabird was brought to the wildlife rescue center, a Northern Gannet, only the second or third record on the west coast, Hiroki said, the bird having been oiled and a frayed plastic rope wrapped around its lower mandible. Hiroki cared for the bird after a team helped cut the bird free, two

hands around the back of the bird's head, scissors making careful work. The shock to the creature was unbelievable, he said. I
remember how Hiroki seemed so distant when he told me, "I
could sense those heartbeats, feel them with mine."

The gannet, he said, grew in strength each day, and I think
about this because of Hiroki's joy with this bird though there
had been so many scoters, hawks, vultures, grebes, even a pair
of Cassin's Auklets to rehabilitate. But the gannet, like a child,
knew Hiroki in its short time there, and he knew the bird, and
I could see their affection growing into a kind of love. I visited
more than once and saw how he nuzzled the bird, how it rubbed
him with its bill. "We shouldn't, I know this," he said. "We're too
close." When it came to release day, Hiroki said he wondered if
he should postpone another week or two, maybe stay away from
the bird altogether. I knew why and told him, "That bird's world
is already a week less." And Hiroki agreed, and was quiet the
morning of the release. And then when he called, seemed like
the phone rang soon as he left, his voice in a kind of shiver, said
the bird had died. And I cried for him because he didn't get to
say goodbye, and somehow knew that one day I wouldn't get to
say goodbye to Hiroki either. Though, I know he knows, *now* he
knows. Hiroki, here, trapped with me, ethereal and blue, knows
that all I ever wanted was to say goodbye, my love.

The water dish has turned milky now like the newt eye. This
creature hasn't moved in some time. I go back inside feeling how
this day passed in a way that makes me want to slip into a quiet,
deep sleep. I don't imagine Risers will knock at my door tonight,
though they could, they always might. If they do I'll sleep with
Hiroki, I tell myself. He'll step from the water new, and though
I'm a different kind of shell, we'll slip toward dim red starlight
and sing something of memories.

Chapter Twenty-Three

WEEKS PASS. BLAS still hasn't seen his brother. He's afraid to walk down streets, to be seen, afraid to enter any hospital ward. He doesn't want to expose himself to stale air, to poor ventilation. All those Risers probably writhing in halls, stairwells, elevators. He doesn't want what they have, doesn't want to breathe the same air. The thought shakes him along with the disturbing feeling that Chango is forever lost in his mind, wandering planetscapes. He can't go see his brother that way. He can't. He can hardly glance at his mother either.

He checks his eBird account. For reasons he can't explain, maybe some randomly working personal hotspot, this is the only part of the internet that sometimes refreshes. His friend Ozziel, who escaped to Santa Maria with Felix before everything got shut down, has been posting birds from a park there, sometimes from other places like the small seaside lake of Oso Flaco. He's birded its boardwalk that bisects the water. Ozziel's latest report was logged from the Santa Maria River Estuary that borders both Santa Barbara and San Luis Obispo counties. It's just south of that little lake, north of Mussel Rock and Rancho Guadalupe Dunes Preserve, also south of the tiny town of Oceano. Due east lies an even smaller town, Guadalupe. Just east of that along the 166, Santa Maria.

Ozziel has listed all kinds of birds at the estuary, including an extremely high number of sandpipers numbering in the tens of thousands. He says birders have been traveling far and wide to see the phenomenon. His list includes a rare Buff-breasted Sandpiper. His report reads:

> Found when flew overhead with several adult breeding Western Sandpipers. Landed on beach ten feet away like it was my best home fries. Foraged amid seaweed. Grey ships on the horizon. Lanky bird, long gait, yellow legs, pale to dull buff on breast, neck, and face. Whitish underside. Wide, pale eye-ring. Medium bill—kinda downward. Scaly-plumaged back and wings with a grey patch between shoulders. Reminded me of the one I saw on the Morro Bay Sandspit close to the harbor mouth, near a danger sign two years ago. Same plumage as that bird though this one appears to be more buffy on chest, lankier, though could just be poor memory. My recollection is that other bird had brighter legs too, while this had greenish-yellow legs if I were to give it a specific color. I'll post photos later today.

The two of them have a game, Blas knows, probably at the direction of Felix, to conceal messages in their reports. Ozziel has been keeping him up to date with possible escape routes, which always come with a reminder of a bird previously seen in an area by a danger sign. This is clearly a warning not to take the sandspit out of the area if trying to escape through Montaña de Oro, and especially not to take any chance to cross the harbor mouth. If anything, it might mean to take the sandspit south, toward the Santa Maria River Estuary. Blas hopes his friend will update

him on a better route out, or be clearer about heading south, but
to be honest, it could be days or weeks, and if he doesn't receive
a clear green light, then no telling if a route could get blocked.
No guarantee anyway with all the drones, with all those ships,
military vehicles, and whatever satellites overhead recording
movements. At least he knows that Ozziel and others are pushing
the boundaries, the trails, seeing where there might be holes in
the perimeter created by the Faceless. If anything, Blas knows the
Faceless might not be able to watch every escape route, especially
during rapidly changing tides, or any possible incoming storms.

Maria tells him she visits Chango every few days—at least
that's where she says she's going when she slips out the door. She
reports back late in the evenings that Chango's fine, he's going to
be okay. Blas doesn't know what to believe when she locks herself
in her room and convulses at the foot of her bed. He thinks she
might not be entering the hospital, that maybe she knows he's
dead. He only hears awful things, like the facility has become a
kind of black hole that even most Risers avoid.

His mother has friends over, a few ladies who used to work
at the salon, who still cut hair, barter for items. They hide in
her room, gossip, try not to be heard. But Blas is used to hearing the tiniest of bird sounds. He presses his ear to the door,
strains to listen. He hears whispers of protesters deading at barricades. Protesting what, he doesn't know. They talk about how
the world needs to be exposed, how everyone on the planet needs
to change. At the same time, those who dead don't want to leave
Baywood, they say. Blas wonders why they care about being
locked in? It's Blas who wants to run. Like most non-deaders, he
wants to find a way out. There's a right time, he thinks. He'll get
out before they get him. Ozziel will let him know.

He soon hears their groans so pulls away from the door, goes
to his bedroom, peers out the window, sees shadows in the street.
Might be his friends, but he hasn't indicated that it's safe to come

over, so he closes the curtains and goes to bed. When his mom leaves the following evening, saying she's off to the hospital, he places a drawing of a crow in the lower left corner of his bedroom window.

Other than Ozziel, his former classmates Chewie Miller and Elisabeth Garcia have been his biggest informants. Kai, Jordan, and a few others do slip him information here and there, though he's starting to get more paranoid about who he can trust. They're some of the last students in his class who don't dead. When they spy his crow drawing they knock. They want him to go out. He grabs his coat, sneaks into the dark.

Tonight they walk the border of Pecho Road Willows, then pass through neighborhoods to a patch of eucalyptus alongside Shark Inlet, an isolated grove of a dozen trees amid shrubs and sand trails in an undeveloped corner of the bay. On the way they shine lights hoping rattlesnakes haven't slithered to this favorite spot, which they find desolate and cold, and empty of reptiles, except one uncommon legless lizard that Blas spots exiting a burrow, a welcome feeling amid the isolation. They sit and whisper on logs cut from the remains of a long-dead eucalyptus, every tree in this grove once a seedling from Australia long ago as part of a speculative scam to grow wood for firebreaks, windbreaks, firewood, and woodworking. They were bought and sold on fears of a timber famine that never came. Either way the wood was unusable. Not to mention those shallow root systems and how easily some blue gums toppled. The thing Blas also knows is the coastal fog belt keeps them alive and that he sometimes sneezes when sitting under them for too long.

When he hears something like laughter he realizes it's a coyote yip, that it's probably pouncing on rabbit burrows. He whispers to his friends, while to the west, a shooting star cuts over the mile-long, seventy-foot-tall sandspit. Also high above, faint in the night sky, the whine of a drone, its shadow spiderlike against a web of star fields. Not alone after all.

"Think it's watching us?" Elisabeth asks.

"It might be," Blas says. "Probably knows we're mostly what's left of the Dead of Night." He thinks of Kaylee, knows she could be with them if she wanted to, if she had a way here. A few others too. But he can't do anything about it. He's not about to walk through the Risers' neighborhoods just to say he likes her, or waste his gas for anything other than food pickup.

"Listening too, you think?" adds Chewie.

"Probably," Blas says. "It might be probing for anyone trying to escape, maybe even analyzing language. It probably won't engage unless we're on the beach stepping foot in water, deep on Coon Creek trails past the barbed wire, or far on the edge of Buchon Point."

"That doesn't sound reassuring."

"I don't know for sure. Do any of us really know?"

Though wary, they soon whisper, sometimes writing in journals, or typing into phones, showing each other their thoughts so the drone won't overhear, so they can maybe plan to get away without being dragged back to Baywood with broken arms or legs. The reality, Elisabeth says, is that they're more worried about the Faceless for now, though they all know about the threat of Risers trying to force them into their strange church. Not to mention those classmates from Black Lace & Bookmarks who sent them all a strange letter trying to get them to join, to dead, to whatever. Either way, it's not like the Risers have all kinds of surveillance they have to worry about. It's the Faceless eavesdropping, spying, listening, keeping them trapped in Baywood.

Chewie tells Blas that they're thinking of dragging kayaks over the steep sandspit slopes where they can paddle south, past the decommissioned Diablo Canyon Nuclear Power Plant and Port San Luis Lighthouse, then through breakwaters into Port San Luis. Maybe even further south past Pismo Beach to Oceano Dunes above the Lost City of Cecil B. DeMille, the City of the

Pharaoh, its sand pits filled with sphinx heads and chopped-off lion arms. That movie set once held twenty-one giant plaster sphinxes and an eight-hundred-foot-wide temple, all ripped apart and shoved into a trench more than a hundred years ago. *If we could get to Oso Flaco boardwalk*, Chewie writes, *escape across the lake into farmland, we could get to the highway. Guadalupe or Santa Maria friends could help us.*

"You mean you hope they help us," Elisabeth says aloud.

"They will," Chewie says. "Blas has his friend there too. And maybe we won't need their help. I got some money."

"He stole it," she says.

Chewie is quick to counter: "Everybody steals lately."

Has your friend said anything about that route? Elisabeth writes.

"Nothing," Blas says. "It's hit-and-miss. I think they're all dangerous. But some, well, some you just shouldn't think about."

Blas reminds them of grey ships they've seen from the top of the sandspit, gargantuan military vessels that have replaced lines of oil tanker convoys. Strange sea lights can be seen cruising up and down the coast. Not to mention recent gunfire heard beyond the surf like staccato oriole chatter. No option feels safe. "And what if there are snails?" he says. "Those goth girls might be wrong. Snails could be everywhere in those waters."

Chewie's eyes turn to dim candles in the star-glow. He grunts then switches to discussing Risers at the barricades. "There's a danger in their constant rallies," he says, "provoking and smashing drones. We've seen them do it. They shoot at them with what few guns they have. What if the Faceless get tired of it and start shooting at all of us? They've already killed three people who were climbing over the barricades."

Elisabeth corrects him. "That's what we heard. We don't know if it's true."

"Right," Chewie adds, "but what if they knock us all out and we wake up in some government facility locked in little rooms? We're caught in the middle, Blas. No one wants to save us so we're going to have to save ourselves."

Blas hasn't gone to the barricades and doesn't know much about the Faceless other than the high school government class he took with Mrs. Palmer where he learned how AI had been implemented in more than eighty-two percent of surveillance technology. He wishes he could sit in that class again and write notes to Kaylee. No one will ever graduate now. He reminds himself that he hardly ever listened when he was there. He was always talking to her. And sometimes caught her gazing at him.

Then, for some reason while there in the dark with his friends, he imagines Chango's emotionless stare, eyes blank and red like he's become a drone. Blas won't go visit his brother. He's gone, he tells himself. You go to the hospital these days to die for real. No pretending. No coming back. Then it hits him that his friends are right, the government probably won't help anyone. "I don't want to see those rallies," he says. "I don't want to get shot."

"Jesus, Blas," Chewie says. "It's getting dangerous but no one's going to shoot you. Not yet, anyway."

"Not funny."

"You need to sneak into town once in a while. Play dead like the rest of us. The Risers can't figure us out."

"I don't know if I can do that," Blas says. "They said they're burying people to see who can survive through deading, that it does something to your breathing and heart rate, but that maybe not everyone can survive buried with little oxygen. So, yeah, everything is getting really dangerous."

"You're right. This is why we all need to get out," Elisabeth says. "Look, we don't know if the drones will ever do anything but watch us and keep us in," she adds. "They spy on everything. But like you said, we can't keep taking the risk that they or the Risers won't bury us. The Faceless government . . ." Elisabeth's throat has gone hoarse from speaking this way for too long. "We can't see them. No one can. They hide behind those barricades and pilot drones. We've seen about ten different kinds, maybe more. If they're not flying, they're crawling across dunes, between shrubs, along houses and barricades. I bet their operators sit in some forward operating base in front of a computer. Might be one crawling around here. Maybe one in the trees above us, or zipping around like a mosquito, all while some jerk monitors us and sips a Diet Coke."

"You don't think they're all run by AI?" Blas says. "Might not even be as many people in that base as you think. Drones can operate on their own. They know we hate to be watched. I mean, everyone has always said that. We don't even know for sure if they're listening. We just have to be careful, assume they're processing our every word, trying to key in on something. We're being safe."

"Not in our criticism."

"Who doesn't criticize drones, or the government? That's old news."

"I hate the eyes on hummingbird and insect drones," Chewie admits. "Tiny drone-wasps mostly. We smashed a few. Kai pulled the wings off one. And that huge bastard in the bay. I don't know who pilots that thing but they're having too much fun. It could tear you apart. That's not cool."

Blas has seen the bay drone too many times swinging along the shore, nipping its pincers at anyone standing for long, or brave enough to poke it with poles and bats. During low tide it patrols only briefly over shores, mostly hovers over water, sometimes crosses all the way over San Luis Bay Boulevard along one of the creeks to quickly patrol Turri Road's tidal ponds where Blas used to check out small flocks of Wilson's Phalaropes and Lesser Yellowlegs. It does seem like it has a personality, like someone with an evil streak might be at the controls.

Maybe it needs water for fuel or something, Blas writes. *Some kind of constant hydro-energy converter after that initial launch from wherever it came from. Maybe that means the mudflats can be navigated during low tide, that we can escape that thing by walking right in front of it.*

No way. The estuary is impossible, Chewie writes, *and those tidal ponds along Turri Road are too in the open, parts of the creek might be too,* then says: "Too many dislocated arms and legs. Surprised no one died besides that dog."

"A cat," Elisabeth says.

Blas knows he doesn't want to run the way of the ocean. At least in the mudflats he can hug the edge of the Elfin Forest bluff, maybe slip beneath San Luis Bay Boulevard bridge north of Los Osos Valley Road. He just needs more information on the Risers, or Risers congregating by the barricades where those roads meet, and of how many drones might be around. Maybe he should be a dronewatcher instead of a birdwatcher. He doesn't want to run into any patrols. And he might need a diversion so he can slip through one of the creeks eastward. He's sure it would all be monitored but maybe a diversion of some kind could help, maybe they could find a way through creek waters. He wishes Ozziel could tell him about those routes specifically.

"I've noticed this too about the Risers," Elisabeth says. "They dead at specific times, day and night, along with random deading too. That was the idea of Kristina Lucas. All those goth girls wear red to symbolize the blood of each death draining into soil. They lie on the ground out by the barriers, form spirals, stars, and other geometric patterns. As if they're doing this for the drones, to show the Faceless how they've created some new society of freaks." She pauses, seems to contemplate the nearby scratching of a rodent in the underbrush. "Your mother is always with them."

"Tell me something I don't know," Blas lies. He didn't know.

But now he understands why his mother always wears red when she leaves the house. He knew she'd been lying about something, that she probably wasn't going to the hospital. *Oh, he's recovering,* she'd say about her visits to Chango. *He's my baby again. He'll be out soon.* Then again, maybe she's been doing both. Maybe she deads at the hospital, though once again, he doubts she even goes there.

Blas thinks about Kaylee again, wishes she were here in the dark.

It's time to get out, Elisabeth writes, then flashes her light into the trees. *Our homes aren't safe. Our friends' homes aren't safe. Yours either. You have to come with us.*

Blas stares into the dark. What does safe mean? He hasn't felt safe since any of this started. Two weeks ago, six of his classmates begged him to join their caravan. They hiked a seldom-used trail into an oak forest on the south side of Los Osos Valley Road, high up near a ridgeline. He didn't trust it and Ozziel sent a warning. He knows Chewie and Elisabeth felt the same. He asks if they know what might have happened.

Maybe captured or eaten by those wild pigs that roam the hills at dusk. They say they're giant, Elisabeth writes.

"They weren't eaten by no Chupacabra pigs," Chewie says.

Blas hums. He's seen wild pigs while searching for Short-eared Owls. They appear at dawn or dusk. Five hundred pounds with deadly tusks, running like freight trains, barreling down slopes, over shrubs. They're scary but never saw one eat anybody.

Chewie laughs, scrawls in his notebook. *We all know you can take those trails all the way to Prefumo Canyon or San Luis Obispo. And you told us your friend says there's a kind of camp by Santa Maria. But we don't know who is there, and you said your friend doesn't know. Another group wanted to take the emergency dirt road that connects Montaña de Oro to Diablo Canyon. Another friend told us that way is blocked for sure.*

"Blocked like much of the Internet," Blas says. "Phones and computers mostly no good anymore. We all know this."

We're glad you can still upload bird data and encode messages to your friend, Elisabeth writes. *Must be some other way to communicate with the outside world. You seem to be the only one.*

Blas doesn't tell them that he's blocked local birders from seeing his eBird data, that he doesn't trust some of them, even tries to throw them off track by posting half-assed bird lists in his window, then reminds his friends that the brightest kids can't even hack their way to an email server, let alone hike through seaside wilderness. *It's a one-way street,* he says. *From what anyone can tell, only my data ever gets out, but it's spotty. I'm the only one. Measurements. Observations. Maybe there are other websites where you can upload scientific numbers, sounds, videos, images. You have to get tricky. Any obvious calls for help embedded within scientific analysis gets washed away by unseen hands, by internet-wide safety protocols. But right now no one has caught on to my being secretive on eBird.*

But what if Ozziel isn't even real anymore? What if he's just AI?

He's not AI, Blas writes, with no explanation. "Have you heard from Kaylee?" he finally asks. He needs to know.

"No one has."

Blas's stomach immediately turns to knots. "What do you mean, no one? I thought she was still one of us."

"We think she might be in their inner circle. You know she sometimes attended Black Lace & Bookmarks. She just refused to dress like them."

"I didn't know." Blas's heart melts in his chest. It hurts to think Kaylee could be wrapped up in all this, which suddenly feels worse than anything.

"It's getting bad," Elizabeth says. "They've established regular deading times. Four times a day wherever you are. They've plastered ordinances throughout town. New clothing requirements too. Funeral-goers dead in all red. Eight a.m. deadings are white, as are ten a.m. and one p.m. Deadings at five and eight at night are the dark hours, the black hours.

"We showed up in secret to a night deading. A circle of torches. Shadows dancing all around us. Lots of hoods. The new leaders, arms raised, chanted 'night fire and night death are an omen to the living, that all will die and enter a realm that only this chosen community has seen.' We didn't see Kaylee, but her face may have been hidden."

Blas feels like he's shrinking into the night. He can see ghosts in the sand and gloom, moving along arterial paths that stretch to the moonlit bay. He imagines Chango with them. He imagines everyone deading, himself too. Even the coyotes and drones. He imagines a deading parade entering their little grove near Shark Inlet, led by Kaylee, dragging him away.

We've been waiting to tell you. We got to get out of here, Chewie writes. *Tonight. We can't take this anymore. Who knows how long this immunity will last?*

Can't leave tonight. Blas shivers at the thought of attempting an escape without any preparation. "Why didn't you say something sooner?"

"I'm saying it now. Right now."

We're going, Elisabeth adds.

Blas doesn't know what to think other than he still hates the idea of an ocean escape.

We gonna take a two-man kayak right now from the bay, take it over the sandspit, Chewie scribbles. *We hid it at a spot they won't be looking, further north. We make our way through Montaña de Oro, hug the coastal arches and sea caves. We get the hell out. I got all my money in my pack.*

I can't . . . the grey ships, is all Blas can pen. He can't just leave without finding food to carry, without leaving at the perfect time. Besides, he thinks they should rule out being in the surf, so obvious to those ships. They could be shot on sight, smashed by waves against rocks in the dark.

"Suit yourself, man," Chewie says to his silence. "We're out."

Before they leave, Blas rips out a drawing he made of a squishy-looking Semipalmated Plover, complete with field notes. *Take it with you. Maybe some good luck. These birds escape everything, I like to think. Dogs and people and drones. Sometimes falcons darting for their little bodies. Maybe you will fly in the wind with more than this one in your wake.*

Chapter Twenty-Four

A RIVER OF snails crosses Baywood. From gardens and coastal scrub where they eat and breed and lay their eggs. They squirm free during a days-long storm, crawl from neighborhoods, from the Preserve where they lurk beneath fallen eucalyptus leaves, amid tangles of oak roots, this wet marsh of reeds, coyote bush, and poison oak being overtaken by swaths of invasive veldt grass.

The snails are endangered Morro shoulderbands. Air-breathing dune snails. Terrestrial pulmonate gastropod molluscs. Spirals mark their large shells like signals. Eyes like starry pinpoints at the end of two of their four tentacles don't allow them to see very far. They cannot hear. Their world is silent. Something else drives them. A smell. A taste. A pulsing. Their pairs of eyeless tentacles pick up a distant scent too. They pull toward the willows.

On oozing, slimy feet, they glide down curbs and dirt roads during a break in the storm, their shells lit by a greenish waning moon. Though some die during their journey, picked at by birds and rodents, most stream into the mouth of Pecho Road Willows, worm their way into its stink and vapor.

In mud-slime they begin to arrange themselves. They form

the primitive outline of a room, slithering upon shells, each secreting a binding mucous that helps their numbers bond into something greater than each individual. The glue is an epiphragm-inspired adhesion mechanism. A polymer gel adhesive that drips and forms complex webs that thicken and harden into translucent, pulsating walls. Within this growing structure they sacrifice their own, tearing slippery bodies apart, spreading and joining bits of living primitive cerebral ganglia, pigmented retina, and optic nerve directly into these walls.

Slowly, through the course of several days, a phantasmagorical beacon and enclosure forms. More walls are soon built. Hallways radiate outward from those.

The snails plant themselves upon these walls like bulbs, forming conduits through the mucous, ganglia, and nerves. They become connected to one another. Through their collective energy they also connect to the thing that dwells within, that which was Bernhard Vestinos. In turn, they bind through the Bernhard host to the deep, to countless creatures unknown to them beyond the bay. They can feel what has happened to them, to ocean biomes, and the waters surrounding Baywood.

A vague familiarity permeates, not dissimilar to the layout of ship's halls that Bernhard's entity once knew. That ship, a home away from home, full of walkways, nests, energy sources pulsing in extraterrestrial thought-rooms capable of traversing plasma-filled wormholes, bisecting space, the spaces between known systems and spiral arms.

Dreams and reality blend into the darkness of these willow rooms, these snail walls, these living translations of reshaped memories. It all comes back, pours back.

The entity, seeing these walls, remembers distant suns through portholes, the remains of a former paradise of room-shapes and hall-shapes, familiar paths, even a scent of love, so distantly familiar, a love that rent, tore into two realities, descending in fire, smashed on land and drowned in sea. It can hear voices. Voices it once knew. Itself. Its own guttural language. Barks and clicks. And others. That love again. A certain face it can't see but knows hangs in ghost shadow, almost there, *here*. Partly touchable. Nearly able to manifest. Now taking the shape of slippery-skinned creatures of the deep, wriggling, eyes like gastropod eyes, secreting mucous, hungry, swallowing others. Choking. Dying because of the people of this planet. So many people consuming, creating waste. How many civilizations have buried their own planets in refuse? How many civilizations thought they were alone on an island in the Great Nothing, or some similar void, where few galaxies exist, where starry nights become lone bands of milk, the rest of the bowl blackness, hopeless, where anxiety turns inward, planets consuming themselves?

The entity has given these shoulderbands what they never had, a hivemind. Along with this new cerebral manifestation, the ability to create, to seethe in unison at dangers to their existence. And now they can project their own primitive will of survival with that of the entity. For they are the last of their kind and must live on though many sacrifice for the walls.

What's left of Bernhard pulls itself through mud, through this construction. His mottled hand touches one of the walls. *What's part of you is part of me. You won't die. You won't ever die.*

Bernhard drags itself further into one of the halls, in a direction it never expects. Outward rather than toward the cockpit. Somehow, the tentacled cerebral mass of its mind feels the pull of something else, its own flaws. It knows not everyone has succumbed to its will. It wants to understand.

It senses these unknowns as it slips through swamp and undergrowth, to the mulched trailhead. Rising on bones, leathery flesh, and skin, it stumbles onto Pecho Road. Here the Bernhard entity falls, slithers not unlike a creature spawned and helpless from a primordial sea. Crawls again, scrabbles on hands and knees, to a corner, and again pushes onto what's left of its bony feet. Walks until it reaches a home where it feels disconnection. A will. Not his. That of the human, Kumi Sato.

Through a window it sees the old woman, young, so infantile compared to it, sitting at a table sipping from a cup. She has grey-black hair, eyes close together, tiny stature compared to his rot. Steam rises into her face when she looks up as if the entity has been expected. She turns pale but doesn't run. Instead, sets down her drink, moves toward the window, runs a finger along the glass as if to touch the bent leather of Bernhard's decomposing cheek, presses her hand to the surface.

"You're not mine," she says. "Hiroki was much smaller than you. Are you the one who has been lost? You're no longer him. But you were lost. I sense you've been isolated a long time, that you've made friends with creatures. I make friends with creatures. Whatever is inside you has enchanted you, kept you somewhat preserved. Though I fear you might not last much longer."

A memory. Buried deep. Like the descent. In the entity's own language. Burns as if falling again. Somehow translated. That face. The one it knew. That love. So different than the face the Bernhard entity stares at but the same expression of wonder and fear.

The entity has not expected this connection through disconnection, this sparked memory of the burning so long ago. The vision arrives as though it were a supernova, overwhelming the entity. The shaking ship. Everything coming apart after the accident. Panicked eyes. Words remembered, different, similar, comparing, two phrases in two epochs. Different, coming through this being on the other side of the glass and inside its tentacled mind. Not, *Are you the one who was lost?* No. Similar. *Are we lost now?* That's what it was. Lost *now*. Terrified. A million years ago. Before everything tore in two. This realization. An acceptance that has taken so long.

Are. We. Lost. Now.

We. Are. Lost. Now.

Something in this voice. Something unexpected. A be-reavement. It wants to hate her. Will hate everyone else. Will transform every last one of them. It thinks this, still staring. It wills her to slip into the *dead* stasis, to join the others, to be like the birds and the snails, to be the people giving in, giving up, slowly, collectively, dying. She doesn't.

"I don't hate you," she says, hand still raised against the glass. She mutters something it doesn't understand.

It sees the burning again. The face. The realization. Everything split and time spreading apart with wings. Wings that come apart, that grow new wings. The entity remembers all now and turns back to the willows. It wonders if it can reach them all in time to save any of this.

Chapter Twenty-Five

THE MEMORY BEGINS with a feeling of closeness I haven't forgotten. Waking tangled in a top sheet while Hiroki snores next to me, not loud like a siren, rather a soft lull that meant he was on an upslope from the deep, but not so far down that he couldn't feel my hand on his back rubbing him to wakefulness, toward the first kiss of morning. Sometimes this happened in the dark, often in early dawn, his eyes sometimes not even open when I kissed him and whispered good morning, or said his name so softly I thought he might hear it within any fading dream. Variations of this memory melt into one. I know this happens. Memories boiled to singular moments, as if they only have to happen once for me to remember, instead of the thousands of times we dawn-kissed. I allow the collective memory to seep into me, let it be what it is, a feeling, a security, something I need to remember, something I've needed daily whether or not I'm locked inside Baywood.

I wear a long red dress that sweeps near to my sandaled feet, a leftover from my thirties, one of only a few I haven't thrown out or given away. I wore this to a banquet with Hiroki then never again. What little I recall, his eyes that night, the way they brightened, how they weren't disappointed, not even for a second, the feeling of his love clinging to me, the prism of his irises, the ever-changing dilation of his pupils, that soft focus that wouldn't let me go even when he wasn't looking at me, in a room where everything glittered and the sound of conversation didn't matter.

The patternless dress fits loose. Ingram, next to me in my small living room—still clean, always clean of dust—has cobbled together a skirt and blouse that don't match, both different shades of red, the top erring toward pink. It feels strange, Ingram pinning my old dress, tightening the waist, the upper back, all the places I've shrunk that I used to worry about for so many years when preserving my youth, not only for my vanity but for Hiroki, who'd fallen in love with that young version of me. Back then when I felt barely a woman, just realizing I could no longer be that girl who didn't want to make friends in my first year of college, to then suddenly having a husband. A wife, with a wife's social obligations, to attend parties, banquets, walk a certain way, act a certain way.

"They say they're slain in the spirit." Ingram cracks through my memories, slips in another safety pin, "though it isn't what you think, isn't what any of us think. I hear it's a purifying ritual, a pain ritual, a burial rite. All of it in one."

"Is it?" I start feeling the need to pull away from Ingram, for once my patience slips. "I think this is fine. I don't want to feel like I can't breathe."

"Then let's set the other piece," Ingram says to my sigh, grabs a black wig and carefully sets it on my head. I instantly feel suffocated, fake hair bunched around my ears, the thickness of it muffling my ability to hear nature the way I'm attuned to: Anna's Hummingbirds singing that final pop through their J-curves, White-crowned Sparrows belting melodies, crows complaining about Scrub-Jays. Or maybe the other way around. Within tangles of the wig, accenting the outline of my face, their bills aimed outward as if about to fly, a dozen dead hummingbirds are pinned. Each has been found near residential feeders, in gardens, where they've dropped dead. The male heads and gorgets, even in the wig, still shine with magenta scales, tiny feathers dipped in bright paint, while the females, with only spots of magenta in the centers of their throats, resemble grey-green leaves.

"How do I look?" I say.

Ingram's eyes turn to points. "Like one of them."

"This is good, no?"

"If we want the Risers to think we're with them we have to do this."

"Then please finalize your look too. I'll wait in the kitchen with Victor."

"He left," Ingram says.

"But he was just here."

"Says he doesn't want to see us like this. Thinks we're going to get caught, and will leave if we do."

"Oh Victor of little faith," I say, wondering if there's something more to why he would leave at a time like this.

Then both of us laugh. I don't know why, can't recall the last time I thought anything was funny, though I grin at the weirdness of what we're about to do, or attempt to do. But the laughter builds. We snort and wheeze and I bend over, tears escaping. Never heard myself or Ingram laugh so hard, and though it rumbles and echoes, our giggling soon ends, we catch our collective breath, and check for any dripping mascara.

I tap the kitchen table, my dress and wig feeling like both anchor and net, hoping to appear the convincing fool. A spoon in my fingers, I gaze into its curvature, at my warped image, rosy cheeks, lipstick, makeup I haven't worn in years, and metallic-green dots of hummers around my cheeks. I nod at my strange inverted image, not doubting, but recalling why I agreed to do this. Ingram had knocked on my door, said we needed to infiltrate the Risers at least once, deep in their hallowed ground, document their rituals. Said that Blas left a note. *Ingram*, it said, *I'm leaving when I get the chance. When I do, you should come, bring Kumi too. I'm tired of this.* Ingram said it made her think that while the drones had seen so much Deader behavior, they might not know what happens behind those Risers' church doors. That if someone documents it, they can transport the images, at least give them to Blas. I admitted not liking the idea of spying, especially since it required us to do more than fall down. We'd have to wear these costumes, behave as if we knew and understood every ritual. We hadn't even seen their manifesto.

"We're ridiculous," I say on our walk to the church, an array of dead sparrows pinned in Ingram's red wig like a flock about to escape a Sharp-shinned Hawk. Neither of us laugh anymore or smile. We have parts to play.

"Call me Our Lady of Baywood," Ingram insists.

"Better than most silly Risers' names I've heard," I say, still wondering about Victor but unwilling for once to say anything. My fears are my own and there are just too many for me to start expressing them while we're off to a lion's den of Risers.

It's a longer stroll than I remember. We amble west on Los Osos Valley Road toward the once-thriving Pentecostal church building. Nothing seems as I recall, not distance, or time, the width of streets, the sound of voices. Everything feels off-kilter, slipping. No face feels recognizable, not ours, not any passing along the street. None make eye contact. Ingram, next to me, walks slowly, perhaps translating birdsong from canopies, bushes, overgrown gardens. I still feel claustrophobic in this wig, wonder what Hiroki would think of me, how maybe he'd try to rescue me like his beloved gannet.

"Still don't know how I let you talk me into this," I say, my voice like a drone.

"Because we need to document," Ingram says.

"I'm thinking, call me the New Sunrise," I add.

Ingram repeats herself: "We have to document this."

We're tired and sweaty by the time we arrive, almost happy to slip to the ground and writhe before filing in, which we do, clenching our teeth, spitting, filling our bodies with tremors, trying not to lose our wigs, or many birds, of which a few detach. I choke again, imagining Hiroki's last moments in the tub.

We're soon up on our feet, trying to dust off, silently re-pinning birds, straightening our wigs, then pass by a door greeter, a teenager I should recognize from Ascendo Coffee over the years, a barista, who nods while we pass into the foyer. That's when I see Ingram slip a smartphone slightly out of a pocket she's sewn into her dress and click the record button. She quickly passes through to the inner sanctuary. I also carry a phone, doubling our chance to pick up sound of whatever's said. We'll write down all we remember. We'll type it into our devices right after, then place both recordings and messages on both phones for two chances to get the information out.

It's a good plan, but in the darkness of the foyer, women crowd around rows of candles, grabbing and lighting them, lighting each other's wicks, chanting words that I can't even understand, am unwilling to hear. It's at this moment, when pulling my phone half from a pocket, that I'm bumped. The phone fumbles out of my fingers, drops, bounces, lands face-up, screen lit, the record button shining like a tiny red sun.

I quickly step toward the light, swing my dress over the phone, and stand like a golem. I'm waiting, it seems like forever, for someone to tell me phones have been banned, that I'm a spy, that I'm not one of them. I imagine myself dragged into the sanctuary, through the center aisle to the altar, forced to my knees, mouth pulled open, the phone shoved into my throat before I'm locked in a casket. I'm standing numb, panicked, thinking I will soon get caught when another wave of dread hits me. I make eye contact with a woman who has been watching. I've been sensing this, yes I think I have, been watched the entire time, and now can see her eyes locked with mine and this woman is coming closer, smiling, not smiling, both at once, squeezing between others, between those sweeping past into the sanctuary. In a moment she leans in. "You dropped something, didn't you?"

"No, no," I say, mouth feeling dry, trying to swallow. "I didn't."

She smiles harder, leans even closer. "I saw you."

"I didn't," I say. "Just waiting for a friend. How are you?"

"I am your friend." The voice isn't warm.

"Of course you are," I say. "I'll be inside in just a moment. Maybe we can come sit with you? Please go ahead."

The woman pulls back, looks at me harder now, eyes slip into a squint in the dim light. She nods. I don't know if it's to me or someone else. She seems to take a breath and I think she may fall right here.

Then she leans in again as if to hug me. I accept the embrace.

"I'm going to get it for you, okay?" she says, kisses me on the cheek.

I'm petrified. And now I can't move. I see Ingram now too, terror drips from dark moons of her eyes. She's helpless to help and all I can mouth is *It's okay*, though none of this is okay, though nothing about this life is okay. This woman stoops in front of me, and in a moment has reached under my dress on the floor, and when she stands, I feel something gentle. So very gentle. She's slipped the phone back into my pocket, and it's then

I feel her brief hug, her trembling, down to her very her very fingers. I realize what happened, and say, "Thank you." She kisses me on the cheek again. "Thank you, obaasan," she whispers.

We find out about two rituals. The first, a pain test, a purification ritual that has already begun. By the altar, two young women, identical twins, adorned in flower crowns, each wearing sleeveless white dresses, each dress pinned with roses and soft, dead tarantulas. The women stand ready to be *slain in the spirit*. Each on the edge of a large hole dug in the front of the sanctuary that could fit multiple caskets side by side. I'm not sure how deep it goes. I see firelight from within, fires on its deep walls. That these young women want to be covered in spiders horrifies me, though this horror feels nothing like the warm, earthy smell of death in the room, so many pelts, so many uncured dead things. I want to vomit. Heads of rats, cats, bats, lizards, small dogs, birds. Tails of everything. More tails than you can imagine, including dismembered baby possum tails wrapped like bracelets. Ingram covers her mouth, wipes her nose, tries not to seem bothered, though I can tell she's probably next to me second-guessing our decision. A woman can tell when another woman wants to vomit. Then I see her, the woman who helped me glancing from the far side of the room, near someone wearing an armband of doll hands, though I can't tell from this distance, from the poor light. What if they're not doll hands, but real stitched skin and fingers? Near them, a group of teenage girls with wild smiles on their faces. One wears a tiara of fragile warbler bones.

Both twins, arms bared, metal protruding from backs of their arms, have been turned away from us. A man painted in red skulls runs needles over a flame next to them. He hands each sharp point to former Jessie Terrell, their leader, the Deadsayer, Queen of the Risers. She talked outside my home one day, bullhorn aimed at my front door. "The Deadsayer has come for truth," she said, repeating this several times, her only words before drifting silently into the marine layer. I remember her former life. She was a bank manager, not this. Just like those teens. I imagine they were all someone special once. Now they worship their obsessions.

I can't stop watching. Blood drips down the twins' arms while they wince at this purification rite. Terrell pushes through folds of bicep skin, each gauge fatter, longer, the wounds higher and closer toward the shoulder. Terrell's quick, doesn't pause to allow even a breath to escape this pain. Only now I can see the whites of her eyes, so I wonder if she's doing this while deading, if this is some new stage of macabre. I've been trying to ignore the smells, the words, to let our recordings capture this, and though I normally can soak in everything, every sound, every word, every twitching leaf, I can't. I begin to shut down my senses, all except what I see, both twins in unimaginable pain, in this slow process of puncturing, creating wounds, creating fanatics.

And then it's over, the needles taken out, or I think they are, not sure, because I'm lightheaded, but I know none of this is done, and we're back to our feet now, most of us with candles, many chanting around me. I hear something Terrell says: "We will soon lower you into the depths of our sanctuary. If you dead correctly, you will survive."

I don't know what she means. I don't think either woman has a choice about their pseudo-funeral. I wonder if they tried to convince the Deadsayer that they were Risers. I think both may die. My heart races. A sickness swells inside my lungs, a sickness for the world, for humanity, for these people. They're all going to suffocate, turn to dust, while the Risers watch. While we watch. While our phone batteries drain.

Altar boys step forward with strings of barbed wire extended between each hand. The women spin in careful choreography, white dresses now dappled in scarlet, faces decorated with tears and dirt. Each casket has been arrayed with stones, ash, bone, wood. Carcasses too. Each woman steps in, tarantulas wriggling, maybe alive after all, and we're allowed to circle the coffins. We see how each lays next to seabird and feline corpses. Snails crawl freely here, hadn't noticed from where I sat, but it's obvious now that some snails follow the scent of death, that human remains must be in the hole, must have been dropped in but never released.

Then the lids close.

I feel the airlessness of the room, the airlessness of boxes and dirt.

Risers lower both coffins into the darkness via a system of pulleys, and then, once lowered, ceremonially cover caskets with shovel loads of dirt. This is death cast in sound, ecstasy, terror. The Risers become fanatical in their movements, swinging and digging wildly, so many shovels, not enough space, not enough dirt.

Suddenly the screams start. Screams from coffins. Screams to let them out. Screams begging not to die. Ingram squeezes my fingers, whispers that we need to leave. I tell her, "We have to see this through."

The Risers up now, sing old hymns stripped of references like Jesus, god, resurrection, lyrics transcribed into frightening verses. "Come Thou Fount of Every Blessing" becomes a new camp-meeting revival chorus:

> *This body of fractals,*
> *vessels like branches,*
> *nerves plucked like strings.*
> *Unending rapturous gelatinous being,*
> *consume me entirely,*
> *a sweetbread for thee.*

Their voices, the other side of grief, unearthly, disharmonious.

Some parishioners hold hands while this goes on. Some merely wail and rock. Others kneel, then prostrate themselves, lick at the dirt. Eventually, the coffins slowly get dragged up. Dirt rains into the hole. Many continue in their writhing, candles long burned out, aisles and pews filled with a putrid stench, as if all of us have been decaying together. I just want to get out of this dress, get the dirt and dust out of my eyes, never again wear a wig.

Then, the woman who picked up my phone, comes over, whispers, "Leave now. This is the time when they search for others among us to bury."

I tug at Ingram while the lids open, see the twins' bodies get dragged out. Moans rise and lights dim further. The teens are up and surrounding the holes, wild, ecstatic. We quickly move to the foyer entrance, only takes a few seconds even while stepping over congregants. When there I turn, take out the phone, snap a single photo, then with Ingram, slip into the night.

Chapter Twenty-Six

WE REMEMBER THE day our city was on the news, many weeks ago but now a memory, cameras aimed from distant hills at the water tower above Baywood High. We remember the long climb, the way we snuck up ladder rungs, the way we painted the banner in the gym. We remember seeing our television ghost images pixelated along the tower railing. We could almost see our smiles. We remember the words before others came and tore them down: SAVE US FROM OURSELVES. We remember the day the TVs went out. We could no longer see outside the barricades looking in, or the replays of our water tower moment. We could never again hear the words *City Under Quarantine, Mystery Illness Strikes Seaside Community,* or *Is There Hope for Baywood, California*? We could no longer count the days with the rest of the world. Since then, many of us have left. Most became Risers. Some tried to escape. Maybe some of them did. Wherever they've gone, we've lost their voice. We feel our own weaknesses, our own trembling and fading.

We remember days when the drones first dropped beneath the marine layer, swimming above us like skeletal fish. We remember the day the tanks came, lining themselves on a distant hill next to the Humvees. We remember when they disappeared.

We remember when Chewie and Elisabeth left us, how we never saw them again, but see the Risers constantly in our neighborhoods, searching for those of us who hide, who used to be part of the Dead of Night. We remember when we became only a few.

And now here we are, wishing we joined those who tried to escape.

And then something else. Something about Kaylee. You know those paths that lead into Elfin Forest over the bay? Some made of sand? Some, dirt? They lead to boardwalks through an ancient shrunken forest. In normal forests these trees are fifty feet tall. Not here. Some of them stand three feet, five feet. They've shrunk. It's all natural, they say. But nothing is natural right now, nothing is normal.

Anyway, Bobby Saramifar tells us we need to drop what we're doing. So a lot of us go to the western edge, not quite inside where a bunch of people live. And that's not where Kaylee has gone anyway. She's not quite inside the forest, rather on the periphery. She's made her way onto a cliff, a slippery ledge high above the estuary.

We have to try to stop her.

When we get there, we race up to the overlook.

"I am one of them," Kaylee screams. "They need me." She hangs on the other side of a barrier fence. The drop, so, so far. She wears a red dress. Bumblebees are pinned or glued in her hair, we can't tell.

We beg her to come back over. We plead. The drop is so, so far. Her eyes glow a shade of vermillion that makes us wish we can turn off the fire inside her. Everything feels surreal, a blur, too much, like we can't process any of this.

"It's eating my insides," she cries. "I can't think, can't breathe, can't exist anymore. I don't want to go there but I have to. I don't care how it feels—this is normal, all normal. Where's Blas?" she cries. "Where is he?" She then mumbles something none of us understand. She only hangs on by a few fingers. We can't get close. We don't know what to say while we creep bit by bit. We don't know where Blas is. We tell her we can find him, bring him. But she loses focus, almost like she forgets her own question, like she's really fighting the thing pulling her inside herself, that she doesn't want to lose.

"My parents wanted me to get perfect grades, to be perfect," she cries. "Now they throw themselves on the ground every day, this nasty yellow froth on their lips. And I think, *They're dead. They're really dead this time.* And I'm no different."

We beg her to come to us but Kaylee's eyes start to roll. "This is what happens to all of us," she spits, fights with herself, begging us, trying to keep focused on us, her eyelids vibrate, her eyes turn.

Kaylee disintegrates in front of us, like her whole body becomes this fragile, shivering thing. "I can do this," she says. "I have to do this while I still have control. They say I will be in the mirrors after I go."

We wonder if she thinks she's to blame for everything.

We tell her she isn't.

But then she smiles. It's wicked. And then she jumps.

After this, almost all of us start deading. Is that what she wanted? It isn't for popularity or to say she's wrong. Not this time. Most of us can't stop if we tried. It's not our fault. It's not her fault.

Those of us who do start looking for her in mirrors.

We chant her name thirteen times.

Chapter Twenty-Seven

"I NEED YOU to do something for me," Blas's mother says. She wears a red dress, red wig, bright red lipstick. Her once-plump round face has thinned, arms noticeably scarred. A fresh scab crawls down her arm like a blind snake.

Blas hates talking to his mother. Hates looking at her. "Okay, Maria," is all he can manage, especially after what happened outside Elfin Forest.

"That letter from the post office you were supposed to pick up weeks ago."

"Months ago."

"I want you to find it."

Blas wants to laugh at the thought. Kaylee's dead, and his mother wants him to pick up a letter? The letter he was supposed to get before all this started? He's long forgotten about that, hasn't been outside in days, hasn't walked across town. He failed Kaylee. Never visited his brother. Not to mention, if there's one place he wants to steer clear from, it's the barricades.

He's not even worried about the drones. It's the people on his side of the fence. Crackpots, ritual seekers, deaders, protesters: the Risers. All one and the same. Elisabeth and Chewie told him enough about deading rituals to make him want to hop a fence and run like hell. For all he knows, they pull knives, sacrifice by drawing real blood, bury guys like him alive with rat heads. He feels paranoia wash through his insides just thinking about it.

Maybe Risers listened that night in the eucalyptus grove. Maybe they captured his friends. He hasn't heard from them, doesn't expect to. Last he saw was their shadows as he helped carry a two-man kayak through scrub in the near-black night. He abandoned them at the sandspit, watched their dissolving forms scramble up a dune while coyotes sang to star-gods. Then a terrifying walk back out of there alone. He heard so much scratching and clawing in the brush he was sure he was going to be eaten.

Maybe if he could remind his mother of a simple reality. "Maria. The post office closed. There's no mail. There's nothing. It's gone."

"Will you stop calling me that? I seen José last time I was around there. You remember him. Everyone knows José. He was creeping around in the dark but I knew it was him. I told him I wouldn't rat him to the Risers." Her eyes widen a little before turning to fire. "Just go knock on the door."

"There's no letter, Mom, all right? The mail is gone, like Kaylee." He tries not to choke up. "Someone probably burned what was left. I would have."

"You would have done no such thing," she says. "You have a good heart, mijo. You have to do this. You understand?"

"No, I don't understand," Blas says. "All I understand is you're over there all the time. You go do it. Be with your crazies."

She pulls at his arm, he wrestles himself free. "You think I can help all this?" she says. "I can't. You know they'll see me if I go in there. We're not allowed. Only the leaders. You're young like some of them. They'll think you're just being curious. They won't do anything to you."

"What's that supposed to mean? If you're afraid of them doing something then stop hanging out with them."

She let's out a whimper as if she wants to cry but can't bring herself to break down in front of him. "Don't you see? It's my last contact with the outside world. I'm going to die," she says. "That letter is my last chance."

He wants to laugh at this too. "I'm your last everything. Chango too. And you're not dead. He's not dead. He just can't wake up from this nightmare. Although you keep saying he's getting better."

"Will you just stop it? Just stop." Her voice transforms into a groan. "I've seen Chango. I go there. His eyes won't close. They won't. Just go. Please. *Please.* Blas."

It's the one p.m. deading. Blas ignores Maria's writhing on the lawn. He stares through binoculars beyond her thrashing, beyond her dirty feet kicking up mud where the grass has long died, logging two Golden-crowned Sparrows, a Yellow-rumped Warbler, two Chestnut-backed Chickadees, and three Lesser Goldfinches into a journal. He quickly sketches a warbler, a butterbun, which he calls the bird because of its yellow rump. He also calls it a Myrtle because of its wide white throat. He thinks for a moment the bird might be a hybrid but his photo doesn't capture any yellow around the white below its chin. He writes, *This Myrtle has a slightly smaller white throat than others I usually see, though my best guess is this butterbun isn't a hybrid at all. This bird has light black striping on its grey back, a wash of yellow on its streaky white flanks, kind of messy white wing bars, and appears mostly drab overall, especially its grey-brown head. The throat is stark white. The eye is ringed with white, and there is a messy white streak almost through the eye. The undertail is white and its tail is medium long.*

The birds forage through a bush at the edge of the yard. A nearby feeder lies empty though a couple birds momentarily perch on it out of habit. He records three additional goldfinches before adding: *One goldfinch drops, twitches, stops moving. Never gets up. Other birds don't even pay attention. They forage and move on. Yesterday's fallen hummingbirds remain still.*

Instead of reading a book or studying his bird guide afterwards he steps outside. His mother has already picked herself up, wandered off. She does this a lot. Just roams. He never follows her. Doesn't want to.

The air still holds a faint chemical scent. Smells better than it has. Doesn't make him nauseous for once. Doesn't make him wish he was dead. He does wish all the birds would carry him away from this mess.

He takes a deeper breath, wants to feel better, to cleanse himself from his mother, from everyone, from what he is about to do. Cold salt air cuts sharp through his nostrils, fills his lungs. He blows out air, can only half swallow his fear. He wishes he could see reports from Ozziel, but the internet is so blocked now that he clings to the last update, its code indicating only one way out. He has it written down, keeps it in his pocket, a crude sort of map to use when he's ready. He's not ready.

Before he begins his trek, he walks over to the fallen goldfinches. Nearby, other dead birds lay in various states of decomposition. Fallen Wilson's, Townsend's and Orange-crowned warblers. Song and White-crowned sparrows with exposed ribcages. Tiny Bushtits. Gull bones from a rare Franklin's lie in a heap with a California Scrub-Jay and crows, even a California Thrasher, its long downcurved bill like a devilish warning that everything grim will pass this way. The gull was dumb luck. Must have fallen straight out of the sky while it sailed over. Deaded and dead. Other dead gulls from three other species, California, Western, and Ring-billed, litter the street. This isn't the kind of fallout he wants to see. He wants to see the High Island fallout in Texas, tired warblers on beaches after their long flights from Mexico, Ecuador, Costa Rica, or something like Observatoire d'oiseaux de Tadoussac in Les Bergeronnes, Quebec. A river of a quarter-million warblers descending on old seal-hunting lands, a fallout of 85,300 Bay-breasted Warblers and 56,900 Cape May Warblers alone. It's a swarm. A lovely warbler blizzard. The most perfect of storms, like the warbler storm in Promontory Point, Chicago, so many hundreds of thousands pushed by rainstorms that a thousand died from striking just one building. He sketches a pile of dead birds, a kind of gesture drawing. He might illustrate something more detailed later so takes a pic through his phone. Then he writes some more field notes. *They fell here as if asleep, as if they couldn't wake up, or didn't want to. What would want to?* He thinks about Chango lying in a coma then closes the book.

He scoops up the goldfinch that just died, a Lesser, strokes its yellow and green feathers and carries it down the street. Two blocks later he pops open a random mailbox and tucks the bird inside. He decides that all mailboxes should be little tombs and promises to lay more birds to rest. He doesn't close the latch all the way, just in case, then heads east on Los Osos Valley Road.

He logs more birds as he goes. Something about this feels freeing. The chemical air not as inhibiting. He notes a kestrel. Doves line wires. A White-tailed Kite hovers, hoping for a vole or mouse. A red-and-green mottled Summer Tanager darts between branches high in a eucalyptus, snacking on bees, then disappears. A beautiful, rare sighting. Holding up his binoculars and peering nearly straight up makes his neck sore. He waits a few minutes to see if it will call or poke its head out. While he does, the last working electric car from the hospital, quiet as a cat, sneaks down the street. He's attuned to slippery birds, the tiniest peeps, so he hears the crunching of car tires on gravel though the engine hums electric, silent.

The car slows next to him. A little whine to the brakes when it stops.

Blas doesn't turn. He stares into the tree where he last spotted reddish leaves wriggling from the tanager's foraging. He wishes the bird would pop its head out, nab another bee with its thick bill. A slight wind kicks up, rattles the leaves. Branches sway. A House Finch darts between clumps of leaves.

The engine buzzes. A window shoots down but no voice. Then a groan. Blas realizes what's happening behind him. He doesn't look and runs into the grove of trees. He knows this area, every ditch, every clump of sage and lupine. He burrows in like the tanager in the canopy. He doesn't move until the car slowly continues down the road as if nothing happened.

Up the street, several bodies line the roadway, stuck in poses of fake death. They've yet to get up from their one p.m. deading. Blas believes they're in some state of bliss, refusing to wake, a state of addictive unconsciousness, because who doesn't want to wake from good dreams, though he doesn't think his visions of his brother's dreams are accurate, that it's really his own fears manifesting dark worlds, but that's beside the point. He's talked to his friends so many times, argued so many times, theorized so many times about where people go when they dead. He's rifled through books and comics, read about so many universes and portals and microchips and micro-transportation devices, and brainwaves that tap into wormholes, and spells, and superheroes with the power to think themselves into other dimensions, and can only lean on the idea that these people merely dream, that's it, *they dream*, they think they go somewhere but it's really just endorphins, like a tidal wave of endorphins, and when they wake, maybe, just maybe those endorphins get blocked, and they can only remember that they went to some happy place, some tunnel of light, to some afterparty, after-death, afterlife, and so, like so many humans that latch onto dreams, have become obsessed to the point where some deaders starve to death these days. Or Risers. He should call them by their stupid name. The Horsemen pick up the dead, he's told, cart them to the new cemetery. Yeah, his same old classmates who carted Chango away have added RISERS to their lettermen sleeves. He's seen the scrawl. And so this all tells him that a society can be built right in front of your eyes, and it can be made of anything, even dark empty dreams, and that's all he can think this is.

Blas finds piles of animals pushed into gutters at the corner of Tenth Street where he used to work. No sign of the electric car so he takes a closer peek. A stench rips at his nostrils, the back of his throat. He pulls his shirt over his nose. More birds. Twenty or so dog corpses. A bare foot protrudes from the pile. He starts to feel sick until a doll head stares at him, plastic hair in a wiry frizz. He thinks about making a sketch then continues.

Ahead, the post office is part of a strip mall close to where barbed wire and metal barricades have been set up. On the other side of the wire no one can be seen. The nearest government vehicles, Humvees with tinted windows, sit a hundred or more yards away in the middle of the road. Along his side of the wire, dozens of protesters hold signs:

DEAD IS DIVINE
SEE INSIDE YOURSELF
THE PARTY IS IN BAYWOOD
WE WILL STAY, TAKE DOWN THE WIRE
GOD IS DEADING
THE HAUNT IS HERE

Blas wonders how food drops go down at the barricades, if more than Humvees and drones accompany trucks, and what kinds of trucks, and whether or not helicopters come in and drop food instead—sometimes he thinks he hears them. He would jump in a helicopter if he could. All he knows: he's been eating beans and rice for days. He always hides when the distribution wagon comes. His mom deals with them.

Some protesters throw rocks at distant drones crawling through brush. Some middle-aged guy with white hair lobs stones at a hovering drone, too high to be reached. The craft soon continues north along the fence line. Blas considers how sneaking under the bridge along the Turri Road tidal pools might leave him face to face with half a dozen such drones, some likely armed with a kind of Taser that can make him sleep. Kumi told him about them. He doesn't want to sleep anymore.

Other drones, like bulbous white spiders, hang in the thermals. Tiny arms, a dozen of them, seem to be collecting things out of thin air. Swifts dart among them. Smaller large-eyed drones the size of apples zip along the barrier now and then. Some run along the wire like sleek, tailless, hairless possums. They leap into the air, shooting straight up the way Anna's Hummingbirds do when about to drop into their J-curve, surveying the scene before zooming back to the barrier and scurrying off. No rock can be zinged close enough to hit one. Their sparkling eyes like holograms, they seem to hover midair.

Blas gets eyed by some of the protesters. Before anyone can talk to him he hurries toward the propped-open post office door, disappears inside. He's been terrified of them for so long, has gotten most of his information from friends, but only a few like him are left. Kai is one. Tatum and Emily too. He saw Jordan deading on top of a red, white, and blue violin that he'd been playing out on a street to one of the goth girls. Blas's eyes drift to where counters have been ripped out, registers smashed. In their stead, piles of wood, lines of cots. Each wall covered with graffiti.

Half a wall, a decree on the "Apocalypse of Death." One line at the end: "And ye shall dead and see the plane." He knows this can't mean an actual airplane or jet. Must be some surreal, sticky landscape in their warped, infected heads, like they've all stolen his Dungeons & Dragons books and created some alternate reality stuck inside a Gelatinous Cube. His own mind continues to concoct what Chango could be experiencing, though he doesn't have it in him to enter that hospital. He again brushes off imagined red landscapes, thinking they're nothing more than a manifestation of all the sci-fi novels and comics he reads.

"What you doing here, boy?" comes a voice from a tangle of blankets. A dirty heap, all beard, sits up. His high forehead, sunburned, peeling, begins to take shape. He isn't José, wears a blue post office shirt, tag with the name PETE hangs by a thread. Pete, for lack of a better name, goes on: "Only the big cheese allowed here. That decree for them to read, not you, though you could be one of them younger ones. They hand it down like the good prophets they are." He falls back into his blankets. "Get the hell out. Let me finish my nap."

"I'm looking for a letter."

Pete lets out a string of raspy laughter. Seems like forever before he sits up again. His eyes dull in a sliver of light. "Case you haven't noticed," he spits, "ain't no more letters."

Blas fingers his binoculars, wonders if this guy is only here to keep someone's nest warm. Pete hunches like he's tucked in his pink rat tail, like this is the best he can do.

"You deaf?" he says. "Ain't a post office no more."

Blas hears a gun go off. He ducks then peeks through his binoculars.

"Hell yes!" Pete jumps to the window, above Blas. "Got another one!" Nearby, a board already scratched to hell with ink and sideways notes. He marks it, tallies up a bunch of black strokes. "Thirty-seven!"

Blas watches someone with a rifle kick at a downed drone while Pete laughs. Before Blas lets his binocs dangle from his neck, he watches the same man zapped unconscious by another drone, his rifle confiscated and flown away.

"Hot damn," Pete says. "We got a couple more for that. He'll wake soon enough."

"Why you wearing that uniform?" Blas asks, eyeing the man outside in the dirt.

Pete seems to chew at nothing. A reflex. An imagined steak. "I used to work in the back if you should know," he says.

"Can we check the back?"

"Ain't nothing there. Burned it all."

"Maybe you missed something."

"Every. Goddam. Letter."

"Why would you do that?" Blas isn't about to leave. "Where's José?"

Pete examines board marks, groans like he doesn't want anything to do with this world except celebrate the destruction of things. He ignores the question.

"Can't you check?" Blas asks.

"Can I check?" Pete grumbles, swipes at his dirty beard. "An old pickup? Something I missed for the fires?" Like a stubborn shopping cart with a bad wheel, his knee joints grind, moves to the back of the room, passes through a curtain.

Blas follows, knocks the curtain aside. "What happened to José?"

"You think that sumbitch Indian still works here?"

"No idea."

"José ain't got a thing to do with the decree."

"I don't know anything about that stuff."

Pete hobbles along a wall, peering in broken cubbyholes and smashed bins. "So, it clear you shouldn't be here." He tosses broken chunks of plastic out of his way. "He don't even go by that name anymore. Where you been, boy? You a no-deader? I don't like no-deaders."

Blas doesn't answer, though he isn't sure why Pete would bother to look. A dim yellow room unfolds: a stale warehouse filled with nasty odors, more cots, dirty blankets, pillows, piles of trash. Blas can't imagine anyone living here. Reminds him of the messes his mother leaves, the detritus she tracks in from deading in an ash pit she's told him is meant to simulate a crematorium or disposal site.

"Shuluwish," Pete says. The name drips out with a strand of spit. "That's what he calls himself these days. He ain't no witch doctor. Not gonna fix nothing. Ain't a single man or woman alive wants to be fixed. You know that if you know anything at all."

Blas mouths the name Shuluwish, wonders if José went crazy or if he just tired of this world and who he was. He wonders what Pete thinks of the hospital, or if everyone there has been dead for a while.

"All the conveyors been ripped out," Pete says about the room.

Blas notices a few unbroken bins shoved against a wall of empty alphabetized slots. He says his last name. *Enriquez.* It sounds strange, as if it's not part of who he is anymore.

"Enriquez," Pete repeats. "That you?"

Blas nods. "Did he leave a long time ago? Shuluwish, I mean."

Pete knocks bins aside, digs in one of the slots, finds a small pile of something under a rag. His eyes brighten. "Man. Sakes alive. Look at these . . . How long you been locked up, anyway?"

"A while."

"A while." Pete starts sorting as if it's born into his blood. Only, most of this sorting ends up on the floor. "Ain't you seen the smoke coming from that forest?"

"Always smoke these days."

"Got that right. Shuluwish gone home to his lookout over the back bay. Cooking things in there that ought not be cooked. Got a compound somewhere in the middle of them dwarf woods. Barricaded himself like a lot of them who don't know how to die right." Pete eyes Blas, seems about to accuse him of some kind of wrongdoing. He sizes him up, spits. "Claims those woods his safe zone, free of government, free of deading. Some say he pay for them dead. Literally. You don't wanna follow that path of bones. You see them motorcycles with skulls painted on them, you go the other way. Best to go to the church, get yourself buried and freed. They'll hang you by your skin, but that's all right."

Pete's legs slip into a jitter. "Now look at this—certified mail. Like a frigging time capsule. Ain't a soul hears from the outside anymore. Not even goddam bill collectors. Maria. That your mother?"

Blas nods.

"I ought to burn this."

"Just give it to me."

"You are one of them no-deaders. I don't see y'all around here. Nope. Don't think one of them would be brave enough to come in here. You been locked up, you say?"

Blas, terrified, catches Pete's dull eyes again. "Something like that."

Pete holds onto the letter, mouth still chewing, licks his beard, lets out a sudden string of laughter.

"You almost got me," he says, starts foaming at the mouth, choking onto his beard.

Blas takes the letter while Pete's eyes roll to the back of his head.

Chapter Twenty-Eight

CHANGO'S EYES FEEL like someone has been pressing thumbs to his sockets for weeks. Any shift side to side, up and down, to scan the room, to see his own skin, crashes with excruciating pain.

The doctor comes in for a second check, this time tells him he's suffered deep, incapacitating extraocular bruises, that the deading has done this, and only to him. The doctor then exits into the hall, deads in front of his nurses, who Chango can hear giggle, then groan against the walls and floor.

Chango feels a pull, wants to slip into a dream, close these lids. For now he can't. He can only blink, lie awake after a lengthy paralysis—a waking coma—and continue staring, listening. No longer in a dream state, anxiety wells until his next calming dose of whatever they're dripping through his IV.

A nurse comes in, tells him his mother has visited, one of the few times she has, that his eyes aren't quite red as they have been. He grunts a reply, tries to close his lids again but can't through the pain.

At the edge of his memory, a burning ocular fluid, a fire that won't go out. His vision, everything he still sees, ringed with a flaming edge. It had been a slow hardening of his body leading up to his paralysis, to these visions. His mother in their living room. Deading together. Him no longer seeing her, hearing her, somehow drifting.

He wills himself to blink out red fluid, not blood, something else filling them. He imagines his mother's face shifting between disgust and wonder.

He remembers her voice, like he was having an out-of-body experience, floating somewhere in the room. He remembers her call to the hospital, before the Horsemen came to cart him off. "I don't know," she said. "He's not deading, not like us . . . No. He's just gone. Worse than his Uncle Antonio who had that Alzheimer's and stared like a fish. You know. Wide-eyed, loose . . . He won't eat. He's dying."

And Blas, his little brother, tears slipping down his dark cheeks, crying, "This is bullshit! Wake up, you asshole!"

Chango remembers not being able to respond, his chest growing heavy, then darkness for a time. He woke here in the hospital, began seeing two places at once: another world, alien sky, yellow hospital ceiling tiles, sixty-four holes to each square. He remembers tying imaginary strings between each tiny hole, at first forming triangles, rectangles, parallelograms, stars. Then complex patterns, organic patterns. Cellular. Unknown. Leaves and flowers. Root systems. Nothing like he'd ever seen, or thought he could imagine. Eventually, creatures too. Crab-like, insect-like. Strange heads. Almost human on some. He connected mindscape ink sketches, imagining innumerable sets of holes on a grid he could zoom into and out of, linking, tying strings, building, creating. Hole to hole. Line to line. All with his mind. They wound through his vision, ethereal storyboards from some distant haunting tale, pulling him further into darkness, closer and closer to the nightmare truth of some story center.

When not connecting strings, he began giving in to a

subconscious desire to visit this other world. He wanted to see more than ceiling holes, to slip among rocks and open spaces, breathe its air, smell its life-forms. Vast landscapes of flowering shrubs, their purple-blue inflorescences of silvery palmate leaves in small spirals like desert lupine. Thick pelts of moss. Carpets of lichen. Creatures with skin and carapace that gave off scents of oil and blood.

And then he went there, to this other world. And he felt like he'd been freed. It wasn't like his hospital bed, his eyes fixed like two red statues, bones unable to move. There, his body and his mind freely roamed. Nothing about the world, or how he felt transported, made sense when he gave into it. He was simply in another place, or inside a dream. And he was willing to give in to this euphoria that felt so ripe for the taking.

He remembers exhilaration, roaming for days, the air, the wild air, him feeding off creatures that crept between rocks and murky tides, their eyes focused on him, an intruder, like the ship, because of that ship.

Their segmented carapaces broke easily apart at grey joints. He tasted blood and belly meat and fingers, making their remains a sanctuary of shells and legs and heads. He piled those near a lean-to that he built from metal slabs, detritus from a debris field scattered over a solid mile and a half. He built that shelter to hide from sudden southwesterlies that blasted across rocks and low vegetation. From the same direction when two moon faces hurtled dead and full, a howl drifted over pale-lit scrub. Some metallic curse he could never make out and didn't want to, something deadly in the lupine, something he didn't want on his scent, perhaps large, maybe giant, he didn't know.

In his hospital room he replays some of these visions. Memory fragments of those last breaths from the other world, an oily residue on his tongue, a taste he can sort of recall, like water or flesh. He reimagines scenes by staring at those ceiling tiles and tying networks of strings between holes again, building from memories, including the debris site, and one portion of it he couldn't climb into, a tangle of sharp metal. At the center, the remains of a cockpit, he remembers, its windows darkened with dust, cracked. He wants to go back, find who or what was inside. Can someone visit this place other than himself? Someone from the spacecraft? Another deader? After some time reconstructing images, perhaps for days, his visions begin to fade. Then his desire to return again overwhelms, causes tremors in his legs, and he allows his mind, or his imagination, or his entire body, to return to that place. There, he roams and feasts, gorges on every creature he can find, and when not eating, begins slowly pulling debris into organized piles. Hull sections, window sections, underbelly, portions of propulsion systems, interior workings, instrument panels. He arranges the puzzle, all the while slowly making his way toward that mysterious cockpit. The ship had begun to take shape.

He wakes again, this time remembers a pink-wash dawn, a humid, heavy morning coated with the scent of shrub, sand, and blood, and most of all, the horror of fingers and legs crawling across his body and face. He'd scrambled out of the shack. Creatures everywhere, hanging on the side of his lean-to, claws scratching over the ground in a writhing mass, and while he made his way to a beach, these same crustaceans seething along an endless shore. A sea dark and boiling. Millions crawled from their mass spawning, legs wriggling, carapace clacking against carapace, tiny minds working as one, ignoring him while he stood amid their numbers that soon piled knee deep. More than a few crawled up his legs. Eyes like his eyes, humanlike, some blinking at him, others determined, gazing at their brethren, at some distant force pulling them.

He knocked them apart in his fury to get back in his lean-to. Eyes glazing at him, Chango thinking he could keep them out of his home. So many already piled against thin walls, the structure slipping apart at the seams. He ran away, pushed through the creatures, scurried up rocks, thinking maybe he could tower over this tide.

The mass thought different.

They crawled upon each other, up the rocks, again up his legs, now his back and shoulders. Smelled like a giant slough of oyster guts hot in the warm ocean sun melting all around him. Putrid, lingering chemicals of these creatures dissolved into mucous, caked in the back of his nasal cavity.

Slipping on them, flinging them off, he forced himself up their slope of wriggling bodies, willing himself atop their heaps, like some kind of god-creature himself, until his feet landed on another protrusion of rock, which he held to, fingers aching. The collective leviathan poured up and over, out of the sea, over his home, the nearby detritus field, and moved southward, trampling moss and shrub, frantic to reach some distant point that he could not imagine, never imagine except for that howl. He wondered if they would all die, or spawn and return to the sea. And he wondered, though they trampled him, if the cockpit was again surrounded by metal shards from the creatures pushing their way through. For all he knew, the cockpit and everything else had been carried away, and he would never see what was inside.

After what seemed days, the last of their numbers passed into the horizon.

Chango, alone on the rocks, untangled himself from the remains of so many trampled creatures. On his feet again, he became transfixed, not by the immense twitching and bleeding still covering the landscape, but those two fast-moving low moons. The moonfaces. Their light was his light. He allowed the glow to fill him until he beamed with energy; the remains of every grey creature seemed to move under ripples of rapidly sinking moon-fire. The universe in the darkness whirled with pulsing stars and a nebulaic web.

And then he saw in the distant past, escaped from an exploded star's silky green threads, so deep into time itself, a ship, unknown and yet familiar, lit like a thousand beacons, ripping between light and darkness, through the atmosphere, burning and descending, thrumming a cacophony of sonic disturbance, not unlike the metallic howl of the unknown creature he sometimes heard from the southern darkness, leaving behind it a great comet-like tail, some history already played out, already soaked in tragedy and death.

He covered his ears until every spark dropped into the sea.

A calm. A red glow. Two moons again. Bright reflections. The ship calls to him. The cockpit. The forms inside. Moonbeams cut through fire-burnt ports while they say his name . . . Only now, slipping away. He can't go back. For weeks he hasn't been able to go back.

Chango blinks easier from his hospital bed. Eyes in less pain. Unable to lift mental black clouds. Like the meds put him under just enough so that he knows he has a consciousness, knows he's wandering in the wrong direction, knows he's alive.

Something isn't right.

A voice. His mother. Maria. That's her name. He never thinks about her name. But she has one. It's not in his culture to use it. He calls her Madre. Mom. Mother. Mama. The Matriarch. The Doña. She wears all red like some kind of Valentine's Day hooker slinking along Bakersfield's Union Avenue in that always polluted Central Valley. She's dirty, her face, her clothes, arms covered in fresh blood.

"Mijo. You awake?"

He bites his tongue, terrified of her.

"Doctor says you fell out of bed this week. They found you standing on your bed. Mijo, you're more awake than I've seen."

Chango can't remember getting out of bed. Or falling down. He can't remember much of anything. Pulses ring in his ears from something falling into the sea. If he tries to remember too far back he recalls the day before Bernhard went missing. He was supposed to go on a date. He can't remember her name.

"Mijo. They're still doing tests on your heart and brain," Maria says. "You don't have a fever, thank god. They already took blood today. Vampiras. Six vials. Why do they need so much blood? Are they drinking it? They say they're running out of supplies. They whisper that your doctor is from the outside, that he can't escape, that his time ran out. He's one of us now but also one of them. He sends information. I promised to keep this secret. Do you trust me?"

Chango sees the IV in his left arm. He wonders if he's fatigued from blood loss, something loss. "What else they give me?" Drifting, he wonders if he can fight this, wants to get out of this bed, go home. His muscles feel no desire to move. Something else, feels something close. Doesn't know what or where. Something besides his mother. He wonders if two of her exist, one he can see, one he can't.

Maria goes on talking. "My friend Fernanda's son Itchy stopped by. You used to play with him all the time. Remember? Practically the size of a VW. He was recruited by Fresno State. Can you believe that? Fresno State. That's like going to USC isn't it? Only, he's trapped. Can't go to university. Said he's going to paddle out to those ships blocking the bay. I think he was joking. You think? He doesn't dead. I didn't turn him in. We're called Risers now. I don't think the people here in the hospital have joined us. This place is strange, mijo. Not sure any of the staff ever leave. I'm one of the only visitors."

Chango can't really make out what's happening. Something shimmering, a slight sparkling, a hum. Here but maybe from another world where things are alive in a different way. A shadow flits. A form with segments. Stalks or arms protrude from thick sides. An ungodly fear pulls at his guts. He doesn't say anything. Can't say anything. Can only think the shadow seems interested in his mother. In his funk he realizes his brain could be making this shit up. These meds. He's drifting, paranoid.

"Nice to see your eyes closing for a change," Maria says.

He can hardly hear her.

"Chango," she says. "Your meds might be kicking in." She holds his hand.

He tries to squeeze back. Feels her hand shiver.

"I'm starting to feel a cold coming on," she says. "A scratchy throat. Think I'll get some lozenges from the gift shop. If they still have any. Okay, mijo? I'll check on you soon." She kisses his forehead. Some of the blood on her arm gets on the sheets. "When I get back I'm going to open something. I'll share it with you. It's a letter. Can you believe it? From the outside world. From before. You know, before all this. Blas picked it up at the post office. I'll show you when I come back tomorrow."

Chango feels a coldness wash over him; then she leaves, watches the shadow follow her, moving close behind like it might inhabit every inch of her soul.

Though he fights the urge, he starts to drift off.

And then a scream. Not his. Someone in the hall. Then someone yelling to get a gurney. Then laughter.

Chapter Twenty-Nine

CHANGO WAKES FOR a second, third, tenth, hundredth time. He knows he's been drifting in and out. Feels like he's died and come back. Feels like he can't handle much more of this. This time when his eyes open, a middle-aged, stinky-breathed vato stands over him, lips curled in half smile. Chango fidgets. This is no normal doctor smile. It hangs on an otherwise blank slate. This doctor exists somewhere else. Some other time zone. Some other reality.

"What happened to my specialist?" Chango asks.

"I'm Greenberg." The doctor flicks a light in Chango's eyes. "You're one of the few who doesn't see a better place, who no longer deads."

"So fucking what?" Chango remembers fragments. He remembers atmosphere, metal, creatures, his lean-to, something else: a noise, a language. He'd never seen another person there. It can't be where people go when they dead. Not that he knows where his mother goes. Like her, something inside tells him never to talk about it, mostly because they can't. No one actually remembers, except him. "I seen another place though," he says. "I don't know if it's better than where you go. You from the outside? How you get in here?"

"It's okay, son. We're here to help you. Ready to go under again?"

"Ain't your fuckin' son." Chango squirms. A memory floods back. A scream. "Hey, what happened to my mom? She all right?"

He really wants to tell this dumbass gringo doctor what he thinks but feels himself melting into the sheets, into darkness. He wants more than anything to be wide awake, raking oysters, making fun of his little brother, going on a date with that woman whose name he can't remember. He can't even see her face.

When he wakes again an hour later, two hours later, ten hours later, he has no idea how time works anymore, he tells himself he's done with this place.

"Ain't shit wrong with me," he mutters, eyes and extremities still sore, pulls out the IV, the catheter. Grunts like a mother-fucker, glad that he hasn't been strapped down.

He slips out of bed. Stiff and shaky. Muscles aching, dick hurting, face damp with sweat. He limps to the bathroom, wets a towel, adds soap, quickly washes his emaciated body. He slips on his T-shirt and jeans. Skin feels thin. So thin. Like he hasn't eaten in days, forgot what food was all about. A tray of moldy something has an unopened cup of applesauce. He sucks it down, not caring that it's lukewarm, then gulps down stale water, rips open two packages of crackers, eats them in seconds.

"What the hell they do with my shoes?" he croaks, search-ing, his voice pained from tubes down his throat, exploring his innards. Wallet is gone too. Sons of bitches either took it, or his mother has it in her purse. Fucking Mom, always taking his shit like he's five years old. He wonders again what's happened to her.

The hall is empty. No noise. No commotion. No moans. No complaining. No nurses at their stations. No sounds from in-tercoms. No phones ringing. No machines buzzing or beeping. Nothing. Just flickering hall lights and the slap of his bare feet on tile.

His mind drifts to the oyster farm and Bernhard. He wonders what happened to his boss. Did the bay swallow him? Or maybe that vato panicked and ran to Mexico? Probably Mexico, he thinks. Bitch is having a margarita in Cabo, laughing about his fat overseas bank account and a new life away from Baywood freaks.

Chango wonders if he's dreaming, sleeping off great sex and blow. He'd prefer that. God he'd prefer that. He tries to clear his throat from another cracker, which feels stuck halfway down his pipe, but only manages to hurt his throat worse. No one comes to investigate.

He wonders about Blas. Always thought his little brother would end up dead along some stream exploring for birds. Killed by a creek tweaker. He's seen those homeless fuckers stalking through woods, gathering in cold mornings along walking paths by their piles of stolen bicycle parts, tents, and junk, tossing hatchets into trees like they were getting ready to invade the neighborhoods and slaughter all those rich folks in their McMansions.

The hospital feels empty, so he checks here and there. Every patient room. Every office. Every station. Every desk. For some reason the facility seems abandoned, though maybe they're all on the third and fourth floors. This makes him even more scared for his little brother. Things must have really turned to shit on the streets. People killing each other. People starving. Had the staff been driven to the brink? Maybe they escaped, or tried to with that doctor what's-his-name. Maybe he'd snuck in, or was dropped in, then had to find his own way out, and took others. Maybe the government helped him out. Maybe he and his staff died. Maybe they turned on each other. If so, then that's it. Hell, either way, that's it. Game over. When people give up on the sick and dying, they give up on each other, on basic humanity. Nothing left but bones, buildings, barbed wire.

Chango heads to an elevator then second-guesses. If he gets trapped, no one will rescue him. He finds a nearby stairwell, and though his knees shake, he descends to the first floor.

An emptiness wracks his insides. A gut feeling. As if he knows something but won't tell himself, won't admit. Something in the hospital air. A hint of burning ash.

He peers through a walkway window. A green-grey sky presses on Baywood. On trees, streets. Everything. It presses on him through the window, against his shoulders, toward the floor.

He sees people out there. None head toward the hospital. One man on all fours, another sprawled on a sidewalk. A woman stops, falls next to the man. Both prone for a solid minute before walking off. What had Greenberg said to him? *One of the few who doesn't see a better place.* What was Greenberg going to help him do? To hell with that. He's done with all that deading, done staring red-eyed at ceiling tiles.

Behind him, sounds.

Shuffling. Grating. Slithering.

A hospital caregiver, scrubs faded and caked with the grime, drags a body across the lobby. Head covered by a pillowcase. Both arms tied. The caregiver, a young woman, tall, thick shoulders, doesn't seem bothered by the corpse's legs dragging along, or that Chango watches.

He doesn't know why but follows her across the lobby to where she pauses, sucks in a breath. Catching up, he presses the elevator button for her. Her eyes, calm. She nods for Chango to step on. She drags the body inside.

Doors close, elevator lights flicker, the basement button gets pressed. Claustrophobic air smells of death, sweat, lives lost, cut apart.

The corpse seems all too familiar. A red blouse. Dark red pants and red leather chanclas. Chango feels like he's in a haze that won't let go. He wants to pull off the pillowcase, see her face, her eyes. Wants to tell her to wake up, to resist being hauled across the floor like this.

Doors open. The caregiver takes a breath, pushes dark braids aside, starts dragging the woman along a narrow corridor, past the laundry room, down an incline where dim greenish-yellow light casts sickness upon every surface. Slow going now. So much weight to pull. They pause at an underground supply station so the worker can take a breath. Few items stacked neatly on shelves. No words spoken. The dragging begins again, takes them down another hallway. Chango doesn't help. Doesn't have the energy to drag a body. It's hard enough to breathe this stale basement air. Hard enough that he has a front seat to this unfolding nightmare. The worker doesn't seem to mind. He wonders how many times she's done this, if some kind of penance is to be had.

Up ahead, a hum. A wetness to the air. And heat. Lots of heat. The light even feels hotter. Less green, turning yellow, a hint of pink along the edges of things.

"I rigged it so it's always on," the caregiver says, her voice a low drone. Whatever love there may have been in her vocal cords seems sucked away, disfigured from her own battle with this place. "Always a fire here now," she says after they come to an incinerator. "Gonna burn a thousand years. Until everything passes through."

Chango doesn't answer. Doesn't know what to think, what to say.

In front of them, a short conveyor.

The worker nods. He knows without being asked. They lift the body.

Feels like they're pulling a sack of rocks from a tank of water. He used to be strong. Now his elbows and knees feel like they're coming apart. He wants to throw up from the exertion, heaves the corpse toward the conveyor.

The worker doesn't wait, presses a button. "Died yesterday," she whispers.

Doors open to an orange glow. A blast of furnace so hot Chango wonders if his beard has been singed off his face. It pains him to peer into this gulf, this endless fire. This is the last stop, he thinks. Any last attachments to this world part ways here, flesh from bone, bone from marrow and aura.

The worker presses another button, corpse jerks forward on the conveyor, toward the open door. Only now can Chango admit the truth—he knows she's held him, cradled him. He knows this the same way you can sense someone watching you. The way you know when someone hides right around the corner, when your best friend is about to call, the scent of familiar skin. He knows this even though she doesn't resemble what he remembers of her. Not these thin, line-scarred arms. He refuses to say her name, refuses to pray.

The body enters, pillowcase and garments combust.

He glimpses her face. Skin melts. He sees bone and gore.

The door closes.

Chango imagines a scene of ash and char.

The worker pours water onto the conveyor as if to cleanse it, then slowly pushes a rag over the uneven surface, though the heat has already done her work.

She then surprises Chango by hopping on. She struggles for a moment to lie back, as if she will never get comfortable, as if it's already burning her. She folds her hands onto her stomach.

"It's done," she says.

"Done? What's done?" he says. "What are you talking about?"

"Press the button. Please. I'd been waiting for you. She was the last."

"Get down. Come on. Let's get out of here."

"Press the button, asshole. I'm already slipping."

Chango doesn't know what to do. He wants to knock her off the conveyor, drag her ass back to some kind of reality he knows doesn't exist for her.

"I can't do this alone," she says.

"Then don't."

"Now." Her eyes dim. She's inside herself. Chango sees that. She's deading.

He doesn't know why but something tells him if he can save one person, even a stranger, he needs to. This is his chance, his one opportunity.

He presses the button.

The doors open. She has no time to take a last breath, only a final shudder of pain and a groan. Heat, dust, vapor, flame, engulf her and the doors re-close.

Chapter Thirty

FOR SEVERAL MOMENTS, Ingram doesn't realize she's been thrown into an ash pit. Dust of bone, innards, and hide slips between her fingers. A circle of torchlight too far away to warm her cold bones licks toward the milky arc.

Ingram coughs and spits, wipes grit from her face. Though it turns her insides, she wonders whether Victor has been strung up like the dogs, raccoons, and a string of pigeons she saw while they pushed and pulled her to this icy, ashen place.

When she moves to get up, a foot pushes her from behind. She crashes again. A cloud rises, blurring flame. She reels and coughs.

Something awful has happened in this place. A stench of death and burnt bone. Shriveled skin. Things coming apart. Things that can never be put back together again. She doesn't want to be here.

She closes her eyes, hums to herself, remembers what it was like, what everything was like. To walk. Breathe. Laugh. Travel. Wander. Eat at restaurants. Sit in parks. Drive down highways, to smell Victor and not this hell. She wonders if returning to that life was ever possible.

NICHOLAS BELARDES

A foot in the back jars her memories. Eyes open again blinking ash. Around her, a circle of torches, lights spaced every five feet or so. She glimpses the people beyond the flames. Lit like ghosts. Two stand in the pit with her. Others have heads wrapped. Hoods cover other faces in the orange glow. She can tell some must be the teenagers she spied at the church with Kumi.

Still a citizen-scientist at heart, Ingram assesses the pit, an indentation scraped a few inches deep. About twenty feet in diameter. Reminds her of the compost pile at her cousin's chicken ranch. She spotted her first Bald Eagle there flinging chicken corpses like playthings. She sees no bird corpses here. Only pale shards. Bones. Twists of hide. Glints from bony material, bits of metal beaming like macabre fool's gold.

Ash beneath her knees feels like an empty heart that pumps dry, frigid air and death. She tries to breathe. No longer choking, she feels claustrophobic from the people and fire, from the foot on her back now flattening her to the ash. She wants to remember again, thinks maybe she can sing to herself, then can't remember any songs.

She senses something else. A drone purring high above. Her scientific mind knows these people are being studied. Everything they do is a data point. Their strange behavior. Their deading rituals—the ones they can see anyway. Even this, what's happening now, an arc, a plot on someone's computer screen. This grounds her in a way, almost makes her laugh.

The first accusation comes from a familiar voice. Sheila Thompson. Former middle school principal. A teen next to Sheila stands silent. Ingram wonders if the girl had been one of Blas's friends. Then she remembers meeting Sheila after pitching a talk on the "Birds of Baywood." Sheila's unwrapped face had been pleasant then, not awful and pale. Not bathed in this sickly glow.

Streaks of shadow scar Sheila's eyes like some kind of creature

228

rose from the pit and scratched its own eyes out. Diaper pins have been used to hook white and grey tern feathers to her robe. Sheila bends toward Ingram. "You pretender," she rasps. "You never deaded."

Ingram feels that foot grind against spine.

"You can't miss the hour marks without us knowing," Sheila continues. "You betray the deading, this community. You betray yourself. How dare you enter the church. How dare you watch our sacred rituals. Where's your friend? She will soon join you."

"My name's Ingram. Don't you people have names anymore?"

Sheila steps away. A third hooded form seems to melt into the pit. Ingram can't make out the face. The voice comes as a terror to her ears, shakes her insides.

"She cannot dead," the voice grunts.

"Help her die. Help her see," the circle responds in unison. One of the teenagers tries not to laugh.

Ingram feels her chest racing. Her heart jumps, lungs gasp. She wants to run. She can't. Her fight or flight won't shift either way, though she already fought these deaders, Risers, these self-proclaimed soothsayers and truthsayers, while they dragged her here. One bleeds from a cheek. A key scrape. That's all Ingram had to fight with. A damn key. And her phone. The one she was supposed to give to Blas.

This bleeder she fought pulls her hood away. Jessie Terrell. Queen of the Risers. The Deadsayer. Ingram remembers the church, the stench, the bodies. Those twins, they died. Both buried alive. Both bled and screamed. For what? Had those goth girls turned them in? She hates how they delight in suffering, even now. She told Victor they had to stay away from the church, from the pit, from the Risers. And so they did. They rarely went outdoors unless they needed food from the passing cart. But now this. Someone betrayed her. Someone wanted her in this pit. She wants to know who.

A voice from the dark, somewhere behind the Deadsayer, beyond the torchlight: "Give her visions!"

Another cries: "Make her one with us. Save her."

The Deathsayer raises a hand to silence any others, arms and neck covered with barbed-wire scars. What did she call Baywood? Hollowed. Lifeless. The Land. Her eyes never stray from Ingram. "Do you wish to see?" she asks.

"Where's Victor?" Ingram only wants him, only wants his touch. She tries to think about the countless times they explored trails. The bright shine of Yellow Warblers. His eagerness to find his first Black-and-white Warbler of the year crawling on a trunk, or the first rare Hammond's Flycatcher of spring: that big grey head, small bill, that sweet little upright body. How she wishes she could hear Victor's voice amid the chattering call of a male Bullock's Oriole flitting to a wire above Third Street.

One of the teens giggles and snorts. "It's time."

The Risers begin to moan. A vicious writhing begins.

Some step into the shallow pit and fall as if wanting to swim in the ash. Others slump beyond the torches. Stiff black forms convulsing in sick firelight.

Some groan, deading even as they stand.

For some reason Ingram's thoughts drift to Blas, how she doubts he will make it out, that Kumi may not be able to hand him a phone with images and recordings to take to the outside world. That poor boy, she thinks. That angry kid. She could have bought him a damn camera, didn't have to be such a pig, such a prissy fool. Those lessons she was trying to teach him about money and ownership don't matter now. She failed him. God, she failed him. That's really all she can think when he pops into her head. She failed that angry brown boy a thousand times, half of that since the deading began. She could have marched over to his house, pounded on his door, insisted he use her spare camera, that they hit the trails for an escape attempt, cut across the volcanic Sisters all the way to Camp

San Luis Obispo on Highway One. They could have counted birds to the safe zone. But they didn't. She didn't say or do a damn thing. Truth is, she got wrapped up in Victor. They hunkered down. They cowered from the get-go. They fake-deaded. Tried to fit in. She always needed Victor more than birds, she tells herself, focusing again on him, on those dirty hands, his rising chest on her bed, now an imaginary bed. More than life, more than anything, she wants him, that whiskey breath-balm sucking into hers. She wishes with all her being that she might taste him one last time before this ritual she's about to endure.

The foot lifts from Ingram's back. She's quick to move to her knees, thinks this might be her chance to get away. Behind her, a form deads in the ash, stirs remains into a choking cloud.

She rises to one foot when others, along with the Deadsayer, surround her. Remains hang from their dresses, robes, and tattered suit jackets. Pelts and legs and tails. These people collect the dead. They carve out skins. They prepare wings and dismembered parts. A vole head, a rat tail, a cat pelt, a dog paw, a raccoon claw, a long-tailed weasel head, gull wings, plover wings, hummingbird corpses, a cat head, the skull of an infant—or perhaps something else, humanlike, skinned and hanging. After all, she'd seen those baby hands in that church.

Ingram's mind sees the worst, imagines the worst for someone's child, for herself, for Victor. She imagines her bones will be dried, broken apart, worn as earrings, used as part of a bone fence, maybe her skull will be set in a window, filled with candles. She wonders if Victor's bones have already burned in a nearby pit. She wants to vomit. Maybe she should, she thinks. Maybe they will take pity. But she doesn't. She doesn't even know what to think when words spill out of her.

"What did you do with him?" she cries.

She misses Victor so much. "At least let us be together," she demands. She needs to feel him close, touch his arms, feel his breath. She'd be braver then. All this pain twisting inside makes it difficult to be defiant, to fight back, save her dignity.

She sees in these people a sick childishness. They're naughty children. Their boldness disgusts her. She allows these feelings to rise like bile, boil over.

"What's wrong with you?" she says. "Fools, rolling around like a bunch of dogs with worms. Look at you. You should be ashamed of yourselves. Children."

The Deadsayer's stare continues to fix on her. Others peer between wrappings, pupils and irises like hot coal. Some eyes liquid from faces painted beneath hoods. Dark skulls. Geometric lines, flaming stars, spirals that offer no meaning.

"Children," Ingram repeats. "With no direction. You're sick bullies."

A voice: "You will either dead or become dead."

Then Ingram feels something. A pinprick in the back of her left shoulder. She groans, flails, like batting away wasps. Glimpses an arm pulling back, the gleam of a syringe needle. "What did you do?" she says. "You have a sickness," she says to no one and everyone. "What have you done?"

Her breathing becomes labored. Her head, light with static. A buzz fills her ears, pain generates, forms out of nothing, spreads through her arms and stomach. "Your rituals mean nothing. You know that? You think they care outside these walls? They don't. They want you to destroy yourselves so they don't have to."

Everything becomes noise, pain. Ingram bows her head, so furious, so helpless, feeling strength drifting outward on back bay tides, scraping over dead oysters, out the harbor mouth. She tries to imagine a kiss, a touch, a bed, that moment close to unconsciousness where she feels love the most. She imagines bird wings, the time she and Victor watched a Sage Thrasher perch upon a roadside post in the Carrizo Plain, its side-eye stare contemplating its own immediate survival.

The Risers, on their feet again, brush themselves off. They begin a new moan, one that feels risen with the moon, blends into light, sound, and vision, poured into each other.

The circle tightens around Ingram. Men, women, teenagers. She whispers: "Where are the children? What did you do to them? I never see children anymore." She feels the shuffle of feet, a collective breath. She's not as afraid though her extremities turn to sharp needles, her head to dull noise. She's handling it though, still reasoning.

"I won't see what you see," she whispers.

When she looks up for the last time, Victor stands there, his sweet hand on her shoulder. They've put us together, she thinks, to die in the pit, bodies soon burned to ash, to forever drift together. At least she has that. At least she has him. She imagines they're inside a room, somewhere, not Baywood, and they're healthy and still wonderfully themselves. People in love, staring out windows into a forest. As long as they stare at the trees they will be safe, and they won't argue, or lose themselves again. There will always be forgiveness, even during cracks of thunder and downpours. They won't let the rain or hail change anything about that moment, but everything will be restored, renewed, resurrected, and they will see themselves in the drops, or in the mushy balls of hail. There will be a fire, a cozy one to their right, swirling in the living room fireplace, and music, the kind that doesn't rattle china on walls or dishes in cabinets. The smell will be of rain and trees, and whatever they had for dinner. They will watch the sun fall into the canopy, and that green flash as if over the sea, between branches, and it will filter light through each window.

"You're here." She slurs this, almost unaware of his robes, almost able to breathe again, even for just this moment.

If she just reaches, she might touch his face, feel the low flames in his eyes. She wants to feel the light in them, their warmth, not this betrayal, not how secretive he must have been in their last days to do this. She wonders how long he's been studying Risers from the inside. How long he's been studying her?

Instead, after he wipes the remains of froth from his lips and straightens his robe, he smashes her phone. She then hears a growl so low, so near that she can almost feel lion's breath on her lips. Losing all strength, she allows herself a kind of numbness amid her terror, and falls into the ash to sleep and sleep, knowing in her final strand of wakefulness that both Victor and the lion pace so very close. She wonders then as everything flickers if she will go somewhere or just see the dark and feel a deep shudder.

Chapter Thirty-One

AIR SWEEPS COLD off the bay. Blas shivers, legs stiff, eyes skyward at the sound. Can't even count these birds, he tells himself. Couldn't draw something like this if he tried.

Forty-five minutes. That's how long Blas has been watching, how long since he realized the roar crashing across Baywood skies while holed up in his dark bedroom wasn't an engine or faceless mothership releasing dronelings over the city.

This constant thunderclap, to his amazement, is a singular bird swarm filling the back bay, blanketing the evening sky, a feathered rowdydow, from sandpiper to albatross, and every bird shape between, filling his mind and the air, screaming, bleating, gawping, gowling, honking every *kuk kuk kuk*, *cack-cack*, *gekgek-gek*, *bek-bek*, *kr-dee kr-dee*, *kree-eed*, and more.

No one in the history of mankind has witnessed this kind of behavior, Blas tells himself while he gawks from a beach next to Pecho Road Willows. Toxic residue, bird bones, and bits of snail shell lines the shore just inches from his feet. Waves lap at the slime like water gods licking to taste mudbank poison. A shoreline of saliva might heal these wounds, clean this wasteland, Blas thinks, though he doesn't know what will heal his community or this sky of shrieking birds.

Whatever reason for this strangeness, whatever caused this apocalyptic sky stampede, he'll never see the sky turn black with feathers again. Not like this. No one will.

And then he sees something else. To the southeast, smoke curls in three black pylons. A string of gunfire cracks like fireworks through the bird noise. Blas instinctively ducks. Who's shooting who is a mystery, though Blas knows it's something to do with the Risers, who he wishes would stop hanging dead shit from their clothes, stop walking around with bullhorns, stop moaning in the streets like the undead, air throbbing around vibrating bodies. His mother, he hates to think, may be somewhere beneath that smoke. Maybe with a gun in her hand, maybe just chanting along, rolling in ash. He doesn't care. He doesn't know her anymore, and she's gone anyway, literally hasn't seen her in days and days—and he's about to be gone himself, standing there with his backpack stuffed with food supplies, his favorite Sibley's West Coast field guide, water, a blanket, a journal, sketchbook, three apples, two soup cans. He's read Ozziel's report, what would be a final message to Blas, about finding a Sharp-tailed Sandpiper. Blas peeled apart clues for an escape route, which makes him think some people might have taken the same route and got through. It was during extremely high tides, nearly seven feet, and those were expected again.

Continuing pot-bellied juvenile rarity visiting from eastern Siberia. Seen with my dad, Felix. Rufous crown, slightly downcurved bill, yellow legs, rusty eyeline, buffy chest and flanks, paler underside, whitish undertail (may have been streaked some), rusty and dark upperside. Its chest had a gradually fading chest buffy/streakiness, different from the chest pattern on the species it often gets confused with: Pectoral Sandpiper. Long, upturned primaries extending nearly to long, upturned tail. Bird flew in while group of

*about twenty-five birders watched. Bird landed near small
group of Long-billed Curlews in shallow tideland water
that included sandpipers, knots, and dowitchers. Solitary,
it walked, dipping its head in the water, then bathed itself,
fluffing its feathers over and over. It dried off, foraged some
more through shallow tidal waters, stepping briefly in pickleweed, then flew off with two Willets, landing on opposite
of canal-like waterway. This bird gave me the same joy as
when I saw a Hooded Warbler in Clark's Valley. We'd birded
nearby creeks before we made our way onto those farm-oak
trails. Or the one I heard about near Diablo Canyon, that
was again seen at Oso Flaco from a kayak. The tides had
been above 6–7 feet, the creeks became backed up with
water. I will post many photos of this sandpiper. I'm stoked to
have seen it. This bird is my new best friend, I swear.*

For now, the swarm has Blas's attention. The eye of sun glows
just beyond the bird-cloud. A dimming horizon illusion. Jetlike
fire burns itself out over the sandspit, propels this stream of shore
and seabirds.

Something Blas can't fathom right now amid all this: the
letter written to his mother. His letter too by familial rights, he's
come to understand. Maria said she would read it to Chango—
that was the last he saw her—right after she gave him a brief
account of what was in there. Said his older brother deserved to
have it read to him in the hospital. He told her he didn't want
her to go, had a feeling she'd disappear.

"He might die in there, fade into the walls," she cried. "He
deserves to know."

True history. Blas remembers her words. Yeah, *true history.*
Not even birds have that anymore. Why did he even have that
conversation with her? Still, he remembers every word.

"Lineages are important to me," she told him. "Two separate

fathers. You boys have two fathers. Chango has forgotten this," she said. "He'd been so young. And later so angry that I think he might have blocked those memories."

Blas didn't care when she said that either, but she went on: "At two different times he called them both that sacred name, you know. Father. Dad. Pops. Old man. One true father, a nobody. The other, stepdad, *padastro*, a cruel parent, a nobody."

"So?" That's all Blas could say to her. But she interrupted, couldn't stop talking about the letter."

"This is proof," she said, "at least something. Chango's inheritance from your biological father who left you both when you were in my belly. Your true father," she added, "left his home to you—that's why this letter is so important. A hill in New Mexico near Santa Rosa. In the Chihuahua Desert. Close to Anaya's stream. *Bless Me, Ultima*. We have that book, you know, for a reason."

She said this like she knew he hadn't read the story when she pushed it in his face so many times. "On the shelf under the painting. The stream flows in and out of an oasis called Blue Hole. I met him there," she said. "I was riding a bus from Texas to California. It broke down. I wandered down the street over the river, found the stream. I walked through the gate. Ruben was diving for coins. You could see them glittering into the water past the scuba divers. You could see his sleek muscles in this eighty-foot-deep water hole that swallowed him, this place where colonizers trekked like aliens."

Blas remembers she took a breath before she went on: "Coronado stopped ten miles away. That other place became a conquistador's puddle some say he named Puerto de Luna. You hate them," she said. "*The colonizers*, you always say. You have their blood in you. From that village. Your father, the son of a bruja whose blood was poisoned by conquistadors.

"So Ruben became one, you know. A brujo. That was your

father. You didn't know. No one knew. A brujo. A spellweaver. We could all move there," she said. "We can be blessed by the brujo ghosts still wandering the Llano Estacado. You can finally get over your hatred of the colonizers."

Blas knows his mother and brother aren't going anywhere. They're lost. Gone. Disappeared in this trap called Baywood.

But *you're* going somewhere, he tells himself. He's leaving, going straight to the address she gave him, the one he tucked into his bird guide. And as much as he didn't listen to her, or pretended not to, he has somewhere to go. Somewhere to aim *this* life. Some hill in a desert, a thousand miles from this broken sea and trapped town.

He'll go to where new birds await. He'll discover them right there in Guadalupe County. Make lists. Find lifebirds. A Canyon Towhee and Mississippi Kite would be nice while he explored the oasis. Not like a colonizer, like a fellow traveler. A fellow migrant, maybe even a fellow brujo. He'll observe their songs and kisses, talk to them, make eye contact when he can, wonder what they wonder. And then maybe, after a time, drift on, fly on, go to college, become someone, an ornithologist, biologist, maybe geobiologist.

Now he turns back to the sky. Multiple bird columns pour over the sandspit, soar to new heights. An invasion from distant ocean shores, from deeper waters where tens of thousands of Sooty Shearwaters, the greatest of all avian travelers, some at nearly fifty-thousand miles, having inspired that old movie *The Birds*, one of Blas's favorites, a cautionary tale filled with cheesy effects that included swarms of insane gulls, through really it had been crazed shearwaters puking and flying into things after gorging on algae in 1961 that might have turned toxic from leaky septic tanks amid a housing boom in Monterey, California. The dark grey birds typically migrate north or south, leg muscles atrophying from flying from nests to years-long journeys over oceans. Their flocks blend in an unearthly mix with the birds he's already seeing, sweeping over the water, dropping low, swinging in a glide before ascending into the sky as if catapulted by invisible cannons.

Gulls, terns, godwits, Willets, Long-billed Curlews all spill over the bay in the avifauna storm. Huge lumbering Black-footed Albatross glide alongside Whimbrels, one like a cat with a squid in its mouth as if it wants to play, wings locked at the shoulder. Innumerable Sanderlings and Least Sandpipers, some of the littlest of shore peeps, in their rush to join, cascade over sand dunes across the bay in tens of thousands alongside their larger brethren, Western Sandpipers, and five rare Semipalmated Sandpipers in tight formation, their stubby short bills and drab plumage obvious to Blas's sharp eyes. The peeps' collective wings shimmer like bright scales along the fast-moving lower edges of this mesocyclone, this organic bird-cloud, churning, turning, spiraling into the thermals.

Captivated, dumbfounded, Blas, more than a little terrified, knows this is as close to a religious experience he will ever get. He should be leaving, escaping while everything has gone nuts. Instead, he wipes tears, wipes images of the letter, tries to ignore the smoke and distant pops. Tries to imagine his new destination isn't a lie.

This is when he knows he's really hurting. He begins to howl at the sky, to really cut loose. He's a dog after all, a mongrel, a thing made of tissue and pain.

When he's done he realizes Kumi Sato has walked up next to him. Where she's come from or how long she's been there, he doesn't know. It's like she's part wolf too, or part skulky bird, skittering silent through shrubs. He should say something but he's too busy wiping his eyes, breathing and taking in this otherworldly sight, too busy feeling sorry for himself, too busy swallowing the remnants of that howl.

"They've been funneling through longer than you've been standing here." Her voice close to drowning in noise. Hundreds of egrets and herons honk their way overhead to join the furious chorus of calls and screams. "I was watching from a dirt lot where I've been hiding. They're looking for me."

Blas strains to listen, like separating birdsong from a morning chorus. Kumi points below the heart of the bird cyclone—Elfin Forest. If there's a focal point, he agrees, that's it. She doesn't have to say. Neither do.

"We go there to find out," she says. "It's not safe for us here."

Blas knows he has choices. He can go to where the fires are, where the smoke rises like fingers, see if his mom has been there, see if she's the cause, if that's where she's been living, or just *run*. Run and don't look back because now he has a chance to get away, when everyone, everything, all the drones, may be watching the smoke and birds.

But these birds.

They call to him. Every feather and wingbeat says to follow Kumi, to find answers in Elfin Forest. It could be like one of their old adventures, when they rose early in the mornings and met on Doris Street. Eyes flicking between them, gripping their binoculars, though Kumi sometimes didn't bring any at all. They would call out the birdsong in the nearby eucalyptus, oak, or lone willows, as if revealing secrets, as if pretending one of them could be a Yellow-throated Vireo calling almost like a chat. Because that's sometimes what birdwatching was, just make believe, though facts always complicated their imaginings, their celebratory wantings, until Blas and Kumi gave in to the reality that they mostly heard only common birds. This common mix of seasonal migrants and year-round restless survivors.

"All right," he says. "I'll go with you."

They're not fast though Kumi moves with determination, a kind of purpose he hasn't seen in her. They make their way from the shore, through his neighborhood, and thirty minutes later, birds still streaming above, slip into an empty stretch of northeast Baywood homes, overgrown yards blossoming with succulent jungles, streets dotted with spruce and Monterey cypress, everywhere lichen and moss. He hasn't been here in forever.

They've been silent, wary. No one deads here that they can see, so Kumi finally talks. "You're smart to leave," she says. "We won't be ignored by the Risers any longer." She seems to pause, like she doesn't know if she wants to reveal the next bit of information. "They took Ingram," she says.

Blas wonders how she knows this but also accepts her doomsaying, the way he accepts that his mother is gone, that Chango is gone, the letter he never read is gone. Nothing is ever coming back. Now, Ingram too. He considers distant deserts. The oasis. Glittering coins descending. That's what she'd said. And scuba divers.

He tells himself he needs to be more like Chewie and Elisabeth, like so many others who turned fear into the propulsion needed to attempt an escape, hopes this new fear will push him across mudflats later tonight when the tide rushes out, when he is to meet up with Kai, Tatum, Torrey, and Emily. They may bring Charlotte. Possibly Jack, who Blas found hiding in the willows of Doris Street. The risk is high from toxins alone. No fair trades exist in this.

"Baywood has destroyed itself," Kumi says. "The tidal mudflats are now submerged by tides of toxins and plastics. You sure you want to go in there? Or maybe you're planning some other route?"

Blas glances, sees her lips move, strains to listen. Her words echo in him, but he has nothing to say. He's already decided to leave. He knows the mudflats went toxic, that the estuary has become a poison wasteland—he can't fix it. He has to get out somehow. Maybe one day he can come back, long after all this, to help rehabilitate the land.

"Silt, bits of shell, bone fragments, crushed shoreline aquatic plants wash in and out along with the remains of all those snails and toxins," Kumi says. "Nutrients feed the biodiversity that dwells there, transformed by what happened at the oyster farm, by what's happened to this place. The land can't hold back the sea," she says in her slow, soft voice. "And the sea can't hold back the land."

Afraid to ask what she means, whether whatever happened here will happen elsewhere, or already has, Blas wonders whether the birds will move on, whether they've already infected the world and returned, or are about to, whether the snails have turned their movements to another oyster farm, or died en masse and their final remnants washed into the mudflats. Either way, he's sure the deading has crept into the hills and beyond. How could it not? Then again, maybe every bird and animal coming out of this area has been killed by drones. He squirms at the thought.

Above them, countless birds soar in a counter-clockwise spiral over Elfin Forest's pygmy oaks. Their collective din makes him feel like a single Snowy Plover, a speck, a thing amid this ethereal swirl of life, grounded, flightless, with injured wings. He wonders why nature has gone to war with itself. A rebellion within a rebellion, that no man can understand, he thinks. One thing he does know, though he's unsure why they're here and what they're doing, he's on the side of the birds, especially the flock of Ruddy Ducks that flies past. But are they on his side?

Just ahead, barricades everywhere in the street. Piles of junk, barriers to the forest. Rows of cars with spikes bolted to hoods and doors. This isn't some Faceless government at work. This is from inside the community, something he hasn't been aware that's been happening, something out of reach of the last of his informers. He wonders how much of Baywood has turned into similar fortresses.

They find a single unblocked route on Eleventh Street bordered by trash and barbed wire. It narrows to an opening at the end of a row of boarded-up homes, a wooden doorway ringed with outward-facing teeth, a violent trap had it been dark, its upper frame covered by more barbed wire.

Once inside, they scurry near a burned-out home that reeks of ash and cinder. He knows this place, Kaylee Jones's house, so stops. Bloody Kaylee, he hears she's referred to now. She's a ghost in a mirror, a haunt to be summoned. He remembers the manicured yard, the constant newness of the two-story home, the wide picture windows, expensive furniture and lamps, even its decorative curtains. This house has nothing that is decades old like the couch in his home, worn and sagging. Once, this house had a midnight-blue BMW out front.

As he wanders past, he imagines Kaylee falling again and again, though he'd never seen her tumble over the ledge, hadn't been there, hadn't known to come and help. He just thought she'd buried herself in her room and music and diaries, like him, and had not become one of them. Then it hits him why he's been so scared, so terrified of everything. That's really what this has been about, he realizes, all of this, *his choices about fear*, his constant decision to block, to deny, to bury himself in birds, music, even books. He sees Kaylee's face; he thinks he sees her in the wreckage; he doesn't even know if her body is somewhere down the cliff, tangled on the side of the bluffs, picked apart by birds and worms. Suddenly he's glad he wasn't there when it happened, glad she stopped coming to the Dead of Night.

He got lost in himself, he knows this, to deal with his own problems, his brother and mother, just staying alive, just staying sane, just wishing he could break into the library for any new reads, which he never does, will never do. Like so many things, it's just a fantasy. He figures all those books were burned anyway.

At least his friends had a chance to stop Kaylee. He didn't run with them every day, and they lived much closer to the forest than he did. But if he's honest with himself, he misses her. He wishes Kaylee were escaping with him. If anyone was going, he wants it to be her. But she's nothing, like the Great Nothing, a void, like this grand middle-class house she used to live in, only ruins that he can't understand, towering glass windows and an arched ceiling transformed into a skeleton of soot-covered walls and blackened beams.

And then movement in the wreckage where he thinks he saw her face. He grabs Kumi by the elbow so she will see too. Through a broken window a ghost-form appears, not a drone, or animal, but a person with a wiry tangled mane, arms like snapped willow branches, bent amid the brokenness of the collapse. For a second he thinks, Bloody Kaylee, then realizes, he knows her. Larisa, Kaylee's younger sister, who appears older now, resembling Kaylee more than ever, fixed on the deafening chorus of *squawks*, *teeps*, *kuks*, *gwaoows*, *tweels* and *screams* from the soaring birds. She doesn't notice Blas, not yet, entranced by feathers spiraling up an imaginary cone toward the heavens.

Then her wild eyes fix on him. Whoever Larisa was, he knows, has been lost in this rubble of ash and bone. He wants to hold out a hand, but she's like one of the dead birds in his yard he left behind or shoved in a mailbox.

"You know her," Kumi says.

"And her sister." Blas carefully steps over a row of sharp metal planted along their path clearly meant to cut through shoe to bone. He doesn't talk about the crush he's had on Kaylee, how at one time he fawned over every social media pic, even the one of her deading in an elevator.

Blas would love to tell Kumi that he wants to cry seeing

Larisa but that wouldn't be true. He's done crying. He's cried himself to sleep, cried himself awake. Cried and vomited. Cried and no one listened. Cried for his brother a dozen times, and cried when his mother never returned. Cried for birds and Kaylee and every feathery corpse piled in a bucket.

He's thinking all this when a pulse shakes the sky.

Larisa scrambles out of view, loses herself in the wreckage.

No one expects this kind of sound, this kind of feeling.

The sky reverberates deep in his bones. He thinks the air itself has erupted.

Kumi has fallen to a knee.

Blas covers his ears when the blast sounds again. Sound stretches beyond what he can understand about bird behavior. This noise from the heavens, maybe the heart of the Milky Way, from every living thing, as if every bird above him has learned a new call from its universe mother, *a pulse call*. It shakes every thing with a heart. He thinks maybe every nearby lizard, toad, and brush rabbit has joined them.

And then a strange quieting. No more calls, no bird screams. Only the collective hum of wingbeats that follow one another in what has turned to a fiery pink-and-orange dusk and rapidly descending night.

Blas helps Kumi to her feet, aims toward a sand path into the forest just up ahead. She grunts and they continue, leaving the ghost of Larisa behind. How they made it this far, Blas can only wonder. Seems like Risers would have stopped them here, just outside the gate to this place. He wants to bring this up, talk about his guilt and fear. Then reminds himself he just wants answers. The forest, he hopes, is hiding them.

They slip between trees, into filtered light cast by the distant bone-bled sun, beneath the continuing dark spiral of wings. To his right a Western Flycatcher hops between tangles of oak branches that only reach shoulder height. The bird quietly moves as he notes it holistically, taking in its group of field marks, the peaked crown, its stubby primaries, medium-length bill, its overall green-and-yellow tones shining through the dimness. The bird peeks from where little light can escape, flashing its white teardrop eye-ring, curious about their movements. Blas thinks this flycatcher fears the birds soaring above, and watches as it shrinks into shadows of foliage. He yearns to draw its expression, hopes he will remember.

This pygmy oak woodland covers sandy hills above the back bay's murky mud-lined estuary, a landscape of rivulets and near-impassable swaths of red-green pickleweed. Stunted by centuries of winds, trees have been reduced to mostly shoulder-height shrubs. The few canopies that grow above Blas's head tower over a distant dune midden at the center of the small forest. He can't see the dune in the dark but knows it's there, ringed by shrubs with furry, apple-like fruit that shrivel and blacken to the color of blood.

A wormlike darkness surrounds them, as does a dull roar of wingbeats from vibrations of collective wing bones and feathers. Blas wonders whether the birds are starving, exhausted from their pulse call alone. Will they soon start falling onto trees, onto *them*? He imagines he and Kumi may soon have to take cover.

They step onto a wooden walkway. Boards creek under each step, warnings that maybe they should turn back.

Somewhere in the woods a generator comes to life, hums, brings a glow to the walkway and trees, small lanterns and lines of lights that brighten the path. Maybe someone wants to bring a kind of meaning to this darkness, transport the very stars to its trees.

They reach an intersection of branches where the smell of gas assaults them. Underneath these boughs, a row of motorcycles with skulls and flames airbrushed onto their tanks, lit by a line of small solar lights; someone perhaps preparing to get away like

Blas, only more daring, willing to start some kind of war against everything and everyone, or simply make a suicidal run that can outpace tanks and Humvees, at least for a little while, until the drones descend.

Then he notices someone among the bikes, still as night, eyes on them the entire time, holding a shotgun. Not pointed at them. Just strapped like it has always been part of her body.

She seems to know they were coming, nods like this has always been this way, spits just in front of her own boots.

"Don't look at me," she says.

"I wouldn't dare." Kumi, in her slow gait, moves past.

A laugh gurgles from the shotgun wielder, then quickly stops. "Have a question though," she says, voice familiar to Blas. She's interested in what they might know, he thinks, then she steps closer, half out of the shadows. "Why ain't birds shitting everywhere? That many in the sky you think we'd be covered in it, yeah?"

Blas knows her now. One of the Miranda girls. Maxine. Always proud to call herself an Indian, she's from the coastal Chumash tribe. Always proud of her motorcycle too. Those airbrushed skulls though, he doesn't remember them. Never bullied Blas for riding a scooter. Always says she's gonna climb Morro Rock and flip off Baywood High while she stands atop its highest curve. Hates school. Hates a lot of things. Otherwise, quiet much of the time.

In the shadows she appears ten years older, a hundred years wiser, and deadly. He wants to talk to her, see how she's been getting on, but doesn't. He can only half smile, shake his head, continue without answering, glance when Maxine secures her shotgun and steps back among the bikes. He wonders why the drones haven't stunned everyone and taken all these guns, can only figure the government knows some need to defend themselves from the Risers. They allow it the way rats might be allowed certain paths in a maze, or food rewards. Blas wonders if he's become a rat himself.

Soon something else. Just around two more bends on the boardwalk, seven people lying end to end. Kumi carefully steps over one of them. Blas nearly stomps a hand when Kumi stops and peers at a young woman, her dirty skin, mouth clear of foam. Face serene. No wriggling or writhing. Just here on the winding boardwalk among trees and lanterns. Kumi squats, touches her on the cheek with the back of her hand. Eyes open. Doesn't seem afraid, or lost, or trying to reach some kind of hell.

Kumi smiles. The woman closes her eyes.

"They aren't deading," Kumi says to Blas. "Aware, but in meditation. Trying to understand. An imitation of the imitation of death. Not a bad idea."

Blas expects hands to grab ankles when they pass, but nothing happens when they step over them. Close to the generator now, it hums and grinds, belting exhaust that collides with sea air. Oaks stretch higher here, fingers of branches in need of touching the Kármán Line, another layer besides birds to block the coming starlight. Blas notices seabirds continue their vocal silence after the pulse. Doesn't mean they're not loud. Wings continue to beat and thrum, at times a constant sibilation, other times a collective thunder.

Some lanterns have been attached to poles above sand and roots. Like symbols and words to interpret, shadows jerk left and right, then flicker from a skip in the generator. Other lights rest on tiered blocks opposite the widest tree where more lanterns hang. Candles around the trunk's base seem sprinkled like stars on this altar to god-light, arbor light, oak light. Blas notes shadows prancing around a glyph on the tree trunk's north side. He feels pulled by this and steps closer. A carving. A lizard-like creature, a tail, or genitalia, maybe three-toed legs, arms spread wide, strange overlapping circles just to the right above its head, and two antennae, or handles.

"Arborglyph," Kumi mutters. She runs her runs fingers along the flesh of the tree above the glyph, which she doesn't touch. "This didn't used to be here. Solar symbols?"

Someone near the tree responds, which jostles Blas from the glyph's hypnotics, a husky voice that could rattle sand. Blas recognizes half in light, half in shadow, that grey-and-black ponytail hanging like a warning. José. Maxine's dad. Forklift driver from the mail facility, the guy his mom wanted him to talk to about the letter. Always stacking pallets like huge piles of Jenga. Used to come watch Maxine play volleyball. He'd sit there for half a set, or until she spiked the ball in some girl's face, step outside the gym, smoke, talk to some other dad who couldn't break the habit either. Blas would go to watch Kaylee, though he never told her that's why he went. He figures now that she knew.

A shotgun like Maxine's strapped over his shoulder, lips strained from sucking cigarettes, jaw and shoulders hardened from working all day, every day, years on end, the kind of work that doesn't break but tires and hardens you. "Kids try to make sense of this shit," José says about the glyph. "Saw it on a website or read in a book. Young Indians want to make their mark. Better to talk about how to get out of here than cut up trunks."

Kumi pulls her hand away from the carving. Blas follows her eyes from the glyph to a gap in the trees where they should see stars. The sky discharges another roll of wingbeat thunder over white noise.

"You can't deny the birds circling this place, maybe this tree," she says.

José appears dark, like the night itself, then awash in orange light. Black shadows and streaks of light run down his jawline. "Guardian stars. That what you want to hear? That why you came? Come to protect the Coyote in the Sky? You're stupid if you think I know what's going on, why they're here, why people been dying but not dying, or starving themselves to death. I don't have answers. No one does."

José's attention switches to Blas. "Get your letter? Saved it when they trashed the facility. I ran in there, you know, tucked a pile away. Told Pete if he burned those last envelopes I'd come back for him. Every once in a while I sneak over there just to remind Pete he better develop eyes in the back of his head."

Blas wants to tell him about the letter, how he gave it to his mom, how she tucked it away, said she would read it to Chango, then disappeared after telling him some kind of broken truth about them being sons of brujos, that maybe they were brujos themselves. Blas didn't buy any of it. He wasn't sure he saw into Chango's dreams, but those visions stopped. What use had they been?

"People don't get those kind of handwritten notes anymore," José says. "Kids' mother used to write me. I remember the way her words leaned to the left, like someone was nudging them, you know?"

Blas wants to drop the subject, assumes José knows more than he lets on. "It's gone."

"Too bad. I was curious about that one."

"What is this place?" Blas asks. "It's changed. Everyone seems immune like us."

"To what though?" José moves to a pit ringed with stones, glances to the dark sky. "Shuluwish." He pokes at the burning wood. Sparks shoot upward. "A name I heard. Or read. Maybe I just know it. Maybe one of the kids told me. Some even call me that. They're always reading me things. Told Pete once. Means 'full of birds,' like this unseen sky filled with feathers. My daughter keeps wondering why the heavens aren't shitting on us. I tell her, just wait, it will come. That's about all the wisdom I have."

Blas glances at Kumi, hoping she might answer for him. She

appears to hardly listen, eyes still peering between trees. Maybe she's gone crazy. He doesn't know. "Stars," she says. "The sun. All falling to earth. Maybe that's what these birds will do."

"You afraid of bird-stars too?" José says to Blas. "Or maybe, me? I'm just an Indian living in the same place we used to. You just can't see the lodges, you know, only the ghosts of them, but they're there. A lot of us see them appear and disappear."

Blas can see that Maxine has followed them to the fire, quiet as a snake.

"Probably better to be judged by us, huh?" José says. "Don't worry, you and the old lady passed inspection. Been judged worse by those Risers. We all know why. You don't dance the way they can. None of us do. Why do you think?"

"I just never feel like I need to," Blas says. "Can't explain it."

"We're not compelled to their ways," Kumi adds.

"Figured you'd eventually show up here," José says. "Too bad it's when we're all about to leave."

Blas swallows, wonders if he should ask to follow José out of Baywood. Then again, he could use them as some kind of cover. They go one way, he slips out another with his friends, quiet as a skulky Yellow-green Vireo. He's got a meet-up spot not too far away. Maybe he could bring his friends here.

"Why haven't they come?" Kumi, still by the tree, seems lucid again.

"The Risers? They tried a few times. Once today." José pats his shotgun. "They'll be back. More next time. Not enough of us. Surprised the drones allowed this. Seems like as long as we kill each other, these might be okay." José's chin lifts, the bird cyclone has quieted its thunder. He points to a gap where Kumi stared a minute ago. Bright dots appear where the birds once blocked starlight.

Blas wonders how so many thousands of birds can just disappear. He's sure Kumi wonders the same thing. Maybe they're all just sitting on the water. Or lining the shore. Maybe they all dropped dead and littered the bay. Then a rustle by a nearby fire pit. Others in the shadows now, among the trees, warming themselves, whispering, waiting it seems. He eyes Maxine longer than he should, her hair longer than he remembers, her entire demeanor older, stronger. She was already tough. He wonders if she watched Kaylee fall, wonders if she calls her Bloody Kaylee. Others he doesn't recognize circle the fire, probably more than a few classmates who were never part of the Dead of Night. Hairs on his arms stand when he sees they all have guns.

"Don't be so paranoid, no one going to shoot you," José says. "Listen. You got two types of people here. The ones who want to run away with us. And those who should have run already."

"We should have run the moment *he* arrived," Kumi says.

"I know that now," José says.

Kumi's eyes light with flame. "You spoke to him then."

"Someone needed to confront that thing," José says. "I knew that at least. He's in most everyone's heads."

"Except ours," Kumi adds.

José nods. "Good for some of us at least."

"You said *he*," Blas says. "Some deader?"

"*The* deader," José says. "Ain't what you think. Not that Deadsayer. Not her. I'm talking Death. The Sun. The Storm. The Spokesman. The Gate. The Bear. I don't know his actual name. Part of him owned that oyster farm at one time. Part of him leapt from the sea into the woods. Part of him crashed down from the sky a million years ago." José pokes at the fire again. "Wasn't much left when I found him in the willows. Head filled with tentacles connected to bones and skin sacs, still thinking, still unleashing his fury. He wondered how so many of us could be immune. I told him that's the problem with people."

"I thought you didn't know what was going on?"

"I don't. Didn't say I understood the why part."

"So then what did you do?" Blas says.

"I shot him."

Blas wonders why Kumi seems so accepting of this story. "You shot someone in Pecho?"

"Don't act so offended," José says. "It's not a someone. Didn't seem to hurt him. Didn't seem to even notice. My mistake for not aiming at his head. Either way, I left. Not my job to fuck with that."

"Maybe I should go there," Kumi says. "Convince him to let us go, to stop this."

"No one needs to go anywhere except the hell out of here," José says. "Welcome to join us. Got a few extra shotguns, though I have a feeling we're on separate paths. Some of us, anyway."

"I don't shoot anything," Kumi says. "But I'm willing to leave."

"Suit yourself."

All Blas wants to do is leave this place and never return. Before he can say he wants to go too, that his friends might want to all go together, José turns to him.

"Only one idiot stupid enough to face off with that thing again," José says. "At least that's what I been told."

Blas hopes he doesn't mean him. He's about to scream that he doesn't want anything to do with Baywood anymore, that he just wants to get out, leave on his own, or with all the rest, not mess with some pendejo who sees through dead eyes, who may be immune to bullets. Then someone familiar steps into the fire-light, right next to José.

Blas recognizes those eyes, seen them a million times, thought they'd turned red for good, thought they'd dimmed and went out in that hospital.

"Hey little brother," Chango says. "You ready to go find this thing? Asshole owes me a few paychecks."

Chapter
Thirty-Two

BLAS HOLDS A broken broom handle so tight his palms sweat. Kumi handed it to him half an hour earlier, telling him, "You better carry something."

She didn't want him to go in there, said he should just find his friends and leave. At the same time she said she didn't want him in the willows unprotected. He didn't want to go either, but now he's crunching snail shells along a narrow trail through willows like he might check the entity with a lacrosse stick and call it good. Only, he doesn't want to call anything good. He's faced with the choice of seeing what's in this swamp he's avoided for months, or leaving without knowing what José and Kumi insist is hiding within its deadfall. He has to follow his brother, has to know about this *thing*, if there is a *thing*.

He kicks himself too, how he hadn't known something was possibly crawling around the trails, something that resembled Chango's boss. He thought firefighters combed through every inch of Pecho in their search for the oyster farmer and Deb. And Kumi, she'd been holding on to secrets. At least she finally told him about her weird experience with the Bernhard creature at her window, how she'd had some kind of vision before she stopped coming here altogether. "I sensed it needed space to grow," she said. He thought that was nuts. All of this is nuts. *Space to grow what?* There are no monsters anyway, only *people*, he mumbled, trying to convince himself, though he wasn't sure what he believed.

She said he was half right.

Chango said he was wrong altogether. Blas could tell his brother had changed, not only becoming a thin doppelgänger of himself, his eyes seemed somewhat clear, more pink than red; more wrapped in thought than before. And he didn't seem angry that Blas hadn't visited the hospital. Just shrugged at his apology. Also, one more thing, Blas realizes after his brother tells him, Chango wasn't deading like the others, not a single instance. And he stopped whatever version of deading he was doing. Blas thinks that if Chango could beat this thing, maybe others can too.

Blas soon reminds his brother he isn't going to hit anyone with a stick, that fighting would only be stupid at this point. Better to try to understand what might be there, document with some field notes and drawings, maybe pics with his no-wifi phone. Treat it like a bird sighting, then leave.

"This ain't no bird, little cabrón." Chango pushes behind Blas with a flashlight, lighting branches and leaves, tangles of webs.

Blas soon realizes how wrong he's been, feels something on the edge of his senses, deep in roots and mud, coughing, curled in the dark. Something could be here. Pale, dying, dead, alive. Infected with yellow light. Swamp yellow. Dim yellow. Emanating not from the diffused moon splintering light through branches, from something else, hidden, or once hidden. He fixes on every shadow, trying to find this thing José claims to have wounded but not wounded.

Death. The Sun. The Storm. The Spokesman. The Gate. The Bear.

The oyster farmer.

Bernhard.

"What's wrong with you?" Chango slips next to his brother. "You're not about to dead are you?"

"I'm just confused about what to believe."

Chango grips the handle of the machete strapped to his side. "Well you still should have brought one of these." Earlier he tried to give a similar knife to Blas instead of that dumb stick Kumi handed him. Blas said he'd only trip over a blade.

Blas can't answer. Something else fills his head now. With every careful step, memories fragment with light and color. He remembers him and his brother surviving their early years. Always beaten, blamed, tossed around, their dad calling them "worthless Mexicans" though they weren't born in Mexico. He can feel every punch, every knuckle scrape. A broken American family long before their machismo-fueled dad, now to find out *stepdad*, was tossed for smacking Mom around too. Old man got his ass whooped soon as Chango grew big enough to shove him into the cold with the fat end of a baseball bat, for all the bruises he'd given them as children.

Chango had been a badass kid. Once he got old enough to throw his weight around, you didn't mess with him or would end up in the dirt. Had he not thrown out their stepdad, Chango would have joined the Army when he was eighteen. Would have turned him into a real killer. And what would that have done to him? Blas feels so glad Chango was a mama's boy. Combat would have really jacked him up. By staying home, Chango could always be around to take care of their mom, bring her groceries, encourage her to be a strong woman. Only recently did he want to move out, board with roommates, let Mom figure herself out.

And their stepdad? Why did that pendejo keep that secret about their real father even after he'd been kicked to the curb? Must have taken some cojones, some serious lip biting to keep his trap shut that he wasn't their dad. Then again, maybe it was his stepdad's way of getting even. Let those sons of a Chihuahua Desert witch-man think some old Baywood drunk was their old man. Don't let *them* know the truth. Let their mom carry the shame of that burden, let her suffer the most, because no mama wants to tell their sons the secret of their birth. Blas wants to say something about the witch-man to Chango here in the willows but doesn't have to. His brother brings it up the way brothers can sometimes read each other's minds.

"Sons of a brujo, huh? That what we are?" Chango says this like their lineage could only be some kind of joke, some kind of mucha-lucha superpower seen only on television or in comic books. "I guess that's why we're going to deal with this S.O.B. Some real magic needed in this town to make things right. What you think, little brother? Got some magic in you, yeah?"

Blas doesn't answer. Doesn't want to. Doesn't want to admit that he might have something in him other than love for a waterthrush he once saw sipping from the very puddle they just stepped over. What's magic anyway? A Wilson's Warbler. That's magic. Reading a few of his brothers thoughts while he was in the hospital? The ability to *not* dead? Maybe those things are magic too. Maybe no magic is magic.

"Hey, how come these deader fucks don't go worship my old boss in this swamp?" Chango says. "Think they'd build their damn shrines all over. I guess that's what's weird about this thing, that it wants to hide from everyone, especially deaders. It just wants to watch."

"He's not your boss anymore."

"Yeah?" Chango says. "Guess not. So what do you think? Should we move to New Mexico after this? I'm thinking Mom would like that. We could take those old paintings she loves. The mesas. The oasis. Hang them up. We could have some parties, esé," he said. "We could learn about some black magic women. Just don't expect me to love those birds."

"We're not taking anything other than what we have," Blas says, stepping on another snail. "We need to leave. José said they'd wait two hours if we want to join them, though I'm not sure their plan is solid. I have to find some of my friends around that time too. I've been thinking to use José's escape party as a diversion. Go our own way. Whether we go with them or not, that's our chance. And I've calculated that it will be high tide, so waters will back-flood the creeks. We carry a kayak, cover it in khaki shit and weeds, dig beneath a fence, fight through mud and bramble, and get floating." He pauses, listens. "We're getting deep now. Might have to move quietly."

"Think it doesn't know we're here?" Chango whips his light into the willows as if any second a face might appear. "It knows, little brother."

Blas hops over a fallen trunk, knows his brother's right, that whatever's here not only knows every snap and crunch of leaf, but knows that one of these two wannabe brujo boys, without a chance, plans to become to be a monster killer.

Chango leaps over the trunk too, takes a swipe into the foliage with his machete. The blade sings. Dismembered branches flop into the mud.

"You probably didn't know," Blas half whispers. "Some old white lady lived across the street from the trailhead, got mad at me a million times for spying on birds in her yard."

"For looking at stupid canaries?"

Blas ignores him. "My friend Elisabeth, who I hope escaped, told me the old lady was a Riser. Said her convulsing got more erratic over the last several weeks. Sometimes she got up, went back inside, turned the lights out. Sometimes she just lay in the gutter for hours, scratching her fingers along the dirt."

"Fuck."

"Then one morning, after she lay out there all night, clawing and creeping outside bedroom windows, Elisabeth peeked out her curtains and saw the old lady's corpse on her back, arms stiff in the air, contorted like she was pushing away some damn ghost. Those Horsemen carted her off. Been happening a lot you know," Blas says. "People deading, then really dying. That's partly why I couldn't visit you . . . I didn't want to know. And I was afraid of that place."

"I didn't actually die." Chango laughs. "If that's what you're wondering."

Blas is about to reply when Chango stops them both. "Look, bro. I did those things, sure—all that mouth foaming. It was some trippy shit, yeah? Don't know if any of it was real. To be honest, I've forgotten where I went, though like I told you, it wasn't where *they* go. I came out of it. Did some bad things after I woke. Guess what? I'm here now." He puts a hand on Blas's shoulder. "I say that whatever is in here we put an end to this. Okay?"

Blas notices a hint of something in his brother's eyes. A glow. Like a bobcat. A splash of orange-yellow amid the pink, he can see it but just keeps nodding, as if the light isn't really there, as if everything will be fine if he just walks deeper into the willows.

"Good," Chango says. "Now make your ass lead the way."

Soon, walking becomes a vague sort of movement through undergrowth, a broken dream lit by a kind of willow light. Instead of growing darker, a kind of bioluminescence appears on edges of leaves, as if something with luminary power brushes against willows when passing through.

"Never seen anything like this," Blas says. "I can see the edges of things."

"I don't see anything," Chango says.

Blas tries to imagine stars, constellations amid points where bioluminescence resemble stars. A bear. A gate. A storm cloud.

Then in the undergrowth a vague shade, almost a grey light, scurries. Then another. All around, small movements. Not lights.

Grey forms. Things crawling, some slithering. There are more snails here too, less on the path, more on trunks and leaves.

Blas stiffens. "You see those?"

"Can hardly make out your ass in front of me," Chango says. "C'mon. Get going."

"I can't."

"You can." Chango shoves him.

Blas forces his feet to move. "This is just a night hunt for owls, for a poorwill," he mutters. "I can do this." He imagines eyes like Chango's, yellow-orange, a reflective glow, wings stretching, a bird body rising from the path. "For owls," he repeats, "for poorwills."

His heart races when he follows a bend in the path. Veins of dim blue light pulse along the mud floor, some thick, some thin along the path and mulch. Broken lines spiral along trunks too, bioluminescent slime left by the creatures he swears he sees crawling, slithering, but can't quite focus. Glowing patterns mark their backs, their eyes. They're not snails. Still so many snails. Blas feels himself tremble though he doesn't think Chango can see his tremors, he's glad for it.

He notices a change in Chango's breathing. A gulping from deep in his throat. A near-constant clearing of airways. The flashlight beam slips close to his feet, slows their forward progress. Before he can complain, Blas ducks a string of yellow light drifting weblike through the dark. He curses, nearly hitting another strand.

"The lights again?" Chango's voice rattles.

"Still don't see them?"

"I don't know." Chango coughs. "Feels like the moon's peering down on us."

Blas imagines Luna's eye turning every leaf and branch to green-grey stone and death. Soon Blas can't tell if he's walking, running, moving, floating. He feels above the canopy, heartbeat wrapped in willow-light, dazed, wet, muddy, slipping through reeds and swamp, back into the willows, following this muddy trail, a trail that never used to stretch this far. The willows were never this deep. Blas wipes at sweat until his face and hands smear with blackened mud, surrounded by roots and arches of sap-bleeding branches.

He slips to his hands and knees, crawls through shadowy passages of underbrush, mud, and filth, still sensing a path, following a path, one that feels alive, aware. He feels that roots could slip around his neck and hold him until he turns to bones. "They're going to strangle me," he says. Another set of creatures wriggle past. He sees segments this time, legs and carapace. Eyes like his eyes, glazed, curious, *human*.

But the path suddenly doesn't want to be found. Blas loses sight of well-trampled ground, or any kind of animal trail. Just mud, tangles, a kind of dark oblivion, tangles of roots, berries, poison oak. He and Chango panic, desperate to orient themselves. This way. No, that way. Under this log. No, around to the left, the path continues here. Then finally, a sliver of trail. Blas drags himself onto a narrow strip of muck, doesn't remember ever taking so long to get anywhere. He leads them on this other narrow line, still crawling, vein-light smearing onto his palms, onto his pants, until covered in a glowing sweat.

"What is this shit?" Chango coughs and spits a sap-like bio-light. "I didn't see this before. I think . . . it's inside me." A luminous jelly oozes from protrusions in the mud, like micro mud-volcanoes along crab-filled shores. "Fuck, man. It burns." Though finally able to stand, he vomits.

Blas waits for Chango to give a signal that he's all right. It takes a minute for his brother to stop breathing so heavy, to wipe his mouth and give a thumbs up. Blas nods, then leads them through an arch of willow light. Chango follows between a fallen trunk that has been sawn in half. Stalky growths cover the path with spindly, severed arms. Thorns tear at their pants, sleeves, and skin. An exposed elbow bleeds. Neither brother whimpers or whines. Not here. Not where they're going. They have to tough this out. They have to end what's happening. Even Blas has started to believe this confrontation can make a difference. Maybe he shouldn't talk to it or broker some deal. Maybe he should just use his primordial instinct to bludgeon, to kill.

Broken lines of yellow light move around them like marching ants, their source, he feels in his goosebumps, emanates from somewhere close, maybe from snails depositing light from their sticky feet.

Chango hisses while they crawl again, this time under thick gelatinous strands of bioluminescence. He splits one of the strands with a single machete hack into two bobbing, churning balls that spill onto his blade, down his hand and arm. "Don't know what this is and don't want it all over me," Chango says.

Blas pulls himself with the broken broomstick, digs into the mud, pulls again. He sees two figures in shadows ahead. Ghosts, he thinks, from somewhere. Not from here. Another time, another dimension, another somewhere. No idea how he knows this. They watch with curiosity while he and Chango return to their feet. In front of the shadows, creatures that look like they've crawled from an ocean nightmare, watching, waiting.

"Those are harmless," Chango says, now able to shine a light onto blanched faces, white as bone, then onto several creatures skittering below them.

"You've seen them?" Blas asks.

"They don't taste so good." Chango's raspy voice scratches the air. "Don't know about those ghosts. Something about them feels familiar. They're not who we're looking for, yet somehow I know this place was built for them to see."

"To see what?"

"Maybe us. Keep going. Don't ask how I know. I just know."

Blas feels his way along the icy skin of earth, unable to avoid any glowing strands squeezed toward them by this pressure built within the swamp, as if something burrowed underground then began releasing strings of light. Hands and legs covered in muck, they duck under branches, crawl over roots, then descend onto a bald slice of cold, acidic earth, where willows border reeds, and those border a sand-and-vegetation-covered shore. They crawl inside a different shade of darkness now, less light. Willows funnel them into tunnels, nothing Blas has ever seen in Pecho, though he enters anyway on his feet again, cramped between vague shapes of mud walls, mud halls, slippery corridors, a complex built of shadowy mimicry, a subterranean recollection of someplace Blas doesn't recognize.

"The walls." Chango cuts at a long web of light about to drip on them. "What are these things in the walls?"

Snails protrude in places, like lightbulbs in hardened glue. In the residue itself, snails meld with their own adhesive. Eye tentacles still free to bend. Halves of spiraled shells and chunks of fleshy matter protrude at odd angles. Snails everywhere, stacks of them, Blas can see, in this fabric, in this living labyrinthine ooze. This was never all mud. The walls have become a life-form, he thinks while they angle downward towards water, not the ocean, but large pools of the swamp itself.

The brothers continue forward, slog through knee-deep water and soaked earth, scramble up mudbanks onto an island in one of the rooms. Here with them, the waterlogged bodies of two Song Sparrows and a Virginia Rail, tucked into balls as if death visited via a volcanic, choking blast.

Blas notes two exits past the dead birds. "I think the one on the left," he says, catching his breath. "Seems like less water anyway."

Chango, breath labored and shallow, holds Blas back from continuing down the island. "Wait," he says. "I know this place." He surveys the room, its shape, the exits and entry.

"You can't know this," Blas says. "This was never here."

"I do know this," Chango says. "It's familiar. All of it. I've *built* this."

"Built this?" Synapses fire, flash images into Blas's mind. He can't grasp why he sees this vision, but embraces thoughts of corridors, long corridors, made of something besides snails.

"Not this place," Chango says. "Believe me, I don't like this swamp. But I know this. We're close to the cockpit."

Blas mouths the word but doesn't say it aloud. He can't get his head around these flashes of visions and the word his brother just said. And he doesn't think of helicopters, fighter jets, commercial planes, or jumbo jets. His mind instead goes to otherworldly explanations, a vessel made for searching the stars, a compartment for piloting a spacecraft, spaceship.

Chango slogs into mud-water, leaving Blas on the island, then finds a split in a wall that resembles a long slat of skin. He tosses the flashlight to Blas, pulls at the opening, exposes shells, snail innards, roots that have grown into the wall itself. He cuts and chops and pulls until he's made a hole large enough to squeeze through.

"This way," he groans. "The cockpit."

"Are you sure?" Blas says. "What if it's just ocean on the other side?"

"Then I'll swim. Come on." Chango leaps headfirst, pushes his thick body, kicks, grabs, swims through skin and mud, growling and grunting until he disappears into the dark.

Alone now, Blas listens to water drip, to mud gurgle. Snails slough along the hole, making slow repairs. He wonders what the cockpit could be, if his brother has gone crazy, or has somehow really seen this place. How could he? He was in the hospital, not in the willows, not in this insane set of catacombs.

Then Blas hears the wet smack of tiny feet on mud, feels his heart jump. Two of the segmented creatures have slipped out of the water. Eyes glisten, fix on him. It's almost familiar, their awareness of him. There's no way these things can know me, Blas thinks, inching away, ready to smash them, end their skittering near his feet. But then they lose interest, at least for the moment, though Blas's senses shoot to a level-ten alert, his terror off the scale, thinking they might try to feed on him—those sharp edges everywhere on them, the way their mouths snap shut and slowly open, their claws. But then each scurries to a sparrow, plucks them from the mud in silvery mandibles. The larger of the two also wants the rail. It creeps closer on spindly legs. Blas, about to strike with his broom handle, chooses a different attack. Quick as the failed youth soccer player he used to be, without thinking, he kicks at its underbelly and sends the creature into the water. The other creature, now afraid of Blas, scurries to the edge of the water, then leaps like a grasshopper to a far wall, where it scrambles for a foothold then slips into the water, losing its sparrow, which now floats at the surface.

A faint sound follows the splash, grabs Blas's attention. A distant whine emanating from a nearby corridor. Close. Too close, whatever it is. There are no signs of the creatures. Not even a bubble. Just that distant whine. Then silence. Still no creatures. The whine gone too. He needs to move, can't abandon his brother like he did at the hospital. Not again. Not this time. He has to go through the hole, always so many choices. This way. That way. Go forward. Go back. Fight the entity. Escape Baywood.

Feeling outside his body, Blas knows he can't stand here. He takes a step, accidentally smashes the dead rail into the muck. Bad luck, yeah? Bones, feathers, skull sink into black. *I'm going to die for sure now* enters his brain as a single pulse. He tries to jerk away but slips down the island, falling forward into the water and mud. Splashing and spitting, he loses all sense of direction, can barely get to his feet. He wants to scream until he finally feels his way along the wall to where Chango disappeared, hand covered in snails, though these aren't Atlantic drillers, some easily fall from his skin. The hole has shrunk. The wall repairing itself. Blas starts pulling off snails, from his arm, from the walls, tearing at the hole, though it doesn't seem to be getting much wider.

He tosses his pack onto the island, pushes into the opening. Blas is thinner and smaller than his brother, he thinks this hole may be just wide enough, and begins pulling himself through. The hole feels tighter than expected. Can't breathe. He loses the broom handle and flashlight in the sludge of the hole. Blas gasps, struggles to find footing, can only kick, swing his arms, reaching, flying, trying to grab something, nostrils filled with stink, anything that can dislodge him.

He spits mud and shell. Feels his lungs gasping. Sludge in his nose, eyes, mouth. I'll die right here, he thinks. A permanent fixture of shell and bone.

Blas feels a hand on the other side, holds him by the wrist. Chango. Blas grabs him. Then, as if birthed from between worlds, he squeezes through roots, mud-wall, and sludge into a room pulsing at the heart of the willows. For a moment, he lies on the hard-packed surface, spitting, trying to catch his breath on a floor of cold, damp mud, a chill up his legs and back where he's already shivered himself near to death.

The walls here feel alive. They wriggle, bioluminous. He can sense and see snail movement, a different species. More so than anywhere else in the corridors. He's never seen so many shoulderbands unlike the garden variety in the outer walls. Outside the willows, shoulderbands mostly live in mulch, sometimes in yards, abundant, though endangered in the nearby nature preserve undergrowth. Exhausted, he reaches toward a spiral, pushes its large round shell. Tiny eye stalks turn toward him, suck inward, disappear, reappear.

Blas sits up. Chango rests next to him.

A sliver of moonlight stares through branches, along with

the luminescence of this place, from the trees, snails, and walls. The glow reveals reddish mud by a serpentlike root, its thickness arching several feet out of the earth, like some kind of control panel mimicry alive with bio-light.

Chango, on his back, gulps air, eyes open, in them a shimmering, burdened by something in the strange hum of the room.

"Blas," Chango says. "I'm sorry. Thought I was stronger. I'm fading. I can feel it. Mom . . ."

Blas feels something too, this strange presence in the dark, more than a feeling or sound, lulling him to pass out, drift away. Not from the snails or reeds, but inside, deep within the tissues of his eyes, his brain, his stomach, from bio-light lodged in front of his spine, from its vibration in the back of his gut, slowly spreading. He knows Chango must feel it too, his labored breathing congested with mud and vapor. He's been through so much at the hospital, seen some other side, Blas thinks, *some other reality*, something they barely talked about, never will. It took a toll. Must have. Still, Chango's mind-altering experiences brought them to this room. He'd seen something while in that stasis, maybe some kind of ship, those creatures.

Blas wonders if the willows or maybe the entity has connected Chango's reality to a kind of disreality. Chango has seen this place, some version of a cockpit, the arching root once again, a control panel, those walls and snails. What had the other version looked like to Chango? Maybe connected to ship propulsion, a tangle of wreckage, connections to a distant solar system, an extraordinary meaning to all of this, maybe something buried somewhere else, maybe the sea of a distant planetoid.

Chango mutters again. Can't finish his words. "Blas . . . Mom . . . I . . ."

"It's okay." Blas knows. He somehow already knows this too. His hands on his brother now, feeling his chest rise and fall. "I love you, you know."

Blas wonders if this is how the deading starts. Will Chango lie here like the birds on mud island? Curl into a ball? Or just sink, like the people at a Riser wedding he heard about, the betrothed deading on an altar of black, destroying themselves intentionally, setting piles of photos alight, along with themselves. Buried within a church sanctuary. Them and their entire photographic histories transported to ash, all disappeared, all burnt. Everyone a witness to the horror. None of this makes sense. He hopes none of this can be true.

The question of death and dying. Blas doesn't even ask anymore: the why, how, the mystery of what it is to be destroyed by the deading. Doesn't matter now, he thinks he's figured it out. This has been nature's payback, a cosmic payback.

He thinks it's in him now too. Blas doesn't want any part of this. This yellow light. The orange-yellow now obvious in Chango's eyes. The answer. The question. Everything. This rupturing. A feeling. A hum. Deep within. The spiral in every snail twirling around and around in his throat like that flock of birds pulsing in the sky. Growing inside his lungs, his stomach, his intestines, his brain. Even so, he fights it. He has to fight it, has to refuse its presence, this cosmic payback.

Chango digs into the mud with his fingers. "It's red, isn't it? Like blood." His eyes, slick and pooling, turning inward. "We're not even here anymore. Back . . . there . . . finally in the cockpit . . . Can you see it," he whispers. "The star falling again. I think I know."

"I can see it," Blas lies, in tears, he can't see anything anymore. Maybe they never were brujo brothers.

"Good. Good. I knew you would. I need to be there. Is that okay? I need to go."

A change to the pulse in the room, snails around edges of walls, vibrating. A brighter light from the control panel area, from a line of snails there, from the root itself. Then from the darkness behind the control panel–root, a face and head takes shape, moonlight now catching its contours. Blas sees the slight movement of a head turning to survey the room through dead eyes. It has been here all along, propped in the dark. Cheeks, hideous and sunken, broken leather. Withered, rotted, eyes—dry blue pits—gazing from a distorted world within, from what was Bernhard Vestinos. Tentacles appear from its mouth, from holes in its cheeks, then disappear back inside. An outline takes human shape. Scintillating form connected to head, arms, legs, sitting on a stump, at this control panel–root, monitoring some kind of pseudo-descent. Blas can feel it, see it, know some of its thoughts.

Blas pushes himself to his feet, picks up Chango's machete from the mud. He thinks about what he could do with it, feels his insides turning loose on themselves. Vibrations and pain strike him in a sudden wave. His mind wants to fall inward, give in to this other consciousness across the room, demanding he join so many others in its revenge from the deep. He feels the need to writhe. There's comfort in the thought, that if he just gives in, lets go, that he will feel a kind of soothing he's never experienced. He has a choice to dead. He doesn't think anyone else has been given this choice.

He glances at his brother. Chango is gone. Lost. Hand clutching red mud, eyes full of golden specks. Tiny reflections of stars.

Blas feels the collective pulse from the snails, from this mind. His own, so weak, can hardly think about what's happening. Can't run. Feet stuck in mud when he stands. His own breathing rapid. Can't carry himself back through the wall, though he can see the hole still there, not closed all the way after all, the mud, the winding maze of trails. He wants to lie down, let his eyes roll back, fall through voids.

He forces himself to continue to stand, this pulse all around like heart rhythms, spirals turning in him, outside, in the walls, the mind boring into him, a frightening whirl of thought demanding now that he choose to slip next to his brother, become one with this collective death, collective infestation, collective encephalopathic burn.

Blas fights the impulse, feels as if he's fallen into the deep, a falling star himself, circling the earth, taking readings of the planet, engine failure a million years ago, then falling, somehow torn into two realities, two places at once.

Then Blas hears something else that pulls him closer to the surface. The whine again. The sound from the other side of the hole. Stronger this time. A familiar machinery *hummm* since this all happened, a *grey ghost*, always in the dark, skimming streets, hovering over homes, outside windows, exploring openings, probably the open doors of his home, his living room, kitchen, bathroom, his bedroom, his mother's paintings.

He hears the drone slowly squeeze through what's left of the hole, engine grinding. That's what he heard from the tunnel island—that drone engine. One followed him and his brother through the willows and halls, watching, spying, collecting data. That's all it ever does, all they ever do. The Faceless. AI controlled. Human controlled.

A beam of light appears from the hole. White arms next, bent, reaching, dripping mud. A phosphorescent eye emerges like the birth of a star, and those rotors humming, the drone floats into this ethereal place, amid walls of flickering snails, eyeing the control panel–root, the shimmering thing that was once Bernhard with its dead blue eyes. Collecting. Always collecting. A probe, Blas now knows. A goddam probe. Bernhard and this drone. Himself too. Probing, unearthing.

Blas being watched by so many unknown eyes. The drone stirs something left in him. Angers him in a way that shakes loose all the humming, burns him in a way that overturns his desire to kill the entity. Pulled from the entity's attention, now awake, he steps toward the drone, swings the machete, catches the machine before it can escape, knocks it sideways into the mud.

Its propellers fill with mulch. They whine and pitch and grind, but can no longer turn. Blas snatches it like he's a male Northern Harrier descending on a squirrel, soaring low along hillsides. The males have the same nickname as some of these drones: *the grey ghost*. Grey. Silent. Hunting. Blas smashes until its phosphorescent light fades, its stoplight eyes, until the whining burns out.

The thing that was Bernhard Vestinos watches from the control panel–root. A corporeal entity. A fragment of life from other worlds, past and present, death and light. For now it stops probing him. Blas realizes this when he looks up. The yellow light inside him fades. Though his insides hurt, Blas can breathe again. He doesn't want to drift away anymore, doesn't want to slip into darkness.

Blas doesn't understand why but feels a sudden compassion toward the entity. He wonders, amid all this pain, if it understands him, feels what he feels in some way. A loss. Some kind of loss on a scale Blas can't understand. Extreme feelings of isolation, buried deep in the sea, a fallen star so lonely, cracked open, having spilled itself in the loneliest black and blue and salt, amid so many nutrients and life-forms; and an acceptance, on a microbial level, or from the smaller, ancient forms, the slithering bottom dwellers, and even then, a collective welcoming, life-forms pulling each other in, even deep in the cold beneath all that pressure.

Blas can hardly see this thing through his tears. Can't speak. His heart becomes full of birds. In his mind, he sees José, Shuluwish, when they parted ways, standing at the edge of the back bay, searching for what bird might land in the shallow tide. Blas backs toward the hole, realizes he's been allowed this chance, this one chance, he knows, to slip free. He does this after discovering the letter in Chango's pocket. It has been carefully wrapped in plastic. He glances one last time to see the tentacles again, having crawled and slithered so much closer, this time pulling against his dead brother's lips. Blas turns and slips into the dark, through the hole, fighting, swimming, pulling through, then wades back to the island, his brother's flashlight, somehow working, lighting the trail, the night.

AFTER

WHEN THE EARTH cracks open from drought, particles spill upwards in little clouds, a kind of film that comes in the night, disintegrates by midday. This isn't dust. Spores, they call them, interconnected sporelings birthed each night, now drifting upward. We see this, our bodies embedded with drugs, experimental vaccines, micro-filters to keep the deading away.

A snake hides in the cracks, slithers into sunlight, twists in curls of pain. Lizards do this too, even a lone House Wren atop nopales. It drops into dust, stirs, sings, and sings again a joyous birdsong of its otherworldly appetite, then falls one last time, feather and bone.

Our encampment has been erected in Guadalupe, just west of Santa Maria. Our tent looks like any other government tent a mile down the highway in what was once farmland. We're not too far from Oso Flaco, where we walked the lagoon to Oso Flaco Creek during our escape, hid in the woods surrounding Lettuce Lake, then walked to freedom. None of that had been easy. We made our way, thanks to Ozziel, along the coast south from Port San Luis, past Pismo Beach, then a lagoon in the south Guadalupe-Nipomo dune complex, where we heard they bury things, things so deep in the sand you'll never see them again. That was after endless trails past Diablo Canyon, where we could hear moaning, and thought we saw workers wanting to restart that nuclear heart there next to the sea. Before that, our path took us through the wilderness southeast of Baywood, kayaking up a creek, then carrying the watercraft through hidden farmland, then cut back west again on deer and lion trails no one has taken for a hundred years. We struggled up and over hills, carrying our kayaks for miles and miles. We had to get away from the epicenter, Blas, Torrey, Emily, Tatum, Kai, and a few others. We knew that, just like we knew we had to get to Guadalupe.

Around the corner from the main encampment a narrow warehouse stretches for dozen of yards. Others in the distance stand where lettuce crops used to be. We call them the Halls of Horrors. Their rooms remind us of the darkness of hill rocks, those granite spires towering above Baywood where we'd hid for some time while winds howled and drones groaned in their search. We hid until we had the nerve to make our next move, until our supplies ran low. We knew our only chance had come, the way some people now sense things, the unimaginable, the faraway drift of stars, interplanetary winds. We talk about it sometimes now, our time up there in the hills, hiding, terrified how any moment we could get caught, how we understood something new about the stars.

Some of us talk about the day we came down from those rocks, when we slipped beneath the buried rock arch Kumi Sato told us about, the one beneath the hill barricades. We're still sad she didn't come with us. Not all of us have seen the photo she took on the phone she gave to Blas, or her strange audio recording and pages of thoughts, but she told us what was on it, and what may have happened to Ingram. Anyway, that was when we decided to cut through Clark's Valley. Ozziel had said to shorten our path that way. We don't like to remember that time, but somehow talking helps us understand each other better, helps us to know that sometimes you have to make tough choices.

We remember winding our way down into scrub and cactus, Baywood miles behind us, then southeast along a rim of hills through oak forests down into a pristine valley. Only one of us had ever been there. We reached a gate, each of its posts a thick tree trunk topped with a steer skull. We asked Blas if this was the right place, if he remembered the code, the one he wasn't supposed to know.

"This is it," he said. "Ozziel and I saw a Hooded Warbler in there."

He'd told us the story the third night we hid in the rocks. Winds screamed so much we could hardly hear his scratched voice. "We spotted the bird at a bend in a creek," he said. "I remember a trough nearby. This was at the last Christmas Bird Count before everything—Ozziel had a tip that there was a special bird in there—we weren't wrong. We had permission from a mushroom hunter, who said he was friends with the landowner. He'd brought these women, a young girl too. We followed them past the gate. That's when I memorized the code. I didn't mean to. It's just something I do. Memorize things, you know? Ozziel said to come through near here, so I knew this was our best chance. Anyway, those women and that girl carried baskets into hillsides for shrooms. Their laughter echoed through the woods while we searched for the bird down along the creek banks. An hour passed before we saw it. I knew the bird right away, that black hood, its yellow face, green wings. That was also when the owner came, scaring this rare jewel back into the creek foliage, terrifying us.

"He chewed us out, said we hadn't asked him to enter his property. 'Now every damn birder in the county gonna want to come pound my gate,' he said. 'They might sneak in, look at what's not theirs to look at.' His eyes bulged. Like every capillary would burst and turn them red. We told him that looking at birds was no big deal, that we visited each other's feeders to see rarities all the time. Cassin's Finch, rare sparrows, one time even a Dickcissel. He wasn't listening. 'Look at this beauty.' He swept his arms toward the creek like we were too stupid to know what we were looking at. 'I don't want a soul to know about this,' he said. 'You got me? Now get out of here. You were never invited.'

"These kinds of property owners are ragers, isolationists, strangely threatened by people like us, thinking we were going to rip this pristine image right from the land and plant it like a dream someplace else, like nature was his and only his, and goddam anyone for even looking at a bird that flew there from god knows where, maybe Washington, D.C. while making its way to southeast Mexico."

This tiny lush valley was a secret, we could tell as soon as we entered the gate. A creek ran through, lush trees almost like aspens, trees we'd never seen anywhere around Baywood, thin trunks, full and leafy and yellow-green, a secret forest of them creekside. Nearby, sharp-rising hills covered in oaks shone like emeralds.

We took our chances though. We had to get through. We walked a dirt road, tired, silent, carrying our kayaks. We camouflaged ourselves in the scrub, draping fishermen's netting and shrubs over ourselves while the Faceless buzzed overhead. We got glimpses of their stoplight eyes, their silver arms. One of them, another grey ghost, hovered, then flew off. Alongside the creek we could see the top of a farmhouse beyond the foliage, beyond the birdsong and gurgling creek water. Blas said the owner had come from the other direction last time, some side road we already passed that crossed on a small creek bridge. He said he'd heard voices in the woods that day, that he hadn't been this far down the road.

It wasn't long before we heard something. A muttering, a

voice emanating from the creek, then from the woods opposite
the bank, drifting through leaves. We couldn't tell what it was
saying or to whom. We could just tell it was angry, that whoever
it was probably wanted us gone, or worse. We were on the open
road at dusk, so kept on at a quick, quiet pace, hoping to move
away from the voice. And soon, we did, though whispers seemed
to hover in the canopy, angry and distant, dwindling so far at
times as to appear miles away. We were all tired and kept on,
pushed on. Beginning to feel confident, a few of us started saying
that we hoped the voice was gone for good, that the farmhouse
we'd seen over the creek trees was now far in the distant valley.
If it was full of deaders or dead things, we didn't want to know.

Until suddenly he stood in front of us, breathing heavy. Just
like Blas described. Eyes bulging in the dim light, throat full of
veins, rifle in his hands. Seemed he could see through most of us.
We set our kayaks down. We just want to pass through, we said.

"Someone following you?" he said. "That whole tribe of
dead? Them skywheels looking down here?"

"No one. Nothing."

"You knew the code. Who gave it to you? Couldn't have been
the ones dead and buried. Ain't a corpse that can talk."

We told him again we just wanted to pass, that we'd be up
and over the hills before he knew it.

Then his eyes fixed on Blas. We thought that rifle would go off.

"I seen you," he spit. "Now I remember. Told you never to
come back. Told you, you're what's wrong with this country. You
and everyone else seeing this place for what it is. You gonna dare
take it. That's why you're here. Gonna dare take all of it. Always
knew you'd come back."

"We're just passing through."

"All kinds been coming here ruining my privacy. Tried to take
my family early on. I put a stop to that. Just like I'll put a stop to
you if you don't turn around."

"Where's your family?" we asked. We had to say something. Anything.

"Where they belong. Where all you deaders belong. Am I starting to make myself clear? You'll soon learn. I'm gonna start with you," he said to Blas.

Some of us know the way of the world before all this, when you didn't have to look twice, or wonder whether or not someone might break in front of you. We find ways to dispose of our thoughts, of the dead and deading. We expel them from our memories, watch them drift into stories and time, expand into something else. Maxine did us one better when she stepped out of the woods where she'd been shadowing us. We were so glad she decided to join us after all. She kissed her dad and her skull-painted motorcycle goodbye and we all slipped into the dark. She'd been in those rocks with us, pissed alongside us on trails. Now she stood on a dim-lit edge of woods, a silhouette and a spark, her face lighting into a shriek, a war cry.

Soon as the landowner turned to hear the crack he must have felt something heavy in his ribs and lungs, something all deaders must feel every time they slip to the ground. We wonder what he thought when we walked past, when we took his rifle, a silent line parallel to the creek, to the world, hunched and hungry. The night wanted to take us so we entered and hid before the drones came back.

Author's Note

A war has arrived in the world of American ornithology that I saw coming long before I completed *The Deading*. It partly has to do with bird names, though it really has to do with intersections of race and ethnicity within birdwatching and ornithology.

Evident to the reader are the obvious differences between the characters Blas and Ingram/Victor. Blas represents new views of the intersections of race and ethnicity within North American birdwatching. He can't afford some of the tools, has no real nurturing birdwatching community, and like all problems with Chicano futurism, has no role model. Where will life take Blas? What does his future hold? You might have more answers than I do. He simply can't see who he might become as a birder, though he has centered his life around the study of birds. When you can't see yourself in the future, then someone/something has erased something about you. This is why we need more brown characters in sci-fi, fantasy, and horror, and this is why we need more brown birdwatchers and ornithologists in the real world. Not to mention more women, more LGBTQ representation, and fewer people saying race, gender, and ethnicity doesn't matter.

Victor and Ingram represent white gatekeeping for their refusal to understand Blas, which aims for some outdated kind of conformity. They represent a kind of paralysis among white birders, ornithologists, and some long-established birding committee group types, with their I-don't-know-how-to-talk-to-brown-people mentality and "we tried" approach in discussions of establishing birding roots within brown communities. Some of these birding communities are exclusively white, though brown communities exist nearby.

The battle goes deeper than inclusivity with non-white birders, because a schism has reached deep into the heart of ornithology itself which has repercussions in *The Deading*, affecting the accuracy of the story's real bird names. On November 1, 2023, the American Ornithological Society announced that it would be changing the English names of more than a hundred North American birds, specifically those deemed harmful or named after people. John James Audubon himself has been proven a racist and a graverobber, and created a fictitious eagle to help sell his infamous *The Birds of America*. So, yes, Audubon's Shearwater will change. John Kirk Townsend robbed skulls from indigenous peoples' graves so he could promote false theories that native peoples were racially inferior. Bye bye, Townsend's Solitaire, etc.

The rollout will take a few years at best, some as soon as 2024. The names that will change in *The Deading* include: Townsend's Warbler, Baird's Sandpiper, Anna's Hummingbird, Wilson's Warbler, Bewick's Wren, Lincoln's Sparrow, Virginia Rail, Cooper's Hawk, Virginia's Warbler, Wilson's Phalarope, Franklin's Gull, Hammond's Flycatcher, Bullock's Oriole, and Cassin's Finch.

In the meantime, I leave you with a thought about the ever-changing nature of bird names, and this bit of wisdom said to me by Cin-Ty Lee, co-author of *Field Guide to North American Flycatchers* and professor in the department of Earth, Environment, and Planetary Sciences at Rice University: "What gives us the right to name any animal, mountain, or plant after a human? I never understood that."

Suggested Reading and Resources

After finishing *The Deading*, readers may be interested in learning more about the topics explored in this book. Below are some further reading suggestions that served as inspiration for this novel.

Environmental & Nature Essays

Elizabeth Kolbert's *New Yorker* essay,[1] "Why Is The Sea So Hot?" provides a startling wake-up call about feverish oceans and off-the-chart sea surface temperatures. Kolbert's quoting of hurricane researcher Brian McNoldy's assessment of 2023 ocean temperatures will haunt you: "It's like the whole climate just fast-forwarded by fifty or a hundred years. That's how strange this looks." During my research, I explored current topics facing our oceans and sea life that you can look up, including the beaching of hundreds of gray whales along the Pacific Coast over the past five or so years and other mass die-offs related to ocean warming, including how massive marine heat waves led to an estimated 1.2 million Common Murre deaths between 2015 and 2016 (62,000 washed ashore). In my own area, I've seen more than a few dead whales during that window, and found seabirds not normally seen from land feeding from their carcasses.

Ornithologist Alvaro Jaramillo's social media posts[2] provided up-to-date concerns on ocean warming, ocean blobs, el niño, and other startling coastal weather phenomena as I wrote this book.

In Alice Walker's short essay,[3] "Am I Blue?" from her 1989 collection *Living by the Word: Selected Writings, 1973–1987*, we meet a horse with that very name and soon come to realize something horrific: "I was shocked that I had forgotten that human animals and nonhuman animals can communicate quite well; if we are brought up around animals as children we take this for granted. By the time we are adults we no longer remember." Walker reminds us that there is a disturbing intrinsic moral superiority to the way many humans treat animals. This important concept informed how I depict animal behavior in the story.

I read John R. Platt's 2021 essay,[4] "I Know Why the Caged Songbird Goes Extinct: A rampant trade in Asian birds for their beautiful songs is emptying forests of sound and life," when I was learning to bird, and Platt's writing had a tremendous impact on me and my creation of Blas and Kumi as characters empathetic to birds. His essay about the disappearance of the Straw-headed Bulbul helped me realize that most every caged bird sold has either been poached, or is a descendent of a poached bird.

Pepper W. Trail's March 2022 essay,[5] "Dying for love: Illegal international trade in hummingbird love charms," in *Conversation Science and Practice*, also details the poaching of hummingbirds in the United States. Multiple species are captured, killed, turned into religious and cultural artifacts, then packaged in little bags and sold as "love charms" in New Mexico and Texas. This includes "chuparrosas" (hummers) with massively declining populations.

In Erin Sharkey's introduction,[6] "More To Be Shaped By" from the anthology *A Darker Wilderness: Black Nature Writing From Soil to Stars,* she writes about being a Black woman experiencing othering while camping or on a national park trail: "I learned that nature is not a place where you can escape the oppressive rules of race." Starkey teaches us about how the genre of nature writing "remains dominated by white, cisgender men with access to resources." She literally has to tell us that Black Americans have related to the natural world since being confined in chains during the Middle Passage, and reminds us of other harsh details, such as how parks were created out of a white desire for open spaces . . . for whites. Let's also not forget that even in urban environments, bird populations have been shaped by redlining and racist loan practices as well.

I get dismissed constantly by white birders who don't want to talk about the intersections between ethnicity and birdwatching. They appear not to care that there are few brown birdwatcher kids in our county. I also wonder if they think ethnicity didn't play into what happened to Christian Cooper in 2020 while birdwatching in Central Park, New York, when a white woman called the police on him for asking her to leash her dog. I'm interested in how white privilege shapes how we talk about and interact in nature.

Notes

1. Elizabeth Kolbert, "Why Is The Sea So Hot?," *New Yorker*, March 14, 2024, https://www.newyorker.com/news/daily-comment/why-is-the-sea-so-hot
2. Alvaro Jaramillo (@alvaros_adventures), https://www.instagram.com/alvaros_adventures/
3. Alice Walker, "Am I Blue?" in *Living by the Word: Selected Writings, 1973-1987*, (United Kingdom: Harcourt Brace Jovanovich, 1989), https://www.sas.upenn.edu/~cavitch/pdf-library/Walker_Blue.pdf
4. John R. Platt, "I Know Why the Caged Songbird Goes Extinct: A rampant trade in Asian birds for their beautiful songs is emptying forests of sound and life," *Revelator*, March 3, 2021, https://therevelator.org/asian-songbird-crisis/

5. P. W. Trail, "Dying for love: Illegal international trade in hummingbird love charms," *Conservation Science and Practice*, vol. 4, iss. 6, (March 2022): e12679, https://doi.org/10.1111/csp2.12679

6. Eric M. Wood, Sevan Esaian, Christian Benitez, Philip J. Ethington, Travis Longcore, Lars Y. Pomara, "Historical racial redlining and contemporary patterns of income inequality negatively affect birds, their habitat, and people in Los Angeles, California," *Ornithological Applications*, vol. 126, iss. 1, (February 2024): duad044, https://doi.org/10.1093/ornithapp/duad044

Birdwatching Resources

Birdwatching/birding in the US has been a part of my life for half a decade. It's tough going, but you can learn the basics with a simple google search. I've even written a "How to" that was published across a dozen or so California newspapers, but I think those are under paywalls. The idea of birding is simple. Birds are *everywhere*. They know no borders. In the US, many species migrate twice per year. And there are many local native and invasive species. I tend to love all of them.

While I use eBird.org to log my species, the moderators can be a bit tone deaf toward new birders, even dismissive. As for birding itself, I tend to shy away from groups, though they can be a great way to learn. And I want nothing to do with Audubon groups. Until they change their name, just consider me like Blas. No, thanks. Though you can do what you want. Join all the groups if you dare!

For me, it's best to bird alone most of the time, to learn alone most of the time, or with a partner who doesn't talk much, who *listens*. Not to me, to *birds*. There's also birdsong, yeah? And you can learn them. Sounds like mud for a year or two. Then something happens. You start to figure them out, start to peel birdsongs apart and ID them without even seeing them scampering about.

Get to know your local patch too. I did and put Meadow Park, San Luis Obispo on the map when I found a Golden-winged Warbler, and recently, a Swainson's Hawk, which was unheard of for the area. So, stay local and learn songs, field marks, body shapes and colors, bill lengths, etc. I find *The Sibley Guide to Birds* most helpful. The illustrations and song/call descriptions are super well done. I also use Cin-Ty Lee's *Field Guide to North American Flycatchers: Empidonax and Pewees* (he also has one on kingbirds). Flycatchers are extremely difficult, so I find his study of fieldmarks, songs, and holistic approach to bills, primary wing extensions, tail length, and head shape a helpful study when these birds are abundant in my area. Don't forget to buy binoculars! I use low-end Zeiss, but you can find birding binos for as low as fifty bucks.

Acknowledgments

Parents break rules. I mean, I don't really even know the rules of parenting. You just kind of make them up, go with your gut. That's the way we all do it. Yet, there are unofficial rules, like how you're not supposed to take little kids to horror movies. But mine did, and that began a slow burn into writing horror that would be decades in the making. Sometime around Christmas 1973, not wanting to lay down any cash for a babysitter, Dad, in his rasquache way of doing things, piled five-year-old me and my siblings into an orange VW pop-top van, then drove us to San Jose's Capitol 6 Drive-In. Dad, because I'm sure Mom always went along with his decision-making machismo, figured we'd fall fast asleep, that our adrenaline for adventure wouldn't kick in. So, he popped the top, we climbed up and into our sleeping bags, and theoretically should have slipped into dreamland before the opening credits could begin to roll.

It wasn't long into the film before my scrawny frame slipped over the edge and hung upside-down to stare at that girl on the screen. She wasn't slimy green. She didn't lock those soon-to-be demonic eyes on me, and she wasn't crawling up the side of the screen to leap onto our van. She was just a girl, and so I didn't think about *The Exorcist* being scary (what did that word mean to me anyway?). Not until I started to hear those demon noises, the grunts, howls, and screams, and though I wasn't brave enough to peek at the screen at that point, that girl's voice haunted me for years, along with Mom's gasps.

Summer 1975, we got a front row seat to the sunny Atlantic Ocean, the fictional town of Amity Island, invading tourists, ugly suits and hair, my eyes on those beachgoers wishing I could sculpt sandcastles in that lovely seaside sand and surf. I was only six, hardly any older than when I heard that demon girl growling at priests. This time the entire family had popcorn, Lifesavers, sodas, maybe licorice too. There was no VW pop-top or hanging upside-down, just movie seats in the Syufy's Century 24 dome, just south of the Winchester Mystery House. What we did still have was Dad's poor parenting, *his* desire for us to be terrified. "Bet you're gonna get so scared that you drop your candy, maybe throw it," I remember him saying, or something like it, which I did, or maybe just said I did to make him happy, because I was afraid of him and wanted to please him, and wanted to be him, to show this Mexican American cowboy of the eighteen wheeler that I could get really freaked out, like when Halloween came around and I tried to stay awake for Creature Feature films to see two-headed monstrosities and vampires. I almost always fell asleep those late nights, though I wanted to be frightened, pretended to be frightened, and had long been terrified of the dark. What I remember about *Jaws* was that fear in Brody's eyes when the shark popped out of the water, Brody's sudden need for a bigger boat, and my sudden feeling that water, any water, even a puddle, wasn't safe, could never be safe.

I'm pretty sure that was my first real jump scare, though that could have come from seeing those hoods and creepy eyes in *The Omega Man* pop out of the dark. Seems like that was always on TV. Either way, I'm pretty sure Dad chuckled when that shark showed itself. I remember already feeling unsettled, that strange music kicking the whole thing off, that nude woman swimming, titillating even for a seventies kid, and then that tug on her legs, like someone had pulled off her covers and grabbed her by the ankle. If there's anything horror works toward, it's a level of fear, constant fear, and it can be conveyed through darkness and mood, through the stillness of water, through music, through eyes, through watching how people react to the hungry mysteries beneath them that nibble on toes and tear apart legs.

It wouldn't be the same if this bad parenting hadn't been the ultimate trifecta of 1970s horror. It was spring, 1979. I was ten by then, an old hat at horror. I'd seen it all, though not really. And either way, had seen nothing like this, and like the other films, hadn't even seen the film trailer. All I knew was the title, and there it was on the screen at the Stockdale 6 Theaters during the opening credits, portions of its letters piecing together slowly, ominously into *Alien*, echoing how the film's alien would slowly grow until it was there, *right there* in front of everyone, this perfect horror lifeform, towering over its victims. Where *Jaws* had me jumping, *Alien* had me frozen and buried deep within myself. I was instantly transported to the gothic, this cinematic setting filled with abject beauty, crumbling gothic architecture, like reading *The Monk* (1796), only this time with rusted outer-space tech. The *Nostromo* felt like it could shake apart. And that crashed nameless alien ship beaming its distress beacon appeared wraithlike in the shadows of a dead world, like some kind of airless cathedral where religion had come to die. And those eggs, *all those eggs*. This wasn't the devil, or a shark, but a sea of chest bursters in the making, things that could grow into monsters so huge and deadly that maybe that shark and devil child would have had a run for their money if confronted with just one of them.

Thanks, Dad. Thanks, Mom.

And I really do think this was mostly Dad's doing, so maybe a little more thanks to him, since he'd been the tough man of the house, that dark-skinned man who believed in assimilation. In that decade I wasn't anything more than a dual ethnic kid told he was white. I had no sense of Chicanismo, no sense of identity, no sense of anything but those childhood forever moments, to have fun, constant fun, to run from the fear of school bullies, but to fear Dad mostly, because you never crossed him, you just did what he said, and if he said to read an old Edgar Rice Burroughs novel set in Pellucidar, I did. If he said to watch horror, I did. So, if he thought horror was fine for his kids, then I thought that was normal. I had to be proud, to brag about seeing those scary movies, even if Dad did sometimes resemble both the heroes and the monsters of those cinematic tales. I mean, who wouldn't show some pride in watching all of *Salem's Lot*, that hovering boy scratching at the window, or *Trilogy of Terror*, that tiki doll with the knife under all our beds? And though I thank Dad again and again, though even his ashes are long gone, spread on atomic Nevada mountains twenty-four years ago, he still deserves these thanks, for he is in Bernhard, and in Blas, and in Victor. And Mom, who has been gone twenty-six years, I thank her too, because she stood up to monsters, though she went along with that trifecta of horror, and is in every bird, her bones just as thin, and in Blas's heartbeat, and in the eyes of those who fight back, even if only for a brief time.

Bad parenting taught me some things, that we need horror, that we need the primordial terror in ourselves to show us that we can face fears, imagine ourselves as the heroes, or the ones who get caught, or the monsters that create fear, or the magic that makes dangerous, human-eating creatures slip into believable/unbelievable worlds. The mirror that horror holds up to us is real. And we are all in the reflections. And we're better for it. And horror writers probably are all thankful for the mirrors they hold up, and so I thank even those mirrors I broke, and the strange luck of the uncanny those reflective shards gave me, because even in my fear of *seven years of bad luck* grew a story of a boy who became a horror writer, who at the same time, wanted to find his way out of the maze of time's dark shadows. Do we ever really find our way out? Or do we use mirrors to help us continue our journey? Doesn't matter, I'm thankful.

Thanks to Jordan, Landen, and Reina for not fussing at me for being a bad parent. Thanks to my birding crew, whose names are scattered throughout the novel, especially KMillyOnTheTrack. We met on Quintana Road chasing an Indigo Bunting, or was it that Lucy's Warbler at Morro Creek? Your swim across Morro Bay from Tidelands Park for that Common Ringed Plover on the sandspit will always be the most epic of bird tales. Your voice is always in my head, on every trail, one with the birdsong, while I attempt to make sense of the muddiness of it all to identify every species. You tell me what I'm hearing. I'm still listening.

Thanks to my editor, Diana Pho, AKA Auntie Editor, for telling me everything straight and always reminding me to keep secrets. You trusted in a weird story, which is your magic to always find them. And now *The Deading* is part of this wonder that you weave into this world over and over. Your edit letter made me realize what was special, and what could be improved. I quickly saw the empty spaces that needed filling. Thanks to the rest of team Erewhon: Marty, Viengsamai, Kasie, Cassandra, and Sarah. Thank you for your expertise, for your infectious enthusiasm for story, for welcoming *The Deading* into your lexicon, and giving an old dual ethnic dude, a Chicano dude, a safe space. Thanks to illustrator Christina Mrozik for your cover art that captures the incredible and unsettling beauty of birds, and their fragility, and for your endpapers, especially your sketches of Goldie, a rare and threatened Golden-winged Warbler I discovered in fall 2021 at San Luis Obispo's Meadow Park. That was the third record for SLO County, around the 68th California record. He stayed four days, then disappeared in a windstorm. Goldie's immortality means everything.

Thanks to my agent, Jud Laghi. You had Diana on your radar, and that nearly turned into an epic bidding war! Erewhon quickly won out, which was the real win for us. I'm so glad for your expertise, for always letting me know how the industry works behind the scenes, for believing in my work. We had that great dinner over at Casa Blanca in Palm Desert with Jane and shared so many stories. What a perfect evening. Thanks for always answering my gazillions of emails, and for caring about all your writers.

Thanks to Stephen Graham Jones for helping rearrange parts of *The Deading*, for teaching me that readers need to see characters make choices on the page, and for making me read, "From Long Shots to X-Rays: Distance and Point of View" by David Jauss. That essay helped me break a code in my writing, opening my mind to looking at sentences in a new way. You encouraged me when we discussed José, recognizing the sensitivity in my desire to get him right, and told me to trust myself, and make sure to add "shotguns and motorcycles," which I did.

Thanks to Tod Goldberg. You asked if I had something else to work on besides my thesis while at UCR Palm Desert Low Residency MFA. That conversation threw me headlong into the world of horror. I'd written a third of *The Deading* around 2018, just before the pandemic, then put it down, locked it away, which in retrospect was a good thing. Two intensive years of pandemic birding meant immersing myself in nature, meant new ideas, new visions, and witnessing new horrors in the Audubon birding world that Blas could face. The new version, and its completion, was ready to happen by the time I joined the UCR program. Your brief curiosity helped give that story a new life.

During that time, I wandered from my actual thesis on family for a couple of quarters, finished *The Deading*, and studied the craft of monsters. Thanks also for ideas about expanding the story's Greek chorus of teens, and that Blas chapter where all hell breaks loose.

Thanks to Jane for reading early drafts of *The Deading* before the pandemic, and for reading other drafts along the way. Any writer would kill for your intense eye for story, for your line edits and impeccable grammar. If you'd read my last draft of *The Deading*, which finally you didn't have to because I was in the UCR program, you would have still caught so much, and would have shaken your head at how much I got wrong. While I worked on final drafts at UCR, and while adding a hundred pages for Erewhon, you were still patient enough to entertain the bits I read from my kitchen table workspace. You heard about every character, every plot point, everything I kept or deleted. You encouraged me. You found truth in what I was saying. Thank you. We are just migrating birds, you and I. We carry the world in us, the past and future. And art, we carry so much *art*, and *love*, and we show the world when we can, and we navigate by the starlight in each other.

Thank you for reading this title from Erewhon Books, publishing books that embrace the liminal and unclassifiable and championing the unusual, the uncanny, and the hard-to-define.

We are proud of the team behind *The Deading* by Nicholas Belardes:

Sarah Guan, Publisher
Diana Pho, Executive Editor
Viengsamai Fetters, Assistant Editor

Martin Cahill, Marketing and Publicity Manager
Kasie Griffitts, Sales Associate

Cassandra Farrin, Director
Leah Marsh, Production Editor
Kelsy Thompson, Production Editor

Seth Lerner, Cover Design
Christine Mrozik, Cover and Endpapers Art
Alice Moye-Honeyman, Interior Map Design

and the whole publishing team at Kensington Books!

Learn more about Erewhon Books and our authors at:
erewhonbooks.com

Find us on most social media at:
@erewhonbooks